THE STORYTELLER

SHORT STORIES FROM AROUND THE WORLD

REFLECTIONS IN FICTION

EDITED BY JAMES BARRY
(BREBEUF COLLEGE SCHOOL)
AND JOSEPH GRIFFIN
(UNIVERSITY OF OTTAWA)

Nelson Canada

© Nelson Canada,
A Division of Thomson Canada Limited, 1992

All rights in this book are reserved.

Published in Canada by
Nelson Canada,
A Division of Thomson Canada Limited
1120 Birchmount Road
Scarborough, Ontario
M1K 5G4

ISBN 0-17-603868-X
Teacher's Guide 0-17-603869-8

Managing Editor: Jean Stinson
Project Manager: Lana Kong
Developmental Editor: David Friend
Copy Editor: Karin Velcheff
Senior Production Editor: Deborah Lonergan
Art Director: Bruce Bond
Designer: Tracy Walker
Cover Design: Tracy Walker
Cover Illustration: Ron Broda
Typesetting: Nelson Canada/Zenaida Merjudio

Printed and bound in Canada

7890 / BG / 1098

Canadian Cataloguing in Publication Data

Main entry under title:

The Storyteller : short stories from around
the world

Includes index.
ISBN 0-17-603868-X

1. Short stories, English.   2. Short stories -
Translations into English.   3. Short stories,
English - Translations from foreign languages.
I. Barry, James, date. II. Griffin, Joseph, date.
PN6120.2.S76 1992   808.83'1   C92-093313-0

Reviewers

The publishers thank the
following people who contributed
their valuable expertise during the
development of this book:

Patti Buchanan, Vancouver, B.C.
Anne Carrier, Toronto, Ont.
Shirley Dale-Easley, Fredericton, N.B.
John Jerome, Orleans, Ont.
P. W. Johnson, Vancouver, B.C.
Dan Kral, Regina, Sask.
John McCuaig, Mississauga, Ont.
Albert Michael, Toronto, Ont.
Jim Petrie, Fredericton, N.B.
Peter Prest, Calgary, Alta.

CONTENTS

III EUROPE

IV LATIN AMERICA

V THE MIDDLE EAST

VI NORTH AMERICA

VII OCEANIA

All the world loves a good story.

Storytelling is as old as the human need to entertain, to comprehend the dynamics of life, and to enter imaginatively into others' experiences.

This anthology of short fiction places the short story within a global framework. The stories have been chosen for their literary excellence, the perspective they provide on the human condition, and the fact that they represent the seven major geographical regions of the world. The geographical designations are a matter of convenience; some writers cross cultural and national boundaries. Some countries as well straddle more than one geographical region.

Among the many internationally respected authors represented are several Nobel Prizewinners for Literature (Lagerkvist, Hemingway, Camus, Garcia Marquez, and Paz). The stories encompass the full range of human experience, male and female, child and adult. As well, they reflect the major writing styles, trends, and narrative voices in modern short fiction.

On this international reading safari we view our world in microcosm. One moment we are in New Zealand giving birth, the next moment in Zimbabwe experiencing the rite of passage to adulthood as we witness the death of a wild animal. We journey back home to our Native roots in America, fall in and out of love in China, confront violence in its many guises in Cyprus, Mexico, and Thailand, and lament for lost childhood innocence in Trinidad. We grimace at the horror of military dictatorship in Korea, cope with the prejudices of class structure in Argentina, place a bouquet of wild roses on a child's grave in Canada.

Meaningful travel delights, but it also teaches. Sharing these stories from different cultures illustrates that the literary map of the world is the map of the human heart. Rejection and alienation wear the same face be it in Latin America or the Middle East. The loss of a loved one brings the same tears in Asia as in Africa. And no country has a monopoly on hardship, materialism, social conscience, or the triumph of the human spirit over adversity.

The selection of stories for this anthology reflects the joint effort of students, educators, publishers, and front-line teachers. We are particularly indebted to the students for reading and rereading stories, and providing their candid opinions and insights. To them we dedicate this book.

The Editors

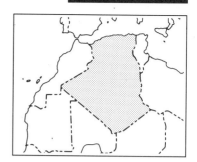

The Guest

BY ALBERT CAMUS

TRANSLATED BY JUSTIN O'BRIEN

The schoolmaster was watching the two men climb toward him. One was on horseback, the other on foot. They had not yet tackled the abrupt rise leading to the schoolhouse built on the hillside. They were toiling onward, making slow progress in the snow, among the stones, on the vast expanse of the high, deserted plateau. From time to time the horse stumbled. Without hearing anything yet, he could see the breath issuing from the horse's nostrils. One of the men, at least, knew the region. They were following the trail although it had disappeared days ago under a layer of dirty white snow. The schoolmaster calculated that it would take them half an hour to get onto the hill. It was cold; he went back into the school to get a sweater.

He crossed the empty, frigid classroom. On the blackboard the four rivers of France, drawn with four different coloured chalks, had been flowing toward their estuaries for the past three days. Snow had suddenly fallen in mid-October after eight months of drought without the transition of rain, and the twenty pupils, more or less, who lived in the villages scattered over the plateau had stopped coming. With fair weather they would return. Daru now heated only the single room that was his lodging, adjoining the classroom and giving also onto the plateau to the east. Like the class windows, his window looked to the south too. On that side the school was a few kilometres from the point where the plateau began to slope toward the south. In clear weather could be seen the purple mass of the mountain range where the gap opened onto the desert.

Somewhat warmed, Daru returned to the window from which he had first seen the two men. They were no longer visible. Hence they must have tackled the rise. The sky was not so dark, for the snow had stopped falling during the night. The morning had opened with a dirty light which had scarcely become brighter as the ceiling of clouds lifted. At two in the afternoon it seemed as if the day were merely beginning. But still this was better than those three days when the thick snow was falling amidst unbroken darkness with little gusts of wind that rattled the double door of the classroom. Then Daru had spent long hours in his room, leaving it only to go to the shed and feed the chickens or get some coal. Fortunately the delivery truck from Tadjid, the nearest village to the north, had brought his supplies two days before the blizzard. It would return in forty-eight hours.

Besides, he had enough to resist a siege, for the little room was cluttered with bags of wheat that the administration left as a stock to distribute to those of his pupils whose families had suffered from the drought. Actually they had all been victims because they were all poor. Every day Daru would distribute a ration to the children. They had missed it, he knew, during these bad days. Possibly one of the fathers or big brothers would come this afternoon and he could supply them with grain. It was just a matter of carrying them over to the next harvest. Now shiploads of wheat were arriving from France and the worst was over. But it would be hard to forget that poverty, that army of ragged ghosts wandering in the sunlight, the plateaus burned to a cinder month after month, the earth shrivelled up little by little, literally scorched, every stone bursting into dust under one's foot. The sheep had died then by thousands and even a few men, here and there, sometimes without anyone's knowing.

In contrast with such poverty, he who lived almost like a monk in his remote schoolhouse, nonetheless satisfied with the little he had and with the rough life, had felt like a lord with his whitewashed walls, his narrow couch, his unpainted shelves, his well, and his weekly provision of water and food. And suddenly this snow, without warning, without the foretaste of rain. This is the way the region was, cruel to live in, even without men—who didn't help matters either. But Daru had been born here. Everywhere else, he felt exiled.

He stepped out onto the terrace in front of the schoolhouse. The two men were now halfway up the slope. He recognized the horseman as Balducci, the old gendarme he had known for a long time. Balducci was holding on the end of a rope an Arab who was walking behind him with hands bound and head lowered. The gendarme waved a greeting to which Daru did not reply, lost as he was in contemplation of the Arab dressed in a faded blue *jellaba*, his feet in sandals but covered with socks of heavy raw wool, his head surmounted by a narrow, short *chèche*. They were approaching. Balducci was holding back his horse in order not to hurt the Arab, and the group was advancing slowly.

Within earshot, Balducci shouted: "One hour to do the three kilometres from El Ameur!" Daru did not answer. Short and square in his thick sweater, he watched them climb. Not once had the Arab raised his head. "Hello," said Daru when they got up onto the terrace. "Come in and warm up." Balducci painfully got down from his horse without letting go the rope. From under his bristling moustache he smiled at the schoolmaster. His little dark eyes, deep-set under a tanned forehead, and his mouth surrounded with wrinkles made him look attentive and studious. Daru took the bridle, led the horse to the shed, and came back to the two men, who were now waiting for him in the school. He led them into his room. "I am going to heat up the classroom," he said. "We'll be more comfortable there." When he entered the room again, Balducci was on the couch. He had undone the rope tying him to the Arab, who had squatted near the stove. His hands still bound, the *chèche* pushed back on his head, he was looking toward the window. At first Daru noticed only his huge lips, fat, smooth, almost Negroid; yet his nose was straight, his eyes were dark and full of fever. The *chèche* revealed an obstinate forehead and, under the weathered skin now rather discoloured by the cold, the whole face had a restless and rebellious look that struck Daru when the Arab, turning his face toward him, looked him straight in the eyes. "Go into the other room," said the schoolmaster, "and I'll make you some mint tea." "Thanks," Balducci said. "What a chore! How I long for retirement." And addressing his prisoner in Arabic: "Come on, you." The Arab got up and, slowly, holding his bound wrists in front of him, went into the classroom.

With the tea, Daru brought a chair. But Balducci was already enthroned on the nearest pupil's desk and the Arab had squatted against the teacher's platform facing the stove, which stood between the desk and the window. When he held out the glass of tea to the prisoner, Daru hesitated at the sight of his bound hands. "He might perhaps be untied." "Sure," said Balducci. "That was for the trip." He started to get to his feet. But Daru, setting the glass on the floor, had knelt beside the Arab. Without saying anything, the Arab watched him with his feverish eyes. Once his hands were free, he rubbed his swollen wrists against each other, took the glass of tea, and sucked up the burning liquid in swift little sips.

"Good," said Daru. "And where are you headed?"

Balducci withdrew his moustache from the tea. "Here, son."

"Odd pupils! And you're spending the night?"

"No. I'm going back to El Ameur. And you will deliver this fellow to Tinguit. He is expected at police headquarters."

Balducci was looking at Daru with a friendly little smile.

"What's this story?" asked the schoolmaster. "Are you pulling my leg?"

"No, son. Those are the orders."

"The orders? I'm not ..." Daru hesitated, not wanting to hurt the old Corsican. "I mean, that's not my job."

"What! What's the meaning of that? In wartime people do all kinds of jobs."

"Then I'll wait for the declaration of war!"

Balducci nodded.

"O.K. But the orders exist and they concern you too. Things are brewing, it appears. There is talk of a forthcoming revolt. We are mobilized, in a way."

Daru still had his obstinate look.

"Listen, son," Balducci said. "I like you and you must understand. There's only a dozen of us at El Ameur to patrol throughout the whole territory of a small department and I must get back in a hurry. I was told to hand this guy over to you and return without delay. He couldn't be kept there. His village was beginning to stir; they wanted to take him back. You must take him to Tinguit tomorrow before the day is over. Twenty kilometres shouldn't faze a husky fellow like you. After that, all will be over. You'll come back to your pupils and your comfortable life."

Behind the wall the horse could be heard snorting and pawing the earth. Daru was looking out the window. Decidedly, the weather was clearing and the light was increasing over the snowy plateau. When all the snow was melted, the sun would take over again and once more would burn the fields of stone. For days, still, the unchanging sky would shed its dry light on the solitary expanse where nothing had any connection with man.

"After all," he said, turning around toward Balducci, "what did he do?" And, before the gendarme had opened his mouth, he asked: "Does he speak French?"

"No, not a word. We had been looking for him for a month, but they were hiding him. He killed his cousin."

"Is he against us?"

"I don't think so. But you can never be sure."

"Why did he kill?"

"A family squabble, I think. One owed the other grain, it seems. It's not at all clear. In short, he killed his cousin with a billhook. You know, like a sheep, *kreezk!*"

Balducci made the gesture of drawing a blade across his throat and the Arab, his attention attracted, watched him with a sort of anxiety. Daru felt a sudden wrath against the man, against all men with their rotten spite, their tireless hates, their bloodlust.

But the kettle was singing on the stove. He served Balducci more tea, hesitated, then served the Arab again, who, a second time, drank avidly. His raised arms made the *jellaba* fall open and the schoolmaster saw his thin, muscular chest.

"Thanks, kid," Balducci said. "And now, I'm off."

He got up and went toward the Arab, taking a small rope from his pocket.

"What are you doing?" Daru asked dryly.

Balducci, disconcerted, showed him the rope.

"Don't bother."

The old gendarme hesitated. "It's up to you. Of course, you are armed?"

"I have my shotgun."

"Where?"

"In the trunk."

"You ought to have it near your bed."

"Why? I have nothing to fear."

"You're crazy, son. If there's an uprising, no one is safe, we're all in the same boat."

"I'll defend myself. I'll have time to see them coming."

Balducci began to laugh, then suddenly the moustache covered the white teeth.

"You'll have time? O.K. That's just what I was saying. You have always been a little cracked. That's why I like you, my son was like that."

At the same time he took out his revolver and put it on the desk.

"Keep it; I don't need two weapons from here to El Ameur."

The revolver shone against the black paint of the table. When the gendarme turned toward him, the schoolmaster caught the smell of leather and horseflesh.

"Listen, Balducci," Daru said suddenly, "every bit of this disgusts me, and first of all your fellow here. But I won't hand him over. Fight, yes, if I have to. But not that."

The old gendarme stood in front of him and looked at him severely.

"You're being a fool," he said slowly. "I don't like it either. You don't get used to putting a rope on a man even after years of it, and you're even ashamed—yes, ashamed. But you can't let them have their way."

"I won't hand him over," Daru said again.

"It's an order, son, and I repeat it."

"That's right. Repeat to them what I've said to you: I won't hand him over."

Balducci made a visible effort to reflect. He looked at the Arab and at Daru. At last he decided.

"No, I won't tell them anything. If you want to drop us, go ahead; I'll not denounce you. I have an order to deliver the prisoner and I'm doing so. And now you'll just sign this paper for me."

"There's no need. I'll not deny that you left him with me."

"Don't be mean with me. I know you'll tell the truth. You're from hereabouts and you are a man. But you must sign, that's the rule."

Daru opened his drawer, took out a little square bottle of purple ink, the red wooden penholder with the "sergeant-major" pen he used for making models of penmanship, and signed. The gendarme carefully folded the paper and put it into his wallet. Then he moved toward the door.

"I'll see you off," Daru said.

"No," said Balducci. "There's no use being polite. You insulted me."

He looked at the Arab, motionless in the same spot, sniffed peevishly, and turned away toward the door. "Goodbye, son," he said. The door shut behind him. Balducci appeared suddenly outside the window and then disappeared. His footsteps were muffled by the snow. The horse stirred on the other side of the wall and several chickens fluttered in fright. A moment later Balducci reappeared outside the window leading the horse by the bridle. He walked toward the little rise without turning around and disappeared from sight with the horse following him. A big stone could be heard bouncing down. Daru walked back toward the prisoner, who, without stirring, never took his eyes off him. "Wait," the schoolmaster said in Arabic and went toward the bedroom. As he was going through the door, he had a second thought, went to the desk, took the revolver, and stuck it in his pocket. Then, without looking back, he went into his room.

For some time he lay on his couch watching the sky gradually close over, listening to the silence. It was this silence that had seemed painful to him during the first days here, after the war. He had requested a post in the little town at the base of the foothills separating the upper plateaus from the desert. There, rocky walls, green and black to the north, pink and lavender to the south, marked the frontier of eternal summer. He had been named to a post farther north, on the plateau itself. In the beginning, the solitude and the silence had been hard for him on these wastelands peopled only by stones. Occasionally, furrows suggested cultivation, but they had been dug to uncover a certain kind of stone good for building. The only ploughing here was to harvest rocks. Elsewhere a thin layer of soil accumulated in the hollows would be scraped out to enrich paltry village gardens. This is the way it was: bare rock covered three quarters of the region. Towns sprang up, flourished, then disappeared; men came by, loved one another or fought bitterly, then died. No one in this desert, neither he nor his guest, mattered. And yet, outside this desert neither of them, Daru knew, could have really lived.

When he got up, no noise came from the classroom. He was amazed at the unmixed joy he derived from the mere thought that the Arab might have fled and that he would be alone with no decision to make. But the prisoner was there. He had merely stretched out between the stove and the desk. With eyes open, he was staring at the ceiling. In that position, his thick lips were particularly noticeable, giving him a pouting look. "Come," said Daru. The Arab got up and followed him. In the bedroom, the schoolmaster pointed to a chair near the table under the window. The Arab sat down without taking his eyes off Daru.

"Are you hungry?"

"Yes," the prisoner said.

Daru set the table for two. He took flour and oil, shaped a cake in a frying pan, and lighted the little stove that functioned on bottled gas. While the cake was cooking, he went out to the shed to get cheese, eggs, dates, and condensed milk. When the cake was done he set it on the window sill to cool, heated some condensed milk diluted with water, and beat up the eggs into an omelette. In one of his motions he knocked against the revolver stuck in his right pocket. He set the bowl down, went into the classroom, and put the revolver in his desk drawer. When he came back to the room, night was falling. He put on the light and served the Arab. "Eat," he said. The Arab took a piece of the cake, lifted it eagerly to his mouth, and stopped short.

"And you?" he asked.

"After you. I'll eat too."

The thick lips opened slightly. The Arab hesitated, then bit into the cake determinedly.

The meal over, the Arab looked at the schoolmaster. "Are you the judge?"

"No, I'm simply keeping you until tomorrow."

"Why do you eat with me?"

"I'm hungry."

The Arab fell silent. Daru got up and went out. He brought back a folding bed from the shed, set it up between the table and the stove, perpendicular to his own bed. From a large suitcase which, upright in a corner, served as a shelf for papers, he took two blankets and arranged them on the camp bed. Then he stopped, felt useless, and sat down on his bed. There was nothing more to do or to get ready. He had to look at this man. He looked at him, therefore, trying to imagine his face bursting with rage. He couldn't do so. He could see nothing but the dark yet shining eyes and the animal mouth.

"Why did you kill him?" he asked in a voice whose hostile tone surprised him.

The Arab looked away.

"He ran away. I ran after him."

He raised his eyes to Daru again and they were full of a sort of woeful interrogation. "Now what will they do to me?"

"Are you afraid?"

He stiffened, turning his eyes away.

"Are you sorry?"

The Arab stared at him open-mouthed. Obviously he did not understand. Daru's annoyance was growing. At the same time he felt awkward and self-conscious with his big body wedged between the two beds.

"Lie down there," he said impatiently. "That's your bed."

The Arab didn't move. He called to Daru:

"Tell me!"

The schoolmaster looked at him.

"Is the gendarme coming back tomorrow?"

"I don't know."

"Are you coming with us?"

"I don't know. Why?"

The prisoner got up and stretched out on top of the blankets, his feet toward the window. The light from the electric bulb shone straight into his eyes and he closed them at once.

"Why?" Daru repeated, standing beside the bed.

The Arab opened his eyes under the blinding light and looked at him, trying not to blink.

"Come with us," he said.

In the middle of the night, Daru was still not asleep. He had gone to bed after undressing completely; he generally slept naked. But when he suddenly realized that he had nothing on, he hesitated. He felt vulnerable and the temptation came to him to put his clothes back on. Then he shrugged his shoulders; after all, he wasn't a child and, if need be, he could break his adversary in two. From his bed he could observe him, lying on his back, still motionless with his eyes closed under the harsh light. When Daru turned out the light, the darkness seemed to coagulate all of a sudden. Little by little, the night came back to life in the window where the starless sky was stirring gently. The schoolmaster soon made out the body lying at his feet. The Arab still did not move, but his eyes seemed open. A faint wind was prowling around the schoolhouse. Perhaps it would drive away the clouds and the sun would reappear.

During the night the wind increased. The hens fluttered a little and then were silent. The Arab turned over on his side with his back to Daru, who thought he heard him moan. Then he listened for his guest's breathing, become heavier and more regular. He listened to that breath so close to him and mused without being able to go to sleep. In this room where he had been sleeping alone for a year, this presence bothered him. But it bothered him also by imposing on him a sort of brotherhood he knew well but refused to accept in the present circumstances. Men who share the same rooms, soldiers or prisoners, develop a strange alliance as if, having cast off their armour with their clothing, they fraternized every evening, over and above their differences, in the ancient community of dream and fatigue. But Daru shook himself; he didn't like such musings, and it was essential to sleep.

A little later, however, when the Arab stirred slightly, the schoolmaster was still not asleep. When the prisoner made a second move, he stiffened, on the alert. The Arab was lifting himself slowly on his arms with almost the motion of a sleepwalker. Seated upright in bed, he waited motionless without turning his head toward Daru, as if he were listening attentively. Daru did not stir; it had just occurred to him that the revolver was still in the drawer of his desk. It was better to act at once. Yet he continued to observe the prisoner, who, with the same slithery motion, put his feet on the ground, waited again, then began to stand up slowly. Daru was about to call out to him when the Arab began to walk, in a quite natural but extraordinarily silent way. He was heading toward the door at the end of the room that opened into the shed. He lifted the latch with precaution and went out, pushing the door behind him but without shutting it. Daru had not stirred. "He is running away," he merely thought. "Good riddance!" Yet he listened attentively. The hens were not fluttering; the guest must be on the plateau. A faint sound of water reached him, and he didn't know what it was until the Arab again stood framed in the doorway, closed the door carefully, and came back to bed without a sound. Then Daru turned his back on him and fell asleep. Still later he seemed, from the depths of his sleep, to hear furtive steps around the schoolhouse. "I'm dreaming! I'm dreaming!" he repeated to himself. And he went on sleeping.

When he awoke, the sky was clear; the loose window let in a cold, pure air. The Arab was asleep, hunched up under the blankets now, his mouth open, utterly relaxed. But when Daru shook him, he started dreadfully, staring at Daru with wild eyes as if he had never seen him and such a frightened expression that the schoolmaster stepped back. "Don't be afraid. It's me. You must eat." The Arab nodded his head and said yes. Calm had returned to his face, but his expression was vacant and listless.

The coffee was ready. They drank it seated together on the folding bed as they munched their pieces of the cake. Then Daru led the Arab under the shed and showed him the faucet where he washed. He went back into the room, folded the blankets and the bed, made his own bed, and put the room in order. Then he went through the classroom and out onto the terrace. The sun was already rising in the blue sky; a soft, bright light was bathing the deserted plateau. On the ridge the snow was melting in spots. The stones were about to reappear. Crouched on the edge of the plateau, the schoolmaster looked at the deserted expanse. He thought of Balducci. He had hurt him, for he had sent him off in a way as if he didn't want to be associated with him. He could still hear the gendarme's farewell and, without knowing why, he felt strangely empty and vulnerable. At that moment, from the other side of the schoolhouse, the prisoner coughed. Daru listened to him almost despite himself and then, furious, threw a pebble that whistled through the air before sinking into the snow. That man's stupid crime revolted him, but to hand him over was contrary to honour. Merely thinking of it made him smart with humiliation. And he cursed at one and the same time his own people who had sent him this Arab and the Arab too who had dared to kill and not managed to get away. Daru got up, walked in a circle on the terrace, waited motionless, and then went back into the schoolhouse.

The Arab, leaning over the cement floor of the shed, was washing his teeth with two fingers. Daru looked at him and said: "Come." He went back into the room ahead of the prisoner. He slipped a hunting-jacket on over his sweater and put on walking-shoes. Standing, he waited until the Arab had put on his *chèche* and sandals. They went into the classroom and the schoolmaster pointed to the exit, saying: "Go ahead." The fellow didn't budge. "I'm coming," said Daru. The Arab went out. Daru went back into the room and made a package of pieces of rusk, dates, and sugar. In the classroom, before going out, he hesitated a second in front of his desk, then crossed the threshold and locked the door. "That's the way," he said. He started toward the east, followed by the prisoner. But, a short distance from the schoolhouse, he thought he heard a slight sound behind them. He retraced his steps and examined the surroundings of the house; there was no one there. The Arab watched him without seeming to understand. "Come on," said Daru.

They walked for an hour and rested beside a sharp peak of limestone. The snow was melting faster and faster and the sun was drinking up the puddles at once, rapidly cleaning the plateau, which gradually dried and vibrated like the air itself. When they resumed walking, the ground rang under their feet. From time to time a bird rent the space in front of them with a joyful cry. Daru breathed in deeply the fresh morning light. He felt a sort of rapture before the vast familiar expanse, now almost entirely yellow under its dome of blue sky. They walked an hour more, descending toward the south. They reached a level height made up of crumbly rocks. From there on, the plateau sloped down, eastward, toward a low plain where there were a few spindly trees and, to the south, toward outcroppings of rock that gave the landscape a chaotic look.

Daru surveyed the two directions. There was nothing but the sky on the horizon. Not a man could be seen. He turned toward the Arab, who was looking at him blankly. Daru held out the package to him. "Take it," he said.

"There are dates, bread, and sugar. You can hold out for two days. Here are a thousand francs too." The Arab took the package and the money but kept his full hands at chest level as if he didn't know what to do with what was being given him. "Now look," the schoolmaster said as he pointed in the direction of the east, "there's the way to Tinguit. You have a two-hour walk. At Tinguit you'll find the administration and the police. They are expecting you." The Arab looked toward the east, still holding the package and the money against his chest. Daru took his elbow and turned him rather roughly toward the south. At the foot of the height on which they stood could be seen a faint path. "That's the trail across the plateau. In a day's walk from here you'll find pasturelands and the first nomads. They'll take you in and shelter you according to their law." The Arab had now turned toward Daru and a sort of panic was visible in his expression. "Listen," he said. Daru shook his head: "No, be quiet. Now I'm leaving you." He turned his back on him, took two long steps in the direction of the school, looked hesitantly at the motionless Arab, and started off again. For a few minutes he heard nothing but his own step resounding on the cold ground and did not turn his head. A moment later, however, he turned around. The Arab was still there on the edge of the hill, his arms hanging now, and he was looking at the schoolmaster. Daru felt something rise in his throat. But he swore with impatience, waved vaguely, and started off again. He had already gone some distance when he again stopped and looked. There was no longer anyone on the hill.

Daru hesitated. The sun was now rather high in the sky and was beginning to beat down on his head. The schoolmaster retraced his steps, at first somewhat uncertainly, then with decision. When he reached the little hill, he was bathed in sweat. He climbed it as fast as he could and stopped, out of breath, at the top. The rock-fields to the south stood out sharply against the blue sky, but on the plain to the east a steamy heat was already rising. And in that slight haze, Daru, with heavy heart, made out the Arab walking slowly on the road to prison.

A little later, standing before the window of the classroom, the schoolmaster was watching the clear light bathing the whole surface of the plateau, but he hardly saw it. Behind him on the blackboard, among the winding French rivers, sprawled the clumsily chalked-up words he had just read: "You handed over our brother. You will pay for this." Daru looked at the sky, the plateau, and, beyond, the invisible lands stretching all the way to the sea. In this vast landscape he had loved so much, he was alone.

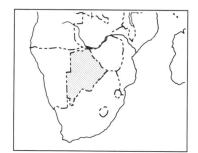

The Wind and a Boy

BY BESSIE HEAD

Like all the village boys, Friedman had a long wind blowing for him, but perhaps the enchanted wind that blew for him filled the whole world with magic.

Until they became ordinary, dull grown men, who drank beer and made babies, the little village boys were a special set all on their own. They were kings whom no one ruled. They wandered where they willed from dawn to dusk and only condescended to come home at dusk because they were afraid of the horrible things in the dark that might pounce on them. Unlike the little girls who adored household chores and drawing water, it was only now and then that the boys showed themselves as useful attachments to any household. When the first hard rains of summer fell, small dark shapes, quite naked except for their loin-cloths, sped out of the village into the bush. They knew that the first downpour had drowned all the wild rabbits, moles, and porcupines in their burrows in the earth. As they crouched down near the entrances to the burrows, they would see a small drowned nose of an animal peeping out; they knew it had struggled to emerge from its burrow, flooded by the sudden rush of storm water and as they pulled out the animal, they would say, pityingly:

"Birds have more sense than rabbits, moles, and porcupines. They build their homes in trees." But it was hunting made easy, for no matter how hard a boy and his dog ran, a wild rabbit ran ten times faster; a porcupine hurled his poisonous quills into the body; and a mole stayed where he thought it was safe—deep under the ground. So it was with inordinate pride that the boys carried home armfuls of dead animals for their families to feast on for many days. Apart from that, the boys lived very much as they pleased, with the wind and their own games.

Now and then, the activities of a single family could captivate the imagination and hearts of all the people of their surroundings; for years and years, the combination of the boy, Friedman, and his grandmother, Sejosenye, made the people of Ga-Sefete-Molemo ward smile, laugh, then cry.

They smiled at his first two phases. Friedman came home as a small bundle from the hospital, a bundle his grandmother nursed carefully near her bosom and crooned to day and night with extravagant care and tenderness.

"She is like that," people remarked, "because he may be the last child she will ever nurse. Sejosenye is old now and will die one of these days; the child is a gift to keep her heart warm."

Indeed, all Sejosenye's children were grown, married, and had left home. Of all her children, only her last-born daughter was unmarried and Friedman was the result of some casual mating she had indulged in, in a town a hundred and sixty kilometres away where she had a job as a typist. She wanted to return to her job almost immediately, so she handed the child over to her mother and that was that; she could afford to forget him as he had a real mother now. During all the time that Sejosenye haunted the hospital, awaiting her bundle, a friendly foreign doctor named Friedman took a fancy to her maternal, grandmotherly ways. He made a habit of walking out of his path to talk to her. She never forgot it and on receiving her bundle she called the baby, Friedman.

They smiled at his second phase, a small dark shadow who toddled silently and gravely beside a very tall grandmother; wherever the grandmother went, there went Friedman. Most women found this phase of the restless, troublesome toddler tedious; they dumped the toddler onto one of their younger girls and were off to weddings and visits on their own.

"Why can't you leave your handbag at home some times, granny?" they said.

"Oh, he's no trouble," Sejosenye would reply.

They began to laugh at his third phase. Almost overnight he turned into a tall, spindly-legged, graceful gazelle with large, grave eyes. There was an odd, musical lilt to his speech and when he teased, or was up to mischief, he moved his head on his long thin neck from side to side like a cobra. It was he who became the king of kings of all the boys in his area; he could turn his hand to anything and made the best wire cars with their wheels of shoe polish tins. All his movements were neat, compact, decisive, and for his age he was a boy who knew his own mind. They laughed at his knowingness and certainty on all things, for he was like the grandmother who had had a flaming youth all her own too. Sejosenye had scandalized the whole village in her days of good morals by leaving her own village ward to live with a married man in Ga-Sefete-Molemo ward. She had won him from his wife and married him and then lived down the scandal in the way only natural queens can. Even in old age, she was still impressive. She sailed through the village, head in the air, with a quiet, almost expressionless face. She had developed large buttocks as time went by and they announced their presence firmly in rhythm with her walk.

Another of Sejosenye's certainties was that she was a woman who could plough, but it was like a special gift. Each season, in drought or hail or sun, she removed herself to her lands. She not only ploughed but nursed and brooded over her crops. She was there all the time till the corn ripened and the birds had to be chased off the land, till harvesting and threshing were done; so that even in drought years with their scanty rain, she came home with some crops. She was the envy of all the women of the surroundings.

"Sejosenye always eats fine things in her house," they said. "She ploughs and then sits down for many months and enjoys the fruits of her labour."

The women also envied her beautiful grandson. There was something special there, so that even when Friedman moved into his bad phase, they forgave him crimes other boys received a sound thrashing for. The small boys were terrible thieves who harassed people by stealing their food and money. It was all a part of the games they played but one which people did not like. Of them all, Friedman was the worst thief, so that his name was mentioned more and more in any thieving that had been uncovered.

"But Friedman showed us how to open the window with a knife and string," the sobbing, lashed boys would protest.

"Friedman isn't as bad as you," the parents would reply, irrationally. They were hypnotized by a beautiful creature. The boy Friedman, who had become a real nuisance by then, also walked around as though he were special. He couldn't possibly be a thief and he added an aloof, offended, disdainful expression to his pretty face. He wasn't just an ordinary sort of boy in Ga-Sefete-Molemo ward. He was ...

It happened, quite accidentally, that his grandmother told him all those stories about the hunters, warriors, and emissaries of old. She was normally a quiet, absent-minded woman, given to dreaming by herself but she liked to sing the boy a little song now and then as they sat by the outdoor fire. A lot of them were church songs and rather sad; they more or less passed as her bedtime prayer at night—she was one of the old church-goers. Now and then she added a quaint little song to her repertoire and as the nighttime fire-light flames flickered between them, she never failed to note that this particular song was always well received by the boy. A little light would awaken in his eyes and he would bend forward and listen attentively.

"Welcome, Robinson Crusoe, welcome," she would sing, in clear, sweet tones. "How could you stay, so long away, Robinson how could you do so?"

When she was very young, Sejosenye had attended the mission school of the village for about a year; made a slight acquaintance with the ABC and one, two, three, four, five, and the little song about Robinson Crusoe. But girls didn't need an education in those days when ploughing and marriage made up their whole world. Yet Robinson Crusoe lived on as a gay and out-of-context memory of her schooldays. One evening the boy leaned forward and asked:

—"Is that a special praise-poem song for Robinson Crusoe, grandmother?"

"Oh yes," she replied, smiling.

"It appears that the people liked Robinson Crusoe much," the boy observed. "Did he do great things for them?"

"Oh yes," she said, smiling.

"What great things did he do?" the boy asked, pointedly.

"They say he was a hunter who went by Gweta side and killed an elephant all by himself," she said, making up a story on the spot. "Oh! In those days, no man could kill an elephant by himself. All the regiments had to join together and each man had to thrust his sword into the side of the elephant before it died. Well, Robinson Crusoe was gone many days and people wondered about him: 'Perhaps he has been eaten by a lion,' they said. 'Robinson likes to be a solitary person and do foolish things. We won't ever go out into the bush by ourselves because we know it is dangerous.' Well, one day, Robinson suddenly appeared in their midst and people could see that he had a great thing on his mind. They all gathered around him. He said: 'I have killed an elephant for all the people.' The people were surprised: 'Robinson!' they said. 'It is impossible! How did you do it? The very thought of an elephant approaching the village makes us shiver!' And Robinson said: 'Ah, people, I saw a terrible sight! I was standing at the feet of the elephant. I was just a small ant. I could not see the world any more. Elephant was above me until his very head touched the sky and his ears spread out like great wings. He was angry but I only looked into one eye which was turning round and round in anger. What to do now? I thought it better to put that eye out. I raised my spear and threw it at the angry eye. People! It went right inside. Elephant said not a word and he fell to one side. Come I will show you what I have done.' Then the women cried in joy: 'Loo-loo-loo!' They ran to fetch their containers as some wanted the meat of the elephant; some wanted the fat. The men made their knives sharp. They would make shoes and many things from the skin and bones. There was something for all the people in the great work Robinson Crusoe did."

All this while, as he listened to the story, the boy's eyes had glowed softly. At the end of it, he drew in a long breath.

"Grandmother," he whispered, adroitly stepping into the role of Robinson Crusoe, the great hunter. "One day, I'm going to be like that. I'm going to be a hunter like Robinson Crusoe and bring meat to all the people." He paused for breath and then added tensely: "And what other great thing did Robinson Crusoe do?"

"Tsaa!" she said, clicking her tongue in exhaustion. "Am I then going away that I must tell *all* the stories at once?"

Although his image of Robinson Crusoe, the great hunter, was never to grow beyond his everyday boyish activities of pushing wire cars, hunting in the fields for wild rabbits, climbing trees to pull down old bird's nests, and yelling out in alarm to find that a small snake now occupied the abandoned abode, or racing against the wind with the spoils of his latest theft, the stories awakened a great tenderness in him. If Robinson Crusoe was not churning up the dust in deadly hand-to-hand combat with an enemy, he was crossing swollen rivers and wild jungles as the great messenger and ambassador of the chief—all his activities were touchingly in aid of, or in defence of, the people. One day Friedman expressed this awakened compassion for life in a strange way. After a particularly violent storm, people found their huts invaded by many small mice and they were hard-pressed to rid themselves of these pests. Sejosenye ordered Friedman to kill the mice.

"But grandmother," he protested. "They have come to us for shelter. They lost all their homes in the storm. It's better that I put them in a box and carry them out into the fields again once the rains are over."

She had laughed in surprise at this and spread the story around among her women friends, who smiled tenderly then said to their own offspring: "Friedman isn't as bad as you."

Life and its responsibilities began to weigh down heavily on Friedman as he approached his fourteenth year. Less time was spent in boyish activities. He grew more and more devoted to his grandmother and concerned to assist her in every way. He wanted a bicycle so that he might run up and down to the shops for her, deliver messages, or do any other chore she might have in mind. His mother, who worked in a town far away, sent him the money to purchase the bicycle. The gift brought the story of his life abruptly to a close.

Towards the beginning of the rainy season, he accompanied his grandmother to her lands which were some thirty kilometres outside the village. They sowed seed together after the hired tractor had turned up the land but the boy's main chore was to keep the household pot filled with meat. Sometimes they ate birds Friedman had trapped, sometimes they ate fried tortoise meat or wild rabbit; but there was always something as the bush abounded with animal life. Sejosenye only had to take a bag of mealie meal, packets of sugar, tea, and powdered milk as provisions for their stay at the lands; meat was never a problem. Midway through the ploughing season, she began to run out of sugar, tea, and milk.

"Friedman," she said that evening, "I shall wake you early tomorrow morning. You will have to take the bicycle into the village and purchase some more sugar, tea, and milk."

He was up at dawn with the birds, a solitary figure cycling on a pathway through the empty bush. By nine, he had reached the village and first made his way to Ga-Sefete-Molemo ward and the yard of a friend of his grandmother, who gave him a cup of tea and a plate of porridge. Then he put one foot on the bicycle and turned to smile at the woman with his beautiful gazelle eyes. His smile was to linger vividly before her for many days as a short while later, hard pounding feet came running into her yard to report that Friedman was dead.

He pushed the bicycle through the winding, sandy pathway of the village ward, reached the high embankment of the main road, peddled vigorously up it, and out of the corner of his eye, saw a small green truck speeding towards him. In the devil-may-care fashion of all the small boys, he cycled right into its path, turned his head, and smiled appealingly at the driver. The truck caught him on the front bumper, squashed the bicycle, and dragged the boy along at a crazy speed for another hundred metres, dropped him, and careered on another twenty metres before coming to a halt. The boy's pretty face was a smear all along the road and he only had a torso left.

People of Ga-Sefete-Molemo ward never forgot the last coherent words Sejosenye spoke to the police. A number of them climbed into the police truck and accompanied it to her lands. They saw her walk slowly and enquiringly towards the truck, they heard the matter-of-fact voice of the policeman announce the death, then they heard Sejosenye say piteously: "Can't you return those words back?"

She turned away from them, either to collect her wits or the few possessions she had brought with her. Her feet and buttocks quivered anxiously as she stumbled towards her hut. Then her feet tripped her up and she fell to the ground like a stunned log.

The people of Ga-Sefete-Molemo ward buried the boy Friedman but none of them would go near the hospital where Sejosenye lay. The stories brought to them by way of the nurses were too terrible for words. They said the old woman sang and laughed and talked to herself all the time. So they merely asked each other: "Have you been to see Mma-Sejosenye?" "I'm afraid I cannot. It would kill my heart." Two weeks later, they buried her.

As was village habit, the incident was discussed thoroughly from all sides till it was understood. In this timeless, sleepy village, the goats stood and suckled their young ones on the main road or lay down and took their afternoon naps there. The motorists either stopped for them or gave way. But it appeared that the driver of the truck had neither brakes on his car nor a driving licence. He belonged to the new, rich civil-servant class whose salaries had become fantastically high since independence. They had to have cars in keeping with their new status; they had to have any car, as long as it was a car; they were in such a hurry about everything that they couldn't be bothered to take driving lessons. And thus progress, development, and a pre-occupation with status and living standards first announced themselves to the village. It looked like being an ugly story with many decapitated bodies on the main road.

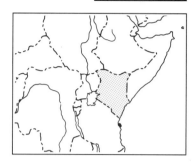

The Rain Came

BY GRACE OGOT

The chief was still far from the gate when his daughter Oganda saw him. She ran to meet him. Breathlessly she asked her father, "What is the news, great Chief? Everyone in the village is anxiously waiting to hear when it will rain." Labong'o held out his hands for his daughter but he did not say a word. Puzzled by her father's cold attitude Oganda ran back to the village to warn the others that the chief was back.

The atmosphere in the village was tense and confused. Everyone moved aimlessly and fussed in the yard without actually doing any work. A young woman whispered to her co-wife, "If they have not solved this rain business today, the chief will crack." They had watched him getting thinner and thinner as the people kept on pestering him. "Our cattle lie dying in the fields," they reported. "Soon it will be our children and then ourselves. Tell us what to do to save our lives, oh great Chief." So the chief had daily prayed with the Almighty through the ancestors to deliver them from their distress.

Instead of calling the family together and giving them the news immediately, Labong'o went to his own hut, a sign that he was not to be disturbed. Having replaced the shutter, he sat in the dimly lit hut to contemplate.

It was no longer a question of being the chief of hunger-stricken people that weighed Labong'o's heart. It was the life of his only daughter that was at stake. At the time when Oganda came to meet him, he saw the glittering chain shining around her waist. The prophecy was complete. "It is Oganda, Oganda, my only daughter, who must die so young." Labong'o burst into tears before finishing the sentence. The chief must not weep. Society had declared him the bravest of men. But Labong'o did not care anymore. He assumed the position of a simple father and wept bitterly. He loved his people, the Luo, but what were the Luo for him without Oganda? Her life had brought a new life in Labong'o's world and he ruled better than he could remember. How would the spirit of the village survive his beautiful daughter? "There are so many homes and so many parents who have daughters. Why choose this one? She is all I have." Labong'o spoke as if the ancestors were there in the hut and he could see them face to face. Perhaps they were there, warning him to remember his promise on the day he was enthroned when he said aloud, before the elders, "I will lay down life, if necessary, and the life of my household, to save this tribe from the hands of the enemy." "Deny! Deny!" he could hear the voice of his forefathers mocking him.

When Labong'o was consecrated chief he was only a young man. Unlike his father, he ruled for many years with only one wife. But people rebuked him because his only wife did not bear him a daughter. He married a second, a third, and a fourth wife. But they all gave birth to male children. When Labong'o married a fifth wife she bore him a daughter. They called her Oganda, meaning "beans," because her skin was very fair. Out of Labong'o's twenty children, Oganda was the only girl. Though she was the chief's favourite, her mother's co-wives swallowed their jealous feelings and showered her with love. After all, they said, Oganda was a female child whose days in the royal family were numbered. She would soon marry at a tender age and leave the enviable position to someone else.

Never in his life had he been faced with such an impossible decision. Refusing to yield to the rainmaker's request would mean sacrificing the whole tribe, putting the interests of the individual above those of the society. More than that. It would mean disobeying the ancestors, and most probably wiping the Luo people from the surface of the earth. On the other hand, to let Oganda die as a ransom for the people would permanently cripple Labong'o spiritually. He knew he would never be the same chief again.

The words of Ndithi, the medicine man, still echoed in his ears. "Podho, the ancestor of the Luo, appeared to me in a dream last night, and he asked me to speak to the chief and the people," Ndithi had said to the gathering of tribesmen. "A young woman who has not known a man must die so that the country may have rain. While Podho was still talking to me, I saw a young woman standing at the lakeside, her hands raised, above her head. Her skin was as fair as the skin of young deer in the wilderness. Her tall slender figure stood like a lonely reed at the riverbank. Her sleepy eyes wore a sad look like that of a bereaved mother. She wore a gold ring on her left ear, and a glittering brass chain around her waist. As I still marvelled at the beauty of this young woman, Podho told me, 'Out of all the women in this land, we have chosen this one. Let her offer herself a sacrifice to the lake monster! And on that day, the rain will come down in torrents. Let everyone stay at home on that day, lest he be carried away by the floods'."

Outside there was a strange stillness, except for the thirsty birds that sang lazily on the dying trees. The blinding midday heat had forced the people to retire to their huts. Not far away from the chief's hut, two guards were snoring away quietly. Labong'o removed his crown and the large eagle head that hung loosely on his shoulders. He left the hut, and instead of asking Nyabog'o the messenger to beat the drum, he went straight and beat it himself. In no time the whole household had assembled under the siala tree where he usually addressed them. He told Oganda to wait a while in her grandmother's hut.

When Labong'o stood to address his household, his voice was hoarse and the tears choked him. He started to speak, but words refused to leave his lips. His wives and sons knew there was great danger. Perhaps their enemies had declared war on them. Labong'o's eyes were red, and they could see he had been weeping. At last he told them. "One whom we love and treasure must be taken away from us. Oganda is to die." Labong'o's voice was so faint, that he could not hear it himself. But he continued. "The ancestors have chosen her to be offered as a sacrifice to the lake monster in order that we may have rain."

They were completely stunned. As a confused murmur broke out, Oganda's mother fainted and was carried off to her own hut. But the other people rejoiced. They danced around singing and chanting, "Oganda is the lucky one to die for the people. If it is to save the people, let Oganda go."

In her grandmother's hut Oganda wondered what the whole family were discussing about her that she could not hear. Her grandmother's hut was well away from the chief's court and, much as she strained her ears, she could not hear what was said. "It must be marriage," she concluded. It was an accepted custom for the family to discuss their daughter's future marriage behind her back. A faint smile played on Oganda's lips as she thought of the several young men who swallowed saliva at the mere mention of her name.

There was Kech, the son of a neighbouring clan elder. Kech was very handsome. He had sweet, meek eyes and a roaring laughter. He would make a wonderful father, Oganda thought. But they would not be a good match. Kech was a bit too short to be her husband. It would humiliate her to have to look down at Kech each time she spoke to him. Then she thought of Dimo, the tall young man who had already distinguished himself as a brave warrior and an outstanding wrestler. Dimo adored Oganda, but Oganda thought he would make a cruel husband, always quarrelling and ready to fight. No, she did not like him. Oganda fingered the glittering chain on her waist as she thought of Osinda. A long time ago when she was quite young Osinda had given her that chain, and instead of wearing it around her neck several times, she wore it round her waist where it could stay permanently. She heard her heart pounding so loudly as she thought of him. She whispered, "Let it be you they are discussing, Osinda, the lovely one. Come now and take me away ..."

The lean figure in the doorway startled Oganda who was rapt in thought about the man she loved. "You have frightened me, Grandma," said Oganda laughing. "Tell me, is it my marriage you were discussing? You can take it from me that I won't marry any of them." A smile played on her lips again. She was coaxing the old lady to tell her quickly, to tell her they were pleased with Osinda.

In the open space outside the excited relatives were dancing and singing. They were coming to the hut now, each carrying a gift to put at Oganda's feet. As their singing got nearer Oganda was able to hear what they were saying: "If it is to save the people, if it is to give us rain, let Oganda go. Let Oganda die for her people, and for her ancestors." Was she mad to think that they were singing about her? How could she die? She found the lean figure of her grandmother barring the door. She could not get out. The look on her grandmother's face warned her that there was danger around the corner. "Grandma, it is not marriage then?" Oganda asked urgently. She suddenly felt panicky like a mouse cornered by a hungry cat. Forgetting that there was only one door in the hut Oganda fought desperately to find another exit. She must fight for her life. But there was none.

She closed her eyes, leapt like a wild tiger through the door, knocking her grandmother flat to the ground. There outside in mourning garments Labong'o stood motionless, his hands folded at the back. He held his daughter's hand and led her away from the excited crowd to the little red-painted hut where her mother was resting. Here he broke the news officially to his daughter.

For a long time the three souls who loved one another dearly sat in darkness. It was no good speaking. And even if they tried, the words could not have come out. In the past they had been like three cooking stones, sharing their burdens. Taking Oganda away from them would leave two useless stones which would not hold a cooking pot.

News that the beautiful daughter of the chief was to be sacrificed to give the people rain spread across the country like wind. At sunset the chief's village was full of relatives and friends who had come to congratulate Oganda. Many more were on their way coming, carrying their gifts. They would dance till morning to keep her company. And in the morning they would prepare her a big farewell feast. All these relatives thought it a great honour to be selected by the spirits to die, in order that the society may live. "Oganda's name will always remain a living name among us," they boasted.

But was it maternal love that prevented Minya from rejoicing with the other women? Was it the memory of the agony and pain of childbirth that made her feel so sorrowful? Or was it the deep warmth and understanding that passes between a suckling babe and her mother that made Oganda part of her life, her flesh? Of course it was an honour, a great honour, for her daughter to be chosen to die for the country. But what could she gain once her only daughter was blown away by the wind? There were so many other women in the land, why choose her daughter, her only child! Had human life any meaning at all—other women had houses full of children while she, Minya, had to lose her only child!

In the cloudless sky the moon shone brightly, and the numerous stars glittered with a bewitching beauty. The dancers of all age groups assembled to dance before Oganda, who sat close to her mother, sobbing quietly. All these years she had been with her people she thought she understood them. But now she discovered that she was a stranger among them. If they loved her as they had always professed why were they not making any attempt to save her? Did her people really understand what it felt like to die young? Unable to restrain her emotions any longer, she sobbed loudly as her age group got up to dance. They were young and beautiful and very soon they would marry and have their own children. They would have husbands to love and little huts for themselves. They would have reached maturity. Oganda touched the chain around her waist as she thought of Osinda. She wished Osinda was there too, among her friends. "Perhaps he is ill," she thought gravely. The chain comforted Oganda—she would die with it around her waist and wear it in the underground world.

In the morning a big feast was prepared for Oganda. The women prepared many different tasty dishes so that she could pick and choose. "People don't eat after death," they said. Delicious though the food looked, Oganda touched none of it. Let the happy people eat. She contented herself with sips of water from a little calabash.

The time for her departure was drawing near, and each minute was precious. It was a day's journey to the lake. She was to walk all night, passing through the great forest. But nothing could touch her, not even the denizens of the forest. She was already anointed with sacred oil. From the time Oganda received the sad news she had expected Osinda to appear any moment. But he was not there. A relative told her that Osinda was away on a private visit. Oganda realized that she would never see her beloved again.

In the late afternoon the whole village stood at the gate to say goodbye and to see her for the last time. Her mother wept on her neck for a long time. The great chief in a mourning skin came to the gate barefooted, and mingled with the people—a simple father in grief. He took off his wrist bracelet and put it on his daughter's wrist, saying, "You will always live among us. The spirit of our forefathers is with you."

Tongue-tied and unbelieving, Oganda stood there before the people. She had nothing to say. She looked at her home once more. She could hear her heart beating so painfully within her. All her childhood plans were coming to an end. She felt like a flower nipped in the bud never to enjoy the morning dew again. She looked at her weeping mother, and whispered, "Whenever you want to see me, always look at the sunset. I will be there."

Oganda turned southward to start her trek to the lake. Her parents, relatives, friends, and admirers stood at the gate and watched her go.

Her beautiful slender figure grew smaller and smaller till she mingled with the thin dry trees in the forest. As Oganda walked the lonely path that wound its way in the wilderness, she sang a song, and her own voice kept her company.

> *The ancestors have said Oganda must die*
> *The daughter of the chief must be sacrificed,*
> *When the lake monster feeds on my flesh.*
> *The people will have rain.*
> *Yes, the rain will come down in torrents.*
> *And the floods will wash away the sandy beaches*

When the daughter of the chief dies in the lake.
My age group has consented
My parents have consented
So have my friends and relatives.
Let Oganda die to give us rain.
My age group are young and ripe,
Ripe for womanhood and motherhood
But Oganda must die young,
Oganda must sleep with the ancestors.
Yes, rain will come down in torrents.

The red rays of the setting sun embraced Oganda, and she looked like a burning candle in the wilderness.

The people who came to hear her sad song were touched by her beauty. But they all said the same thing. "If it is to save the people, if it is to give us rain, then be not afraid. Your name will forever live among us."

At midnight Oganda was tired and weary. She could walk no more. She sat under a big tree, and having sipped water from her calabash, she rested her head on the tree trunk and slept.

When Oganda woke up in the morning the sun was high in the sky. After walking for many hours, she reached the *tong'*, a strip of land that separated the inhabited part of the country from the sacred place (*kar lamo*). No layman could enter this place and come out alive—only those who had direct contact with the spirits and the Almighty were allowed to enter this holy of holies. But Oganda had to pass through this sacred land on her way to the lake, which she had to reach at sunset.

A large crowd gathered to see her for the last time. Her voice was now hoarse and painful, but there was no need to worry anymore. Soon she would not have to sing. The crowd looked at Oganda sympathetically, mumbling words she could not hear. But none of them pleaded for life. As Oganda opened the gate, a child, a young child, broke loose from the crowd, and ran toward her. The child took a small earring from her sweaty hands and gave it to Oganda saying, "When you reach the world of the dead, give this earring to my sister. She died last week. She forgot this ring." Oganda, taken aback by the strange request, took the little ring, and handed her precious water and food to the child. She did not need them now. Oganda did not know whether to laugh or cry. She had heard mourners sending their love to their sweethearts, long dead, but this idea of sending gifts was new to her.

Oganda held her breath as she crossed the barrier to enter the sacred land. She looked appealingly at the crowd, but there was no response. Their minds were too preoccupied with their own survival. Rain was the precious medicine they were longing for, and the sooner Oganda could get to her destination the better.

A strange feeling possessed Oganda as she picked her way in the sacred land. There were strange noises that often startled her, and her first reaction was to take to her heels. But she remembered that she had to fulfill the wish of her people. She was exhausted, but the path was still winding. Then suddenly the path ended on sandy land. The water had retreated kilometres away from the shore leaving a wide stretch of sand. Beyond this was the vast expanse of water.

Oganda felt afraid. She wanted to picture the size and shape of the monster, but fear would not let her. The society did not talk about it, nor did the crying children who were silenced by the mention of its name. The sun was still up, but it was no longer hot. For a long time Oganda walked ankle-deep in the sand. She was exhausted and longed desperately for her calabash of water. As she moved on, she had a strange feeling that something was following her. Was it the monster? Her hair stood erect, and a cold paralyzing feeling ran along her spine. She looked behind, sideways, and in front, but there was nothing, except a cloud of dust.

Oganda pulled up and hurried but the feeling did not leave her, and her whole body became saturated with perspiration.

The sun was going down fast and the lake shore seemed to move along with it.

Oganda started to run. She must be at the lake before sunset. As she ran she heard a noise coming from behind. She looked back sharply, and something resembling a moving bush was frantically running after her. It was about to catch up with her.

Oganda ran with all her strength. She was now determined to throw herself into the water even before sunset. She did not look back, but the creature was upon her. She made an effort to cry out, as in a nightmare, but she could not hear her own voice. The creature caught up with Oganda. In the utter confusion, as Oganda came face with the unidentified creature, a strong hand grabbed her. But she fell flat on the sand and fainted.

When the lake breeze brought her back to consciousness, a man was bending over her. "..........!!" Oganda opened her mouth to speak, but she had lost her voice. She swallowed a mouthful of water poured into her mouth by the stranger.

"Osinda, Osinda! Please let me die. Let me run, the sun is going down. Let me die, let them have rain." Osinda fondled the glittering chain around Oganda's waist and wiped the tears from her face.

"We must escape quickly to the unknown land," Osinda said urgently. "We must run away from the wrath of the ancestors and the retaliation of the monster."

"But the curse is upon me, Osinda, I am no good to you anymore. And moreover the eyes of the ancestors will follow us everywhere and bad luck will befall us. Nor can we escape from the monster."

Oganda broke loose, afraid to escape, but Osinda grabbed her hands again.

"Listen to me, Oganda! Listen! Here are two coats!" He then covered the whole of Oganda's body, except her eyes, with a leafy attire made from the twigs of *Bwombwe*. "These will protect us from the eyes of the ancestors and the wrath of the monster. Now let us run out of here." He held Oganda's hand and they ran from the sacred land, avoiding the path that Oganda had followed.

The bush was thick, and the long grass entangled their feet as they ran. Halfway through the sacred land they stopped and looked back. The sun was almost touching the surface of the water. They were frightened. They continued to run, now faster, to avoid the sinking sun.

"Have faith, Oganda—that thing will not reach us."

When they reached the barrier and looked behind them trembling, only a tip of the sun could be seen above the water's surface.

"It is gone! It is gone!" Oganda wept, hiding her face in her hands.

"Weep not, daughter of the chief. Let us run, let us escape."

There was a bright lightning. They looked up, frightened. Above them black furious clouds started to gather. They began to run. Then the thunder roared, and the rain came down in torrents.

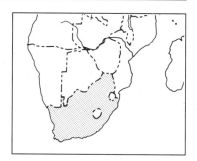

Ha'penny

BY ALAN PATON

Of the six hundred boys at the reformatory, about one hundred were from ten to fourteen years of age. My Department had from time to time expressed the intention of taking them away, and of establishing a special institution for them, more like an industrial school than a reformatory. This would have been a good thing, for their offences were very trivial, and they would have been better by themselves. Had such a school been established, I should have liked to have been Principal of it myself, for it would have been an easier job; small boys turn instinctively towards affection, and one controls them by it, naturally and easily.

Some of them, if I came near them, either on parade or in school or at football, would observe me watchfully, not directly or fully, but obliquely and secretly; sometimes I would surprise them at it, and make some small sign of recognition, which would satisfy them so that they would cease to observe me, and would give their full attention to the event of the moment. But I knew that my authority was thus confirmed and strengthened.

These secret relations with them were a source of continuous pleasure to me. Had they been my own children I would no doubt have given a greater expression to it. But often I would move through the silent and orderly parade, and stand by one of them. He would look straight in front of him with a little frown of concentration that expressed both childish awareness of and manly indifference to my nearness. Sometime I would tweak his ear, and he would give me a brief smile of acknowledgment, or frown with still greater concentration. It was natural I suppose to confine these outward expressions to the very smallest, but they were taken as symbolic, and some older boys would observe them and take themselves to be included. It was a relief, when the reformatory was passing through times of turbulence and trouble, and when there was danger of estrangement between authority and boys, to make these simple and natural gestures, which were reassurances both to me and them that nothing important had changed.

On Sunday afternoons when I was on duty, I would take my car to the reformatory and watch the free boys being signed out at the gate. This simple operation was also watched by many boys not free, who would tell each other "in so many weeks I'll be signed out myself." Amongst the watchers were always some of the small boys, and these I would take by turns in the car. We would go out to the Potchefstroom Road with its ceaseless stream of traffic, and to the Baragwanath crossroads, and come back by the Van Wyksrus Road to the reformatory. I would talk to them about their families, their parents, their sisters and brothers, and I would pretend to know nothing of Durban, Port Elizabeth, Potchefstroom, and Clocolan, and ask them if these places were bigger than Johannesburg.

One of the small boys was Ha'penny, and he was about twelve years old. He came from Bloemfontein and was the biggest talker of them all. His mother worked in a white person's house, and he had two brothers and two sisters. His brothers were Richard and Dickie and his sisters Anna and Mina.

"Richard and Dickie?" I asked.

"Yes, *meneer.*"

"In English," I said, "Richard and Dickie are the same name."

When we returned to the reformatory, I sent for Ha'penny's papers; there it was plainly set down, Ha'penny was a waif, with no relatives at all. He had been taken in from one home to another, but he was naughty and uncontrollable, and eventually had taken to pilfering at the market.

I then sent for the Letter Book, and found that Ha'penny wrote regularly, or rather that others wrote for him till he could write himself, to Mrs. Betty Maarman, of 48 Vlak Street, Bloemfontein. But Mrs. Maarman had never once replied to him. When questioned, he had said, perhaps she is sick. I sat down and wrote at once to the Social Welfare Officer at Bloemfontein, asking him to investigate.

The next time I had Ha'penny out in the car, I questioned him again about his family. And he told me the same as before, his mother, Richard and Dickie, Anna and Mina. But he softened the "D" of "Dickie," so that it sounded now like Tickie.

"I thought you said Dickie," I said.

"I said Tickie," he said.

He watched me with concealed apprehension, and I came to the conclusion that this waif of Bloemfontein was a clever boy, who had told me a story that was all imagination, and had changed one single letter of it to make it safe from any question. And I thought I understood it all too, that he was ashamed of being without a family, and had invented them all, so that no one might discover that he was fatherless and motherless, and that no one in the world cared whether he was alive or dead. This gave me a strong feeling for him, and I went out of my way to manifest towards him the fatherly care that the State, though not in those words, had enjoined upon me by giving me this job.

Then the letter came from the Social Welfare Officer in Bloemfontein, saying that Mrs. Betty Maarman of 48 Vlak Street was a real person, and that she had four children, Richard and Dickie, Anna and Mina, but that Ha'penny was no child of hers, and she knew him only as a derelict of the streets. She had never answered his letters, because he wrote to her as *mother*, and she was no mother of his, nor did she wish to play any such role. She was a decent woman, a faithful member of the church, and she had no thought of corrupting her family by letting them have anything to do with such a child.

But Ha'penny seemed to me anything but the usual delinquent, his desire to have a family was so strong, and his reformatory record was so blameless, and his anxiety to please and obey so great, that I began to feel a great duty towards him. Therefore I asked him about his "mother."

He could not speak enough of her, nor with too high praise. She was loving, honest, and strict. Her home was clean. She had affection for all her children. It was clear that the homeless child, even as he had attached himself to me, would have attached himself to her; he had observed her even as he had observed me, but did not know the secret of how to open her heart, so that she would take him in, and save him from the lonely life that he led.

"Why did you steal when you had such a mother?" I asked.

He could not answer that; not all his brains nor his courage could find an answer to such a question, for he knew that with such a mother he would not have stolen at all.

"The boy's name is Dickie," I said, "not Tickie."

And then he knew the deception was revealed. Another boy might have said, "I told you it was Dickie," but he was too intelligent for that; he knew that if I had established that the boy's name was *Dickie*, I must have established other things too. I was shocked by the immediate and visible effect of my action. His whole brave assurance died within him, and he stood there exposed, not as a liar, but as a homeless child who had surrounded himself with mother, brothers, and sisters who did not exist. I had shattered the very foundations of his pride, and his sense of human significance.

He fell sick at once, and the doctor said it was tuberculosis. I wrote at once to Mrs. Maarman, telling her the whole story, of how this small boy had observed her, and had decided that she was the person he desired for his mother. But she wrote back saying that she could take no responsibility for him. For one thing, Ha'penny was a Mosuto, and she was a coloured woman; for another, she had never had a child in trouble, and how could she take such a boy?

Tuberculosis is a strange thing; sometimes it manifests itself suddenly in the most unlikely host, and swiftly sweeps to the end. Ha'penny withdrew himself from the world, from all Principals and mothers, and the doctor said there was little hope. In desperation I sent money for Mrs. Maarman to come.

She was a decent homely woman, and seeing that the situation was serious, she, without fuss or embarrassment, adopted Ha'penny for her own. The whole reformatory accepted her as his mother. She sat the whole day with him, and talked to him of Richard and Dickie, Anna and Mina, and how they were all waiting for him to come home. She poured out her affection on him, and had no fear of his sickness, nor did she allow it to prevent her from satisfying his hunger to be owned. She talked to him of what they would do when he came back, and how he would go to the school, and what they would buy for Guy Fawkes night.

He in his turn gave his whole attention to her, and when I visited him he was grateful, but I had passed out of his world. I felt judged in that I had sensed only the existence and not the measure of his desire. I wished I had done something sooner, more wise, more prodigal.

We buried him on the reformatory farm, and Mrs. Maarman said to me, "When you put up the cross, put he was my son."

"I'm ashamed," she said, "that I wouldn't take him."

"The sickness," I said, "the sickness would have come."

"No," she said, shaking her head with certainty. "It wouldn't have come. And if it had come at home, it would have been different."

So she left for Bloemfontein, after her strange visit to a reformatory. And I was left too, with the resolve to be more prodigal in the task that the State, though not in so many words, had enjoined on me.

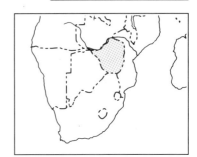

Sunrise on the Veld

BY DORIS LESSING

Every night that winter he said aloud into the dark of the pillow: Half-past four! Half-past four! till he felt his brain had gripped the words and held them fast. Then he fell asleep at once, as if a shutter had fallen; and lay with his face turned to the clock so that he could see it first thing when he woke.

It was half-past four to the minute, every morning. Triumphantly pressing down the alarm-knob of the clock, which the dark half of his mind had outwitted, remaining vigilant all night and counting the hours as he lay relaxed in sleep, he huddled down for a last warm moment under the clothes, playing with the idea of lying abed for this once only. But he played with it for the fun of knowing that it was a weakness he could defeat without effort; just as he set the alarm each night for the delight of the moment when he woke and stretched his limbs, feeling the muscles tighten, and thought: Even my brain—even that! I can control every part of myself.

Luxury of warm rested body, with the arms and legs and fingers waiting like soldiers for a word of command! Joy of knowing that the precious hours were given to sleep voluntarily!—for he had once stayed awake three nights running, to prove that he could, and then worked all day, refusing even to admit that he was tired; and now sleep seemed to him a servant to be commanded and refused.

The boy stretched his frame full-length, touching the wall at his head with his hands, and the bedfoot with his toes; then he sprang out, like a fish leaping from water. And it was cold, cold.

He always dressed rapidly, so as to try and conserve his night-warmth till the sun rose two hours later; but by the time he had on his clothes his hands were numbed and he could scarcely hold his shoes. These he could not put on for fear of waking his parents, who never came to know how early he rose.

As soon as he stepped over the lintel, the flesh of his soles contracted on the chilled earth, and his legs began to ache with cold. It was night: the stars were glittering, the trees standing black and still. He looked for signs of day, for the greying of the edge of a stone, or a lightening in the sky where the sun would rise, but there was nothing yet. Alert as an animal he crept past the dangerous window, standing poised with his hand on the sill for one proudly fastidious moment, looking in at the stuffy blackness of the room where his parents lay.

Feeling for the grass-edge of the path with his toes, he reached inside another window further along the wall, where his gun had been set in readiness the night before. The steel was icy, and numbed fingers slipped along it, so that he had to hold it in the crook of his arm for safety. Then he tiptoed to the room where the dogs slept, and was fearful that they might have been tempted to go before him; but they were waiting, their haunches crouched in reluctance at the cold, but ears and swinging tails greeting the gun ecstatically. His warning undertone kept them secret and silent till the house was a hundred metres back: then they bolted off into the bush, yelping excitedly. The boy imagined his parents turning in their beds and muttering: Those dogs again! before they were dragged back in sleep; and he smiled scornfully. He always looked back over his shoulder at the house before he passed a wall of trees that shut it from sight. It looked so low and small, crouching there under a tall and brilliant sky. Then he turned his back on it, and on the frowsting sleepers, and forgot them.

He would have to hurry. Before the light grew strong he must be six kilometres away; and already a tint of green stood in the hollow of a leaf, and the air smelled of morning and the stars were dimming.

He slung the shoes over his shoulder, veld *skoen* that were crinkled and hard with the dews of a hundred mornings. They would be necessary when the ground became too hot to bear. Now he felt the chilled dust push up between his toes, and he let the muscles of his feet spread and settle into the shapes of the earth; and he thought: I could walk a hundred kilometres on feet like these! I could walk all day, and never tire!

He was walking swiftly through the dark tunnel of foliage that in daytime was a road. The dogs were invisibly ranging the lower travelways of the bush, and he heard them panting. Sometimes he felt a cold muzzle on his leg before they were off again, scouting for a trail to follow. They were not trained, but free-running companions of the hunt, who often tired of the long stalk before the final shots, and went off on their own pleasure. Soon he could see them, small and wild-looking in a wild strange light, now that the bush stood trembling on the verge of colour, waiting for the sun to paint earth and grass afresh.

The grass stood to his shoulders; and the trees were showering a faint silvery rain. He was soaked; his whole body was clenched in a steady shiver.

Once he bent to the road that was newly scored with animal trails, and regretfully straightened, reminding himself that the pleasure of tracking must wait till another day.

He began to run along the edge of a field, noting jerkily how it was filmed over with fresh spiderweb, so that the long reaches of great black clods seemed netted in glistening grey. He was using the steady lope he had learned by watching the natives, the run that is a dropping of the weight of the body from one foot to the next in a slow balancing movement that never tires, nor shortens the breath; and he felt the blood pulsing down his legs and along his arms, and the exultation and pride of body mounted in him till he was shutting his teeth hard against a violent desire to shout his triumph.

Soon he had left the cultivated part of the farm. Behind him the bush was low and black. In front was a long *vlei*, hectares of long pale grass that sent back a hollowing gleam of light to a satiny sky. Near him thick swathes of grass were bent with the weight of water, and diamond drops sparkled on each frond.

The first bird woke at his feet and at once a flock of them sprang into the air calling shrilly that day had come; and suddenly, behind him, the bush woke into song, and he could hear the guinea fowl calling far ahead of him. That meant they would now be sailing down from their trees into thick grass, and it was for them he had come: he was too late. But he did not mind. He forgot he had come to shoot. He set his legs wide, and balanced from foot to foot, and swung his gun up and down in both hands horizontally, in a kind of improvised exercise, and let his head sink back till it was pillowed in his neck muscles, and watched how above him small rosy clouds floated in a lake of gold.

Suddenly it all rose in him: it was unbearable. He leapt up into the air, shouting and yelling wild, unrecognizable noises. Then he began to run, not carefully, as he had before, but madly, like a wild thing. He was clean crazy, yelling mad with the joy of living and a superfluity of youth. He rushed down the *vlei* under a tumult of crimson and gold, while all the birds of the world sang about him. He ran in great leaping strides, and shouted as he ran, feeling his body rise into the crisp rushing air and fall back surely on to sure feet; and thought briefly, not believing that such a thing could happen to him, that he could break his ankle any moment, in this thick tangled grass. He cleared bushes like a duiker, leapt over rocks; and finally came to a dead stop at a place where the ground fell abruptly away below him to the river. It had been a three-kilometre-long dash through waist-high growth, and he was breathing hoarsely and could no longer sing. But he poised on a rock and looked down at stretches of water that gleamed through stooping trees, and thought suddenly, I am fifteen! Fifteen! The words came new to him; so that he kept repeating them wonderingly, with swelling excitement; and he felt the years of his life with his hands, as if he were counting marbles, each one hard and separate and compact, each one a wonderful shining thing. That was what he was: fifteen years of this rich soil, and this slow-moving water, and air that smelt like a challenge whether it was warm and sultry at noon, or as brisk as cold water, like it was now.

There was nothing he couldn't do, nothing! A vision came to him, as he stood there, like when a child hears the word "eternity" and tries to understand it, and time takes possession of the mind. He felt his life ahead of him as a great and wonderful thing, something that was his; and he said aloud, with the blood rising to his head: all the great men of the world have been as I am now, and there is nothing I can't become, nothing I can't do; there is no country in the world I cannot make part of myself, if I choose. I contain the world. I can make of it what I want. If I choose, I can change everything that is going to happen: it depends on me, and what I decide now.

The urgency, and the truth and the courage of what his voice was saying exulted him so that he began to sing again, at the top of his voice, and the sound went echoing down the river gorge. He stopped for the echo, and sang again: stopped and shouted. That was what he was!—he sang, if he chose; and the world had to answer him.

And for minutes he stood there, shouting and singing and waiting for the lovely eddying sound of the echo; so that his own new strong thoughts came back and washed round his head, as if someone were answering him and encouraging him; till the gorge was full of soft voices clashing back and forth from rock to rock over the river. And then it seemed as if there was a new voice. He listened, puzzled, for it was not his own. Soon he was leaning forward, all his nerves alert, quite still: somewhere close to him there was a noise that was no joyful bird, nor tinkle of falling water, nor ponderous movement of cattle.

There it was again. In the deep morning hush that held his future and his past, was a sound of pain, and repeated over and over: it was a kind of shortened scream, as if someone, something, had no breath to scream. He came to himself, looked about him, and called for the dogs. They did not appear: they had gone off on their own business, and he was alone. Now he was clean sober, all the madness gone. His heart beating fast, because of that frightened screaming, he stepped carefully off the rock and went towards a belt of trees. He was moving cautiously, for not so long ago he had seen a leopard in just this spot.

At the edge of the trees he stopped and peered, holding his gun ready; he advanced, looking steadily about him, his eyes narrowed. Then, all at once, in the middle of a step, he faltered, and his face was puzzled. He shook his head impatiently, as if he doubted his own sight.

There, between two trees, against a background of gaunt black rocks, was a figure from a dream, a strange beast that was horned and drunken-legged, but like something he had never even imagined. It seemed to be ragged. It looked like a small buck that had black ragged tufts of fur standing up irregularly all over it, with patches of raw flesh beneath ... but the patches of rawness were disappearing under moving black and came again elsewhere; and all the time the creature screamed, in small gasping screams, and leaped drunkenly from side to side, as if it were blind.

Then the boy understood: it *was* a buck. He ran closer, and again stood still, stopped by a new fear. Around him the grass was whispering and alive. He looked wildly about, and then down. The ground was black with ants, great energetic ants that took no notice of him, but hurried and scurried towards the fighting shape, like glistening black water flowing through the grass.

And, as he drew in his breath and pity and terror seized him, the beast fell and the screaming stopped. Now he could hear nothing but one bird singing, and the sound of the rustling, whispering ants.

He peered over at the writhing blackness that jerked convulsively with the jerking nerves. It grew quieter. There were small twitches from the mass that still looked vaguely like the shape of a small animal.

It came into his mind that he should shoot it and end its pain; and he raised the gun. Then he lowered it again. The buck could no longer feel; its fighting was a mechanical protest of the nerves. But it was not that which made him put down the gun. It was a swelling feeling of rage and misery and protest that expressed itself in the thought: if I had not come it would have died like this: so why should I interfere? All over the bush things like this happen; they happen all the time; this is how life goes on, by living things dying in anguish. He gripped the gun between his knees and felt in his own limbs the myriad swarming pain of the twitching animal that could no longer feel, and set his teeth, and said over and over again under his breath: I can't stop it. I can't stop it. There is nothing I can do.

He was glad that the buck was unconscious and had gone past suffering so that he did not have to make a decision to kill it even when he was feeling with his whole body: this is what happens, this is how things work.

It was right—that was what he was feeling. *It was right and nothing could alter it.*

The knowledge of fatality, of what has to be, had gripped him and for the first time in his life; and he was left unable to make any movement of brain or body, except to say: "Yes, yes. That is what living is." It had entered his flesh and his bones and grown in to the furthest corners of his brain and would never leave him. And at that moment he could not have performed the smallest action of mercy, knowing as he did, having lived on it all his life, the vast unalterable, cruel *veld*, where at any moment one might stumble over a skull or crush the skeleton of some small creature.

Suffering, sick, and angry, but also grimly satisfied with his new stoicism, he stood there leaning on his rifle, and watched the seething black mound grow smaller. At his feet, now, were ants trickling back with pink fragments in their mouths, and there was a fresh acid smell in his nostrils. He sternly controlled the uselessly convulsing muscles of his empty stomach, and reminded himself: the ants must eat too! At the same time he found that the tears were streaming down his face, and his clothes were soaked with the sweat of that other creature's pain.

The shape had grown small. Now it looked like nothing recognizable. He did not know how long it was before he saw the blackness thin, and bits of white showed through, shining in the sun—yes, there was the sun, just up, glowing over the rocks. Why, the whole thing could not have taken longer than a few minutes.

He began to swear, as if the shortness of the time was in itself unbearable, using the words he had heard his father say. He strode forward, crushing ants with each step, and brushing them off his clothes, till he stood above the skeleton, which lay sprawled under a small bush. It was clean-picked. It might have been lying there years, save that on the white bone were pink fragments of gristle. About the bones ants were ebbing away, their pincers full of meat.

The boy looked at them, big black ugly insects. A few were standing and gazing up at him with small glittering eyes.

"Go away!" he said to the ants, very coldly. "I am not for you—not just yet, at any rate. Go away." And he fancied that the ants turned and went away.

He bent over the bones and touched the sockets in the skull; that was where the eyes were, he thought incredulously, remembering the liquid dark eyes of a buck. And then he bent the slim foreleg bone, swinging it horizontally in his palm.

That morning, perhaps an hour ago, this small creature had been stepping proud and free through the bush, feeling the chill on its hide even as he himself had done, exhilarated by it. Proudly stepping the earth, tossing its horns, frisking a pretty white tail, it had sniffed the cold morning air. Walking like kings and conquerors it had moved through this free-held bush, where each blade of grass grew for it alone, and where the river ran pure sparkling water for its slaking.

And then—what had happened? Such a swift sure-footed thing could surely not be trapped by a swarm of ants?

The boy bent curiously to the skeleton. Then he saw that the back leg that lay uppermost and strained out in the tension of death, was snapped midway in the thigh, so that broken bones jutted over each other uselessly. So that was it! Limping into the ant-masses it could not escape, once it had sensed the danger. Yes, but how had the leg been broken? Had it fallen, perhaps? Impossible, a buck was too light and graceful. Had some jealous rival horned it?

What could possibly have happened? Perhaps some Africans had thrown stones at it, as they do, trying to kill it for meat, and had broken its leg. Yes, that must be it.

Even as he imagined the crowd of running, shouting natives, and the flying stones, and the leaping buck, another picture came into his mind. He saw himself, on any one of these bright ringing mornings, drunk with excitement, taking a snap shot at some half-seen buck. He saw himself with the gun lowered, wondering whether he had missed or not; and thinking at last that it was late, and he wanted his breakfast, and it was not worthwhile to track kilometres after an animal that would very likely get away from him in any case.

For a moment he would not face it. He was a small boy again, kicking sulkily at the skeleton, hanging his head, refusing to accept the responsibility.

Then he straightened up, and looked down at the bones with an odd expression of dismay, all the anger gone out of him. His mind went quite empty: all around him he could see trickles of ants disappearing into the grass. The whispering noise was faint and dry, like the rustling of a cast snakeskin.

At last he picked up his gun and walked homewards. He was telling himself half-defiantly that he wanted his breakfast. He was telling himself that it was getting very hot, much too hot to be out roaming the bush.

Really, he was tired. He walked heavily, not looking where he put his feet. When he came within sight of his home he stopped, knitting his brows. There was something he had to think out. The death of that small animal was a thing that concerned him, and he was by no means finished with it. It lay at the back of his mind uncomfortably.

Soon, the very next morning, he would get clear of everybody and go to the bush and think about it.

II ASIA

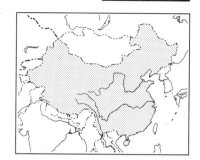

Love Must Not Be Forgotten

BY ZHANG JIE

TRANSLATED BY GLADYS YANG

I am thirty, the same age as our People's Republic. For a republic thirty is still young. But a girl of thirty is virtually on the shelf.

Actually, I have a bona fide suitor. Have you seen the Greek sculptor Myron's Discobolus? Qiao Lin is the image of that discus thrower. Even the padded clothes he wears in winter fail to hide his fine physique. Bronzed, with clear-cut features, a broad forehead, and large eyes, his appearance alone attracts most girls to him.

But I can't make up my mind to marry him. I'm not clear what attracts me to him, or him to me.

I know people are gossiping behind my back: "Who does she think she is, to be so choosy?"

To them, I'm a nobody playing hard to get. They take offence at such preposterous behaviour.

Of course, I shouldn't be captious. In a society where commercial production still exists, marriage like most other transactions is still a form of barter.

I have known Qiao Lin for nearly two years, yet still cannot fathom whether he keeps so quiet from aversion to talking or from having nothing to say. When, by way of a small intelligence test, I demand his opinion of this or that, he says "good" or "bad" like a child in kindergarten.

Once I asked, "Qiao Lin, why do you love me?" He thought the question over seriously for what seemed an age. I could see from his normally smooth but now wrinkled forehead that the little grey cells in his handsome head were hard at work cogitating. I felt ashamed to have put him on the spot.

Finally he raised his clear childlike eyes to tell me, "Because you're good!"

Loneliness flooded my heart. "Thank you, Qiao Lin!" I couldn't help wondering, if we were to marry, whether we could discharge our duties to each other as husband and wife. Maybe, because law and morality would have bound us together. But how tragic simply to comply with law and morality! Was there no stronger bond to link us?

When such thoughts cross my mind I have the strange sensation that instead of being a girl contemplating marriage I am an elderly social scientist.

Perhaps I worry too much. We can live like most married couples, bringing up children together, strictly true to each other according to the law.... Although living in the seventies of the twentieth century, people still consider marriage the way they did millenia ago, as a means of continuing the race, a form of barter, or a business transaction in which love and marriage can be separated. As this is the common practice, why shouldn't we follow suit?

But I still can't make up my mind. As a child, I remember, I often cried all night for no rhyme or reason, unable to sleep and disturbing the whole household. My old nurse, a shrewd though uneducated woman, said an ill wind had blown through my ear. I think this judgement showed prescience, because I still have that old weakness. I upset myself over things which really present no problem, upsetting other people at the same time. One's nature is hard to change.

I think of my mother too. If she were alive, what would she say about my attitude to Qiao Lin and my uncertainty about marrying him?

My thoughts constantly turn to her, not because she was such a strict mother that her ghost is still watching over me since her death. No, she was not just my mother but my closest friend. I loved her so much that the thought of her leaving me makes my heart ache.

She never lectured me, just told me quietly in her deep, unwomanly voice about her successes and failures, so that I could learn from her experience. She had evidently not had many successes—her life was full of failures.

During her last days she followed me with her fine, expressive eyes, as if wondering how I would manage on my own and as if she had some important advice for me but hesitated to give it. She must have been worried by my naiveté and sloppy ways. She suddenly blurted out, "Shanshan, if you aren't sure what you want, don't rush into marriage—better live on your own!"

Other people might think this strange advice from a mother to her daughter, but to me it embodied her bitter experience. I don't think she underestimated me or my knowledge of life. She loved me and didn't want me to be unhappy.

"I don't want to marry, mum!" I said, not out of bashfulness or a show of coyness. I can't think why a girl should pretend to be coy. She had long since taught me about things not generally mentioned to girls.

"If you meet the right man, then marry him. Only if he's right for you!"

"I'm afraid no such man exists!"

"That's not true. But it's hard. The world is so vast, I'm afraid you may never meet him." Whether I married or not was not what concerned her, but the quality of the marriage.

"Haven't you managed fine without a husband?"

"Who says so?"

"I think you've done fine."

"I had no choice...." She broke off, lost in thought, her face wistful. Her wistful lined face reminded me of a withered flower I had pressed in a book.

"Why did you have no choice?"

"You ask too many questions," she parried, not ashamed to confide in me but afraid that I might reach the wrong conclusion. Besides, everyone treasures a secret to carry to the grave. Feeling a bit put out, I demanded bluntly, "Didn't you love my dad?"

"No, I never loved him."

"Did he love you?"

"No, he didn't."

"Then why get married?"

She paused, searching for the right words to explain this mystery, then answered bitterly, "When you're young you don't always know what you're looking for, what you need, and people may talk you into getting married. As you grow older and more experienced you find out your true needs. By then, though, you've done many foolish things for which you could kick yourself. You'd give anything to be able to make a fresh start and live more wisely. Those content with their lot will always be happy, they say, but I shall never enjoy that happiness." She added self-mockingly, "A wretched idealist, that's all I am."

Did I take after her? Did we both have genes which attracted ill winds?

"Why don't you marry again?"

"I'm afraid I'm still not sure what I really want." She was obviously unwilling to tell me the truth.

I cannot remember my father. He and Mother split up when I was very small. I just recall her telling me sheepishly that he was a fine handsome fellow. I could see she was ashamed of having judged by appearances and made a futile choice. She told me, "When I can't sleep at night, I force myself to sober up by recalling all those stupid blunders I made. Of course it's so distasteful that I often hide my face in the sheet for shame, as if there were eyes watching me in the dark. But distasteful as it is, I take some pleasure in this form of atonement."

I was really sorry that she hadn't remarried. She was such a fascinating character, if she'd married a man she loved, what a happy household ours would surely have been. Though not beautiful, she had the simple charm of an ink landscape. She was a fine writer too. Another author who knew her well used to say teasingly, "Just reading your works is enough to make anyone love you!"

She would retort, "If he knew that the object of his affection was a white-haired old crone, that would frighten him away."

At her age, she must have known what she really wanted, so this was obviously an evasion. I say this because she had quirks which puzzled me.

For instance, whenever she left Beijing on a trip, she always took with her one of the twenty-seven volumes of Chekhov's stories published between 1950 and 1955. She also warned me, "Don't touch these books. If you want to read Chekhov, read that set I bought you." There was no need to caution me. Having a set of my own why should I touch hers? Besides, she'd told me this over and over again. Still she was on her guard. She seemed bewitched by those books.

So we had two sets of Chekhov's stories at home. Not just because we loved Chekhov, but to parry other people like me who loved Chekhov. Whenever anyone asked to borrow a volume, she would lend one of mine. Once, in her absence, a close friend took a volume from her set. When she found out she was frantic, and at once took a volume of mine to exchange for it.

Ever since I can remember, those books were on her bookcase. Although I admire Chekhov as a great writer, I was puzzled by the way she never tired of reading him. Why, for over twenty years, had she had to read him every single day?

Sometimes, when tired of writing, she poured herself a cup of strong tea and sat down in front of the bookcase, staring raptly at that set of books. If I went into her room then it flustered her, and she either spilt her tea or blushed like a girl discovered with her lover.

I wondered: Has she fallen in love with Chekhov? She might have if he'd still been alive.

When her mind was wandering just before her death, her last words to me were: "That set...." She hadn't the strength to give it its complete title. But I knew what she meant. "And my diary ... 'Love Must Not Be Forgotten' .... Cremate them with me."

I carried out her last instruction regarding the works of Chekhov, but couldn't bring myself to destroy her diary. I thought, if it could be published, it would surely prove the most moving thing she had written. But naturally publication was out of the question.

At first I imagined the entries were raw material she had jotted down. They read neither like stories, essays, a diary, or letters. But after reading the whole I formed a hazy impression, helped out by my imperfect memory. Thinking it over, I finally realized that this was no lifeless manuscript I was holding, but an anguished, loving heart. For over twenty years one man had occupied her heart, but he was not for her. She used these diaries as a substitute for him, a means of pouring out her feelings to him, day after day, year after year.

No wonder she had never considered any eligible proposals, had turned a deaf ear to idle talk whether well-meant or malicious. Her heart was already full, to the exclusion of anybody else. "No lake can compare with the ocean, no cloud with those on Mount Wu." Remembering those lines I often reflected sadly that few people in real life could love like this. No one would love me like this.

I learned that towards the end of the thirties, when this man was doing underground work for the Party in Shanghai, an old worker had given his life to cover him, leaving behind a helpless wife and daughter. Out of a sense of duty, of gratitude to the dead and deep class feeling, he had unhesitatingly married the girl. When he saw the endless troubles caused by "love" of couples who had married for "love," he may have thought, "Thank Heaven, though I didn't marry for love, we get on well, able to help each other." For years, as man and wife they lived through hard times.

He must have been my mother's colleague. Had I ever met him? He couldn't have visited our home. Who was he?

In the spring of 1962, Mother took me to a concert. We went on foot, the theatre being quite near.

A black limousine pulled up silently by the pavement. Out stepped an elderly man with white hair in a black serge tunic-suit. What a striking shock of white hair! Strict, scrupulous, distinguished, transparently honest—that was my impression of him. The cold glint of his flashing eyes reminded me of lightning or swordplay. Only ardent love for a woman really deserving his love could fill cold eyes like those with tenderness.

He walked up to Mother and said, "How are you, Comrade Zhong Yu? It's been a long time."

"How are you!" Mother's hand holding mine suddenly turned icy cold and trembled a little.

They stood face to face without looking at each other, each appearing upset, even stern. Mother fixed her eyes on the trees by the roadside, not yet in leaf. He looked at me. "Such a big girl already. Good, fine—you take after your mother."

Instead of shaking hands with Mother he shook hands with me. His hand was as icy as hers and trembling a little. As if transmitting an electric current, I felt a sudden shock. Snatching my hand away I cried, "There's nothing good about that!"

"Why not?" he asked with a surprised expression grown-ups always have when children speak out frankly.

I glanced at Mother's face. I did take after her, to my disappointment. "Because she's not beautiful!"

He laughed, then said teasingly, "Too bad that there should be a child who doesn't find her own mother beautiful. Do you remember in '53, when your mum was transferred to Beijing, she came to our ministry to report for duty? She left you outside on the verandah, but like a monkey you climbed all the stairs, peeped through the cracks in doors, and caught your finger in the door of my office. You sobbed so bitterly that I carried you off to find her."

"I don't remember that." I was annoyed at his harking back to a time when I was still in open-seat pants.

"Ah, we old people have better memories." He turned abruptly and remarked to Mother, "I've read that last story of yours. Frankly speaking, there's something not quite right about it. You shouldn't have condemned the heroine.... There's nothing wrong with falling in love, as long as you don't spoil someone else's life.... In fact, the hero might have loved her too. Only for the sake of a third person's happiness, they had to renounce their love...."

A policeman came over to where the car was parked and ordered the driver to move on. When the driver made some excuse, the old man looked round. After a hasty "Goodbye" he strode to the car and told the policeman, "Sorry. It's not his fault, it's mine...."

I found it amusing watching this old cadre listening respectfully to the policeman's strictures. When I turned to Mother with a mischievous smile, she looked as upset as a first-form primary schoolchild standing forlornly in front of the stern headmistress. Anyone would have thought she was the one being lectured by the policeman.

The car drove off, leaving a puff of smoke. Very soon even this smoke vanished with the wind, as if nothing at all had happened. But the incident stuck in my mind.

Analyzing it now, he must have been the man whose strength of character won Mother's heart. That strength came from his firm political convictions, his narrow escapes from death in the Revolution, his active brain, his drive at work, his well-cultivated mind. Besides, strange to say, he and Mother both liked the oboe. Yes, she must have worshipped him. She once told me that unless she worshipped a man, she couldn't love him even for one day.

But I could not tell whether he loved her or not. If not, why was there this entry in her diary?

"This is far too fine a present. But how did you know that Chekhov's my favourite writer?"

"You said so."

"I don't remember that."

"I remember. I heard you mention it when you were chatting with someone."

So he was the one who had given her the *Selected Stories of Chekhov*. For her that was tantamount to a love letter.

Maybe this man, who didn't believe in love, realized by the time his hair was white that in his heart was something which could be called love. By the time he no longer had the right to love, he made the tragic discovery of this love for which he would have given his life. Or did it go deeper than that?

This is all I remember about him.

How wretched Mother must have been, deprived of the man to whom she was devoted! To catch a glimpse of his car or the back of his head through its rear window, she carefully figured out which roads he would take to work and back. Whenever he made a speech, she sat at the back of the hall watching his face rendered hazy by cigarette smoke and poor lighting. Her eyes would brim with tears, but she swallowed them back. If a fit of coughing made him break off, she wondered anxiously why no one persuaded him to give up smoking. She was afraid he would get bronchitis again. Why was he so near yet so far?

He, to catch a glimpse of her, looked out of the car window every day, straining his eyes to watch the streams of cyclists, afraid that she might have an accident. On the rare evenings on which he had no meetings, he would walk by a roundabout way to our neighbourhood, to pass our compound gate. However busy, he would always make time to look in papers and journals for her work.

His duty had always been clear to him, even in the most difficult times. But now confronted by this love he became a weakling, quite helpless. At his age it was laughable. Why should life play this trick on him?

Yet when they happened to meet at work, each tried to avoid the other, hurrying off with a nod. Even so, this would make Mother blind and deaf to everything around her. If she met a colleague named Wang she would call him Guo and mutter something unintelligible.

It was a cruel ordeal for her. She wrote:

> We agreed to forget each other. But I deceived you, I have never forgotten. I don't think you've forgotten either. We're just deceiving each other, hiding our misery. I haven't deceived you deliberately, though; I did my best to carry out our agreement. I often stay far away from Beijing, hoping time and distance will help me to forget you. But on my return, as the train pulls into the station, my head reels. I stand on the platform looking round intently, as if someone were waiting for me. Of course there is no one. I realize then that I

have forgotten nothing. Everything is unchanged. My love is like a tree the roots of which strike deeper year after year—I have no way to uproot it.

At the end of every day, I feel as if I've forgotten something important. I may wake with a start from my dreams wondering what has happened. But nothing has happened. Nothing. Then it comes home to me that you are missing! So everything seems lacking, incomplete, and there is nothing to fill up the blank. We are nearing the ends of our lives, why should we be carried away by emotion like children? Why should life submit people to such ordeals, then unfold before you your lifelong dream? Because I started off blindly I took the wrong turning, and now there are insuperable obstacles between me and my dream.

Yes, Mother never let me go to the station to meet her when she came back from a trip, preferring to stand alone on the platform and imagine that he had met her. Poor mother with her greying hair was as infatuated as a girl.

Not much space in the diary was devoted to their romance. Most entries dealt with trivia: Why one of her articles had not come off; her fear that she had no real talent; the excellent play she missed by mistaking the time on the ticket; the drenching she got by going out for a stroll without her umbrella. In spirit they were together day and night, like a devoted married couple. In fact, they spent no more than twenty-four hours together in all. Yet in that time they experienced deeper happiness than some people in a whole lifetime. Shakespeare makes Juliet say, "I cannot sum up half my sum of wealth." And probably that is how Mother felt.

He must have been killed in the Cultural Revolution. Perhaps because of the conditions then, that section of the diary is ambiguous and obscure. Mother had been so fiercely attacked for her writing, it amazed me that she went on keeping a diary. From some veiled allusions I gathered that he had queried the theories advanced by that "theoretician" then at the height of favour, and had told someone, "This is sheer Rightist talk." It was clear from the tear-stained pages of Mother's diary that he had been harshly denounced; but the steadfast old man never knuckled under to the authorities. His last words were, "When I go to meet Marx, I shall go on fighting my case!"

That must have been in the winter of 1969, because that was when Mother's hair turned white overnight, though she was not yet fifty. And she put on a black arm-band. Her position then was extremely difficult. She was criticized for wearing this old-style mourning, and ordered to say for whom she was in mourning.

"For whom are you wearing that, mum?" I asked anxiously.

"For my lover." Not to frighten me she explained, "Someone you never knew."

"Shall I put one on too?" She patted my cheeks, as she had when I was a child. It was years since she had shown me such affection. I often felt that as she aged, especially during these last years of persecution, all tenderness had left her, or was concealed in her heart, so that she seemed like a man.

She smiled sadly and said, "No, you needn't wear one."

Her eyes were as dry as if she had no more tears to shed. I longed to comfort her or do something to please her. But she said, "Off you go."

I felt an inexplicable dread, as if dear Mother had already half left me. I blurted out, "Mum!"

Quick to sense my desolation, she said gently, "Don't be afraid. Off you go. Leave me alone for a little." I was right. She wrote:

> You have gone. Half my soul seems to have taken flight with you.
>
> I had no means of knowing what had become of you, much less of seeing you for the last time. I had no right to ask either, not being your wife or friend.... So we are torn apart. If only I could have borne that inhuman treatment for you, so that you could have lived on! You should have lived to see your name cleared and take up your work again, for the sake of those who loved you. I knew you could not be a counter-revolutionary. You were one of the finest men killed. That's why I love you—I am not afraid now to avow it.
>
> Snow is whirling down. Heavens, even God is such a hypocrite, he is using this whiteness to cover up your blood and the scandal of your murder.
>
> I have never set store by my life. But now I keep wondering whether anything I say or do would make you contract your shaggy eyebrows in a frown. I must live a worthwhile life like you, and do some honest work for our country. Things can't go on like this— those criminals will get what's coming to them.
>
> I used to walk alone along that small asphalt road, the only place where we once walked together, hearing my footsteps in the silent night.... I always paced to and fro and lingered there, but never as wretchedly as now. Then, though you were not beside me, I knew

you were still in this world and felt that you were keeping me company. Now I can hardly believe that you have gone.

At the end of the road I would retrace my steps, then walk along it again.

Rounding the fence I always looked back, as if you were still standing there waving goodbye. We smiled faintly, like casual acquaintances, to conceal our undying love. That ordinary evening in early spring, a chilly wind was blowing as we walked silently away from each other. You were wheezing a little because of your chronic bronchitis. That upset me. I wanted to beg you to slow down, but somehow I couldn't. We both walked very fast, as if some important business were waiting for us. How we prized that single stroll we had together, but we were afraid we might lose control of ourselves and burst out with "I love you"—those three words which had tormented us for years. Probably no one else could believe that we never once even clasped hands!

No, Mother, I believe it. I am the only one able to see into your locked heart.

Ah, that little asphalt road, so haunted by bitter memories. We shouldn't overlook the most insignificant spots on earth. For who knows how much secret grief and joy they may hide.

No wonder that when tired of writing, she would pace slowly along that little road behind our window. Sometimes at dawn after a sleepless night, sometimes on a moonless, windy evening. Even in winter during howling gales which hurled sand and pebbles against the window pane.... I thought this was one of her eccentricities, not knowing that she had gone to meet him in spirit.

She liked to stand by the window too, staring at the small asphalt road. Once I thought from her expression that one of our closest friends must be coming to call. I hurried to the window. It was a late autumn evening. The cold wind was stripping dead leaves from the trees and blowing them down the small empty road.

She went on pouring out her heart to him in her diary as she had when he was alive. Right up to the day when the pen slipped from her fingers. Her last message was:

I am a materialist, yet I wish there were a Heaven. For then, I know, I would find you there waiting for me. I am going there to join you, to be together for eternity. We need never be parted again or keep at a distance for fear of spoiling someone else's life. Wait for me, dearest, I am coming—

I do not know how Mother, on her deathbed, could still love so ardently with all her heart. To me it seemed not love but a form of madness, a passion stronger than death. If undying love really exists, she reached its extreme. She obviously died happy, because she had known true love. She had no regrets.

Now these old people's ashes have mingled with the elements. But I know that, no matter what form they may take, they still love each other. Though not bound together by earthly laws or morality, though they never once clasped hands, each possessed the other completely. Nothing could part them. Centuries to come, if one white cloud trails another, two grasses grow side by side, one wave splashes another, a breeze follows another ... believe me, that will be them.

Each time I read that diary "Love Must Not Be Forgotten" I cannot hold back my tears. I often weep bitterly, as if I myself experienced their ill-fated love. If not a tragedy it was too laughable. No matter how beautiful or moving I find it, I have no wish to follow suit!

Thomas Hardy wrote that "the call seldom produces the comer, the man to love rarely coincides with the hour for loving." I cannot censure them from conventional moral standards. What I deplore is that they did not wait for a "missing counterpart" to call them.

If everyone could wait, instead of rushing into marriage, how many tragedies could be averted!

When we reach communism, will there still be cases of marriage without love? Maybe, because since the world is so vast, two kindred spirits may be unable to answer each other's call. But how tragic! However, by that time, there may be ways to escape such tragedies.

Why should I split hairs?

Perhaps after all we are responsible for these tragedies. Who knows? Maybe we should take the responsibility for the old ideas handed down from the past. Because if someone never marries, that is a challenge to these ideas. You will be called neurotic, accused of having guilty secrets or having made political mistakes. You may be regarded as an eccentric who looks down on ordinary people, not respecting age-old customs—a heretic. In short they will trump up endless vulgar and futile charges to ruin your reputation. Then you have to knuckle under to those ideas and marry willy-nilly. But once you put the chains of a loveless marriage around your neck, you will suffer for it for the rest of your life.

I long to shout: "Mind your own business! Let us wait patiently for our counterparts. Even waiting in vain is better than willy-nilly marriage. To live single is not such a fearful disaster. I believe it may be a sign of a step forward in culture, education, and the quality of life."

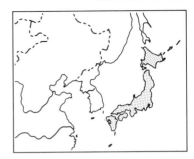

Swaddling Clothes

BY YUKIO MISHIMA

TRANSLATED BY IVAN MORRIS

He was always busy, Toshiko's husband. Even tonight he had to dash off to an appointment, leaving her to go home alone by taxi. But what else could a woman expect when she married an actor—an attractive one? No doubt she had been foolish to hope that he would spend the evening with her. And yet he must have known how she dreaded going back to their house, unhomely with its Western-style furniture and with the bloodstains still showing on the floor.

Toshiko had been oversensitive since girlhood: that was her nature. As the result of constant worrying she never put on weight, and now, an adult woman, she looked more like a transparent picture than a creature of flesh and blood. Her delicacy of spirit was evident to her most casual acquaintance.

Earlier that evening, when she had joined her husband at a night club, she had been shocked to find him entertaining friends with an account of "the incident." Sitting there in his American-style suit, puffing at a cigarette, he had seemed to her almost a stranger.

"It's a fantastic story," he was saying, gesturing flamboyantly as if in an attempt to outweigh the attractions of the dance band. "Here this new nurse for our baby arrives from the employment agency, and the very first thing I notice about her is her stomach. It's enormous—as if she had a pillow stuck under her kimono! No wonder, I thought, for I soon saw that she could eat more than the rest of us put together. She polished off the contents of our rice bin like that...." He snapped his fingers. " 'Gastric dilation'—that's how she explained her girth and her appetite. Well, the day before yesterday we heard groans and moans coming from the nursery. We rushed in and found her squatting on the floor, holding her stomach in her two hands, and moaning like a cow. Next to her our baby lay in his cot, scared out of his wits and crying at the top of his lungs. A pretty scene, I can tell you!"

"So the cat was out of the bag?" suggested one of their friends, a film actor like Toshiko's husband.

"Indeed it was! And it gave me the shock of my life. You see, I'd completely swallowed that story about 'gastric dilation.' Well, I didn't waste any time. I rescued our good rug from the floor and spread a blanket for her to lie on. The whole time the girl was yelling like a stuck pig. By the time the doctor from the maternity clinic arrived, the baby had already been born. But our sitting room was a pretty shambles!"

"Oh, that I'm sure of!" said another of their friends, and the whole company burst into laughter.

Toshiko was dumbfounded to hear her husband discussing the horrifying happening as though it were no more than an amusing incident which they chanced to have witnessed. She shut her eyes for a moment and all at once she saw the newborn baby lying before her: on the parquet floor the infant lay, and his frail body was wrapped in bloodstained newspapers.

Toshiko was sure that the doctor had done the whole thing out of spite. As if to emphasize his scorn for this mother who had given birth to a bastard under such sordid conditions, he had told his assistant to wrap the baby in some loose newspapers, rather than proper swaddling. This callous treatment of the newborn child had offended Toshiko. Overcoming her disgust at the entire scene, she had fetched a brand-new piece of flannel from her cupboard and, having swaddled the baby in it, had laid him carefully in an armchair.

This all had taken place in the evening after her husband had left the house. Toshiko had told him nothing of it, fearing that he would think her oversoft, oversentimental; yet the scene had engraved itself deeply in her mind. Tonight she sat silently thinking back on it, while the jazz orchestra brayed and her husband chatted cheerfully with his friends. She knew that she would never forget the sight of the baby, wrapped in stained newspapers and lying on the floor—it was a scene fit for a butchershop. Toshiko, whose own life had been spent in solid comfort, poignantly felt the wretchedness of the illegitimate baby.

I am the only person to have witnessed its shame, the thought occurred to her. The mother never saw her child lying there in its newspaper wrappings, and the baby itself of course didn't know. I alone shall have to preserve that terrible scene in my memory. When the baby grows up and wants to find out about his birth, there will be no one to tell him, so long as I preserve silence. How strange that I should have this feeling of guilt! After all, it was I who took him up from the floor, swathed him properly in flannel, and laid him down to sleep in the armchair.

They left the night club and Toshiko stepped into the taxi that her husband had called for her. "Take this lady to Ushigomé," he told the driver and shut the door from the outside. Toshiko gazed through the window at her husband's smiling face and noticed his strong, white teeth. Then she leaned back in the seat, oppressed by the knowledge that their life together was in some way too easy, too painless. It would have been difficult for her to put her thoughts into words. Through the rear window of the taxi she took a last look at her husband. He was striding along the street toward his Nash car, and soon the back of his rather garish tweed coat had blended with the figures of the passers-by.

The taxi drove off, passed down a street dotted with bars, and then by a theatre, in front of which the throngs of people jostled each other on the pavement. Although the performance had only just ended, the lights had already been turned out and in the half-dark outside it was depressingly obvious that the cherry blossoms decorating the front of the theatre were merely scraps of white paper.

Even if that baby should grow up in ignorance of the secret of his birth, he can never become a respectable citizen, reflected Toshiko, pursuing the same train of thoughts. Those soiled newspaper swaddling clothes will be the symbol of his entire life. But why should I keep worrying about him so much? Is it because I feel uneasy about the future of my own child? Say twenty years from now, when our boy will have grown up into a fine, carefully educated young man, one day by a quirk of fate he meets the other boy, who then will also have turned twenty. And say that the other boy, who has been sinned against, savagely stabs him with a knife....

It was a warm, overcast April night, but thoughts of the future made Toshiko feel cold and miserable. She shivered on the back seat of the car.

No, when the time comes I shall take my son's place, she told herself suddenly. Twenty years from now I shall be forty-three. I shall go to that young man and tell him straight out about everything—about his newspaper swaddling clothes, and about how I went and wrapped him in flannel.

The taxi ran along the dark wide road that was bordered by the park and by the Imperial Palace moat. In the distance Toshiko noticed the pinpricks of light which came from the blocks of tall office buildings.

Twenty years from now that wretched child will be in utter misery. He will be living a desolate, hopeless, poverty-stricken existence—a lonely rat. What else could happen to a baby who has had such a birth? He'll be wandering through the streets by himself, cursing his father, loathing his mother.

No doubt Toshiko derived a certain satisfaction from her sombre thoughts: she tortured herself with them without cease. The taxi approached Hanzomon and drove past the compound of the British Embassy. At that point the famous rows of cherry trees were spread out before Toshiko in all their purity. On the spur of the moment she decided to go and view the blossoms by herself in the dark night. It was a strange decision for a timid and unadventurous young woman, but then she was in a strange state of mind and she dreaded the return home. That evening all sorts of unsettling fancies had burst open in her mind.

She crossed the wide street—a slim, solitary figure in the darkness. As a rule when she walked in the traffic Toshiko used to cling fearfully to her companion, but tonight she darted alone between the cars and a moment later had reached the long narrow park that borders the Palace moat. Chidorigafuchi, it is called—the Abyss of the Thousand Birds.

Tonight the whole park had become a grove of blossoming cherry trees. Under the calm cloudy sky the blossoms formed a mass of solid whiteness. The paper lanterns that hung from wires between the trees had been put out; in their place electric light bulbs, red, yellow, and green, shone dully beneath the blossoms. It was well past ten o'clock and most of the flower-viewers had gone home. As the occasional passers-by strolled through the park, they would automatically kick aside the empty bottles or crush the waste paper beneath their feet.

Newspapers, thought Toshiko, her mind going back once again to those happenings. Bloodstained newspapers. If a man were ever to hear of that piteous birth and know that it was he who had lain there, it would ruin his entire life. To think that I, a perfect stranger, should from now on have to keep such a secret—the secret of a man's whole existence....

Lost in these thoughts, Toshiko walked on through the park. Most of the people still remaining there were quiet couples; no one paid her any attention. She noticed two people sitting on a stone bench beside the moat, not looking at the blossoms, but gazing silently at the water. Pitch black it was, and swathed in heavy shadows. Beyond the moat the sombre forest of the Imperial Palace blocked her view. The trees reached up, to form a solid dark mass against the night sky. Toshiko walked slowly along the path beneath the blossoms hanging heavily overhead.

On a stone bench, slightly apart from the others, she noticed a pale object—not, as she had at first imagined, a pile of cherry blossoms, nor a garment forgotten by one of the visitors to the park. Only when she came closer did she see that it was a human form lying on the bench. Was it, she wondered, one of those miserable drunks often to be seen sleeping in public places? Obviously not, for the body had been systematically covered with newspapers, and it was the whiteness of those papers that had attracted Toshiko's attention. Standing by the bench, she gazed down at the sleeping figure.

It was a man in a brown jersey who lay there, curled up on layers of newspapers, other newspapers covering him. No doubt this had become his normal night residence now that spring had arrived. Toshiko gazed down at the man's dirty, unkempt hair, which in places had become hopelessly matted. As she observed the sleeping figure wrapped in its newspapers, she was inevitably reminded of the baby who had lain on the floor in its wretched swaddling clothes. The shoulder of the man's jersey rose and fell in the darkness in time with his heavy breathing.

It seemed to Toshiko that all her fears and premonitions had suddenly taken concrete form. In the darkness the man's pale forehead stood out, and it was a young forehead, though carved with the wrinkles of long poverty and hardship. His khaki trousers had been slightly pulled up; on his sockless feet he wore a pair of battered gym shoes. She could not see his face and suddenly had an overmastering desire to get one glimpse of it.

She walked to the head of the bench and looked down. The man's head was half-buried in his arms, but Toshiko could see that he was surprisingly young. She noticed the thick eyebrows and the fine bridge of his nose. His slightly open mouth was alive with youth.

But Toshiko had approached too close. In the silent night the newspaper bedding rustled, and abruptly the man opened his eyes. Seeing the young woman standing directly beside him, he raised himself with a jerk, and his eyes lit up. A second later a powerful hand reached out and seized

Toshiko by her slender wrist.

She did not feel in the least afraid and made no effort to free herself. In a flash the thought had struck her. Ah, so the twenty years have already gone by! The forest of the Imperial Palace was pitch dark and utterly silent.

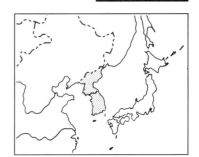

The Non-revolutionaries

BY YU-WOL CHONG-NYON

TRANSLATED BY THE AUTHOR AND DANIEL L. MILTON

> Revolution, counterrevolution, nonrevolution.
> The revolutionaries are executed by the counterrevolutionaries and the counterrevolutionaries by the revolutionaries.
> The nonrevolutionaries are sometimes taken for revolutionaries and executed by the counterrevolutionaries, sometimes taken for counterrevolutionaries and executed by either the revolutionaries or the counterrevolutionaries for no apparent reason at all.
>
> *–Lu Hsun (1881–1936)*
> *Translated from Chinese by Chi-chen Wang*

Cursed be the men of the East. Cursed be the men of the West. Cursed be those who have left my beloved homeland bleeding and torn.

They banged on the doors. They hammered at the walls. Out! *Out!* Everybody out! Everybody to the playfield.

With fear and with trembling we all got up, we got up out of our blankets into the chilly dawn. My father and my mother, my sisters and my brother. Out. *Out.* The shouting and the hammering continued. Out to the playfield.

"What about Ok-Sun?" my mother said to my father, pointing to me.

"They don't know she's here. Maybe she should hide?"

"No, no," said my father. "They'll surely find her."

"But why? If we keep her hidden in the back, no one will see her."

"They will, they will. They're breaking in without warning. Only the night before they broke into twelve houses in our district. In the middle of the night, at two and three in the morning. They banged at the doors and pushed their way in, stamped into the houses with their muddy boots on, and dragged the men away.

"With their boots on!" My mother was silent for a moment, shocked at this revelation of incredible boorishness. The poorest rag-picker, the most unlearned peasant, would never dream of entering another's home without removing his footwear.

But she returned to the argument. "I'm sure we can hide her safely—"

"No! No!" my father again protested. "Too dangerous. Better she go with all of us."

"But—"

But there was no time to argue. Out! *Out!* The shouting and the banging went on. They were still there, rounding up every man, woman, and child. Out I went, too, with my sisters and brother, my father and mother, out to the playfield.

I had returned home only a month ago. My year's scholarship had ended, and I was coming back to bring the wisdom of the West to my "underdeveloped" homeland. The boat had arrived at Seoul a day earlier than expected, but late at night. When I had reached home after midnight, none of the neighbours had seen me come. My father, glad as he and all the family were to see me, had said, "Enough. We'll go to bed and talk in the morning. She must be tired."

Tired I was, tired of the long, long voyage, still ill-adjusted to the many-houred change in time, so tired that I developed a fever of exhaustion that night. It was as though I had been holding it in until I could get back to my own bed before letting it go. For weeks I lay there sick.

It was at the beginning of my illness that the armies suddenly and without warning swarmed down from the north, blasting their way through my homeland, leaving us overnight under a strange regime, ruled by men of our own nation, but men warped and twisted by their training in a foreign land, by the rule of an oppressive hand, of cruel and unfeeling heart and mind.

In a faraway country on the other side of the globe, the President of the United States, the Prime Minister of His Majesty's Government, and the chairman of the Supreme Soviet, accompanied by their Chiefs of Staff and other experts on human welfare, had met. The map had glistened brightly before them with its greens and reds and yellows and blues. The fate of the world was decided. Here a cut, there a snip, and here a line. "For purposes of military convenience," the history books say, my beloved homeland was cut in two. Our minds and hearts, our families and lives, were cut into shreds.

My beloved homeland! Will your rice and your wine ever taste the same again? Will your flutes and your harps ever sound the same again?

We were at the playfield once more. The playfield of so many mixed memories, now to be the site of the most sharply etched memory of them all. The playfield where with the girls of my class I had spent so many happy hours of childhood and adolescence. The playfield which had been built during the days of our Japanese lords, the days where here as everywhere in Korea we were taught to speak, write, and think only in a foreign tongue, when a phrase spoken in our mother tongue in a public place brought a slap on the face from the lords or their Korean vassals. The playfield where my father with all the other fathers had had to go so often to prostrate himself before the Shinto shrines. The playfield where our masters revealed a change of heart to us, where they suddenly called us brothers, members of the same race, fruit of the same cultural heritage, and "invited" our young men to join their armies to fight for the glory of our "common primordial ancestors." Then we knew that the war was truly going badly for them, that their men were dying.

The playfield! We waited in the chilly dawn for our new lords to guide us. We were there by the thousand, fathers and mothers, children and elders. I saw many neighbours I hadn't seen for well over a year, but they were too preoccupied to be surprised at my sudden reappearance. We waited in the chilly dawn for our new lords to guide us.

They came. They came with their heavy boots and their heavy rifles. They came dragging twelve men behind them. Twelve men we all knew. Twelve men we had grown up with.

The men with the boots and the rifles distributed themselves among the crowd. A hundred men or more. A man here, a man there. Everyone felt the alien presence close to his skin, everyone felt the gnawing cancer digging into his soul.

Their leader climbed up on the platform and slowly turned his eyes over us, at the sea of faces all around him. A signal, and one of the twelve men was set up next to him, one of the twelve men we knew. He was a clerk in our municipal office, a man as inoffensive as he was inefficient, a man who did his insignificant work as well as his limited abilities permitted him, a man whose main interest in his job consisted in receiving his pay regularly and going home to his family at the end of each day.

I had noticed his wife and children in the crowd.

"Comrades!" bellowed the leader. "Behold a traitor to the people. As you all know, the man you see before you has for years held in his hands the lives and well-being of all the people of this community. It is he who handles the rationing records, he who can decide how much rice you are to receive and when you are to get it. Comrades, an investigation of his records has revealed gross mismanagement of the rationing system of our community. When this treacherous criminal was directed to mend his ways, he offered nothing but resistance and reactionary proposals. For ten days now he has deliberately and malevolently sabotaged every effort on our part to establish the system of food distribution in this community on a rational and an honest basis. Comrades," he cried out again to the crowd, "what shall we do with this traitor?"

"*Kill him!*" The hundred men who had distributed themselves among the crowd had raised their fists and roared out this response with a single voice: "*Kill him!*"

The leader on the platform nodded in approval. "Thank you, comrades. That is indeed the only proper treatment for traitors."

He took his heavy pistol out of its holster, held it against the man's temple, and pulled the trigger. The clerk slumped to the boards of the platform. The crowd gasped.

"*Death to traitors!*" roared the hundred men. The man's blood trickled through the cracks between the boards and stained the soil of the playfield.

Another man was hoisted up onto the platform to take his place.

"Comrades," again cried the leader, "behold a traitor to the people...."

An excited murmur went through the crowd as we recognized the man. I heard my brother whisper to my father, "Daddy! Isn't he the leader of the Communists?"

"Yes!"

"Then why?"

"Three kinds—Communists who've been in South Korea all the time; those trained in Russia and China; those trained in North Korea since the partition. They're fighting among themselves already."

The leader had finished his charges. Again he cried to the crowd: "Comrades, what shall we do with this traitor?"

"*Kill him!*" the hundred shouted as before.

But this time the leader looked displeased. "Comrades, I ask you what to do with a traitor and there is hardly any response! Comrades, think it over well. Take your time and reflect on the matter. I will ask once again a minute from now."

The hundred men glared at us, swung around in their places, and looked us each in the eye in turn. "I wonder if there could be any traitors here among us," they said for all to hear.

Then again the leader turned to the crowd. "Comrades," he bellowed once more, "What shall we do with this traitor to the people?"

"*Kill him!*" roared the hundred.

"*Kill him!*" we cried with our lips.

The leader looked pleased. He again unholstered his pistol, pressed it to the man's head, and his blood joined that of the other, dripping down to the soil of the playfield.

Ten more times did the leader harangue us. Ten more times did we shudder as we cried aloud with our lips, "*Kill him!*" Ten more times did the blood of a Korean stain the soil of Korea.

We watched and we trembled as the chilly dawn unfolded into the chilly day.

My beloved homeland!
Will your rice and your wine
    ever taste the same again?
Will your flutes and your harps
    ever sound the same again?

Cursed be the men of the East.
Cursed be the men of the West.
Cursed be those
    who have left my beloved homeland
    bleeding and torn.

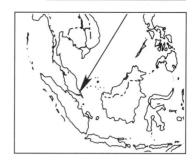

Paper

BY CATHERINE LIM

He wanted it, he dreamed of it, he hankered after it, as an addict after his opiate. Once the notion of a big beautiful house had lodged itself in his imagination, Tay Soon nurtured it until it became the consuming passion of his life. A house. A dream house such as he had seen on his drives with his wife and children along the roads bordering the prestigious housing estates on the island, and in the glossy pages of *Homes* and *Modern Living*. Or rather, it was a house which was an amalgam of the best, the most beautiful aspects of the houses he had seen. He knew every detail of his dream house already, from the aluminium sliding doors to the actual shade of the dining room carpet to the shape of the swimming pool. Kidney. He rather liked the shape. He was not ashamed of the enthusiasm with which he spoke of the dream house, an enthusiasm that belonged to women only, he was told. Indeed, his enthusiasm was so great that it had infected his wife and even his children, small though they were. Soon his wife Yee Lian was describing to her sister Yee Yeng, the dream house in all its perfection of shape and decor, and the children were telling their cousins and friends, "My daddy says that when our house is ready ..."

They talked of the dream house endlessly. It had become a reality stronger than the reality of the small terrace house which they were sharing with Tay Soon's mother, to whom it belonged. Tay Soon's mother, whose little business of selling bottled curries and vegetable preserves which she made herself, left her little time for dreams, clucked her tongue and shook her head and made sarcastic remarks about the ambitiousness of young people nowadays.

"What's wrong with this house we're staying in?" she asked petulantly. "Aren't we all comfortable in it?"

Not as long as you have your horrid ancestral altars all over the place, and your grotesque sense of colour—imagine painting the kitchen wall bright pink. But Yee Lian was tactful enough to keep the remarks to herself, or to make them only to her sister Yee Yeng, otherwise they were sure to reach the old lady, and there would be no end to her sharp tongue.

The house—the dream house—it would be a far cry from the little terrace house in which they were all staying now, and Tay Soon and Yee Lian talked endlessly about it, and it grew magnificently in their imaginations, this dream house of theirs with its timbered ceiling and panelled walls and sunken circular sitting room which was to be carpeted in rich amber. It was no empty dream, for there was much money in the bank already. Forty thousand dollars had been saved. The house would cost many times that, but Tay Soon and Yee Lian with their good salaries would be able to manage very well. Once they took care of the down payment, they would be able to pay back monthly over a period of ten years—fifteen, twenty—what did it matter how long it took as long as the dream house was theirs? It had become the symbol of the peak of earthly achievement, and all of Tay Soon's energies and devotion were directed towards its realization. His mother said, "You're a show-off; what's so grand about marble flooring and a swimming pool? Why don't you put your money to better use?" But the forty thousand grew steadily, and after Tay Soon and Yee Lian had put in every cent of their annual bonuses, it grew to forty-eight thousand, and husband and wife smiled at the smooth way their plans were going.

It was a time of growing interest in the stock market. The quotations for stocks and shares were climbing the charts, and the crowds in the rooms of the broking houses were growing perceptibly. Might we not do something about this? Yee Lian said to her husband. Do you know that Dr. Soo bought Rustan Banking for four dollars and today the shares are worth seven dollars each? The temptation was great. The rewards were almost immediate. Thirty thousand dollars' worth of NBE became fifty-five thousand almost overnight. Tay Soon and Yee Lian whooped. They put their remaining eighteen thousand in Far East Mart. Three days later the shares were worth twice that much. It was not to be imagined that things could stop here. Tay Soon secured a loan from his bank and put twenty thousand in OHTE. This was a particularly lucky share; it shot up to four times its value in three days.

"Oh, this is too much, too much," cried Yee Lian in her ecstasy, and she sat down with pencil and paper, and found after a few minutes' calculation that they had made a cool one hundred thousand in a matter of days.

And now there was to be no stopping. The newspapers were full of it, everybody was talking about it, it was in the very air. There was plenty of money to be made in the stock exchange by those who had guts—money to be made by the hour, by the minute, for the prices of stocks and shares were rising faster than anyone could keep track of them! Dr. Soo was said—he laughingly dismissed it as a silly rumour—Dr. Soo was said to have made two million dollars already. If he sold all his shares now, he would be a millionaire twice over. And Yee Yeng, Yee Lian's sister, who had been urged with sisterly good will to come join the others make money, laughed happily to find that the shares she had bought for four twenty on Tuesday had risen to seven ninety-five on Friday—she laughed and thanked Yee Lian who advised her not to sell yet, it was going further, it would hit the ten dollar mark by next week. And Tay Soon both laughed and cursed—cursed that he had failed to buy a share at nine dollars which a few days later had hit seventeen dollars! Yee Lian said reproachfully, "I thought I told you to buy it, darling," and Tay Soon had beaten his forehead in despair and said, "I know, I know, why didn't I! Big fool that I am!" And he had another reason to curse himself—he sold five thousand West Parkes at sixteen twenty-three per share, and saw, to his horror, West Parkes climb to eighteen ninety the very next day!

"I'll never sell now," he vowed. "I'll hold on. I won't be so foolish." And the frenzy continued. Husband and wife couldn't talk or think of anything else. They thought fondly of their shares—going to be worth a million altogether soon. A million! In the peak of good humour, Yee Lian went to her mother-in-law, forgetting the past insults, and advised her to join the others by buying some shares; she would get her broker to buy them immediately for her, there was sure money in it. The old lady refused curtly, and to her son later, she showed great annoyance, scolding him for being so foolish as to put all his money in those worthless shares. "Worthless!" exploded Tay Soon. "Do you know, Mother, if I sold all my shares today, I would have the money to buy fifty terrace houses like the one you have?"

His wife said, "Oh, we'll just leave her alone. I was kind enough to offer to help her make money. But since she's so nasty and ungrateful, we'll leave her alone." The comforting, triumphant thought was that soon, very soon, they would be able to purchase their dream house; it would be even more magnificent than the one they had dreamed of, since they had made almost a—Yee Lian preferred not to say the sum. There was the old superstitious fear of losing something when it is too often or too directly referred to, and Yee Lian had cautioned her husband not to make mention of their gains.

"Not to worry, not to worry," he said jovially, not superstitious like his wife, "After all, it's just paper gains so far."

The downward slide, or the bursting of the bubble as the newspapers dramatically called it, did not initially cause much alarm, for the speculators all expected the shares to bounce back to their original strength and thence continue the phenomenal growth. But that did not happen. The slide continued.

Tay Soon said nervously, "Shall we sell? Do you think we should sell?" but Yee Lian said stoutly, "There is talk that this decline is a technical thing only—it will be over soon, and then the rise will continue. After all, see what is happening in Hong Kong and London and New York. Things are as good as ever."

"We're still making, so not to worry," said Yee Lian after a few days. Their gains were pared by half. A few days later their gains were pared to marginal.

There is talk of a recovery, insisted Yee Lian. Do you know, Tay Soon, Dr. Soo's wife is buying up some OHTE and West Parkes now? She says these two are sure to rise. She has some inside information that these two are going to climb past the forty-dollar mark—

Tay Soon sold all his shares and put the money in OHTE and West Parkes. OHTE and West Parkes crashed shortly afterwards. Some began to say the shares were not worth the paper of the certificates.

"Oh, I can't believe, I can't believe it," gasped Yee Lian, pale and sick. Tay Soon looked in mute horror at her.

"All our money was in OHTE and West Parkes," he said, his lips dry.

"That stupid Soo woman!" shrieked Yee Lian. "I think she deliberately led me astray with her advice! She's always been jealous of me—ever since she knew we were going to build a house grander than hers!"

"How are we going to get our house now?" asked Tay Soon in deep distress, and for the first time he wept. He wept like a child, for the loss of all his money, for the loss of the dream house that he had never stopped loving and worshipping.

The pain bit into his very mind and soul, so that he was like a madman, unable to go to his office to work, unable to do anything but haunt the broking houses, watching with frenzied anxiety for OHTE and West Parkes to show him hope. But there was no hope. The decline continued with gleeful rapidity. His broker advised him to sell, before it was too late, but he shrieked angrily, "What! Sell at a fraction at which I bought them! How can this be tolerated!"

And he went on hoping against hope.

He began to have wild dreams in which he sometimes laughed and sometimes screamed. His wife Yee Lian was afraid and she ran sobbing to her sister who never failed to remind her curtly that all her savings were gone, simply because when she had wanted to sell, Yee Lian had advised her not to.

"But what is your sorrow compared to mine," wept Yee Lian, "see what's happening to my husband. He's cracking up! He talks to himself, he doesn't eat, he has nightmares, he beats the children. Oh, he's finished!"

Her mother-in-law took charge of the situation, while Yee Lian, wide-eyed in mute horror at the terrible change that had come over her husband, shrank away and looked to her two small children for comfort. Tight-lipped and grim, the elderly woman made herbal medicines for Tay Soon, brewing and straining for hours, and got a Chinese medicine man to come to have a look at him.

"There is a devil in him," said the medicine man, and he proceeded to make him a drink which he mixed with the ashes of a piece of prayer paper. But Tay Soon grew worse. He lay in bed, white, haggard, and delirious, seeming to be beyond the touch of healing. In the end, Yee Lian, on the advice of her sister and friends, put him in hospital.

"I have money left for the funeral," whimpered the frightened Yee Lian only a week later, but her mother-in-law sharply retorted, "You leave everything to me! I have the money for his funeral, and I shall give him the best! He wanted a beautiful house all his life; I shall give him a beautiful house now!"

She went to the man who was well-known on the island for his beautiful houses, and she ordered the best. It would come to nearly a thousand dollars, said the man, a thin, wizened fellow whose funereal gauntness and pallor seemed to be a concession to his calling.

That doesn't matter, she said, I want the best. The house is to be made of superior paper, she instructed, and he was to make it to her specifications. She recollected that he, Tay Soon, had often spoken of marble flooring, a timbered ceiling, and a kidney-shaped swimming pool. Could he simulate all these in paper?

The thin, wizened man said, "I've never done anything like that before. All my paper houses for the dead have been the usual kind—I can put in paper furniture and paper cars, paper utensils for the kitchen and paper servants, all that the dead will need in the other world. But I shall try to put in what you've asked for. Only it will cost more."

The house when it was ready, was most beautiful to see. It stood two metres tall, a delicate framework of wire and thin bamboo strips covered with finely worked paper of a myriad colours. Little silver flowers, scattered liberally throughout the entire structure, gave a carnival atmosphere. There was a paper swimming pool (round, as the man had not understood "kidney") which had to be fitted inside the house itself, as there was no provision for a garden or surrounding grounds. Inside the house were paper figures; there were at least four servants to attend to the needs of the master who was posed beside two cars, one distinctly a Chevrolet and the other a Mercedes.

At the appointed time, the paper house was brought to Tay Soon's grave and set on fire there. It burned brilliantly, and in three minutes was a heap of ashes on the grave.

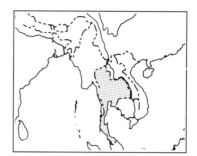

Who Needs It?

BY VILAS MANIVAT

TRANSLATED BY JENNIFER DRASKAU

Nai Phan was one of the neighbourhood celebrities. Not because he was a dancer with feet as light as stardust; nor had he distinguished himself in the fields of politics or literature. Perhaps a talent for concocting a good dish of fried rice was his claim to immortality, but even if his culinary gifts had not been outstanding, he would have been famous, for he was ready to allow his customers unlimited credit.

He liked to give children sweets without asking for money. Of course this always caused his wife to complain, but he would reply: "Twenty satangs worth of sweets won't reverse the family fortunes." The Than Khun, a high official who lived in the lane, used to say to his boy when he fancied a good cup of coffee: "Go and bring coffee from Nai Phan's. He puts in plenty of milk; you'd think he kept a cow for the purpose!"

There lived in the same lane a drunkard who loved to turn up at the cook shop and recite verses from the tale of Khun Chang and Khun Phaen; Nai Phan would listen with rapt attention. After the performance the drunkard would ask for a glass of free iced tea, which Nai Phan would gladly supply, with a doughnut thrown in for good measure.

During the rains Nai Phan would say to the young girl students, "Young ladies, you have been wading in mud with difficulty. From now on you can carry your shoes to my shop to put them on." He would always give them clean water to wash their feet.

But at eight p.m. sharp every night, he would shut up his shop. His friends would say to him, "You should start serving at night; business is good then, and you will get rich quicker."

Nai Phan would laugh good-humouredly saying, "It's better to go to bed than to get rich quick!"

This retort touched something in the hearts of listeners who were richer than Nai Phan, yet were still not satisfied with their wealth, but were struggling to amass even greater fortunes.

People who lived in the lane, returning home late at night after a long day spent chasing money, would see Nai Phan reclining in his little deck chair, chatting contentedly with his wife. Then they would think to themselves: "How happy they look, free from hankering after wealth. They are better off than us."

One evening his wife went to a cinema, and Nai Phan was alone. It was getting dark and he was preparing to close his shop, when a young man rushed in.

"What can I do for you, sir?" Nai Phan asked.

Instead of replying, the stranger produced a gun and levelled it at his heart. Nai Phan did not understand, but he felt that matters were getting out of hand.

"Hand over your cash," the young man snapped roughly, "all of it; whatever you have. Murder seems to be the fashion nowadays; people shoot each other every day. If I kill you, it will not be anything special, and if you kill me, that would not be very strange either, so be quick about it. If I don't get the money, I'll let you have a taste of bullets."

Nai Phan did not tremble. He stood quite calmly and said in a conversational tone: "I'll give you the money, but not because of your gun, I'll give it to you because you seem to need it so badly. Perhaps it is a matter of life and death. Here … all the money I have is here. Take it and hurry home. Who knows? Perhaps your mother is ill; perhaps she has not touched food for days. Hurry home; perhaps many people are waiting there, wondering whether you will bring back money or not. Many lives may depend on your return with this money. I won't tell the police. There is about nine hundred here in cash; there may be more … take it."

He placed the money on the table but the young gunman did not seem able to get up enough courage to touch it.

"Why don't you take it?" Nai Phan asked. "Look here, why would I trick you? I know you're hard up. We're all hard up these days. I don't believe you are a bad man. Who would choose to be a thief if he could afford not to? Perhaps your father has had a stroke and you have to look after him. Take him this money, but don't spend it all on medicine. Believe me, a doctor can cure the body, but a man needs a cure for his mind and soul as well. Buy some sweet-smelling flowers, a garland for your mother to place before the sacred image at home. That's what I do every night. You don't have to know what holiness is or where it lives. It is enough to feel at peace with yourself. That's heaven. Oh!— and put away your gun—you will feel better at once. A man who carries a gun cannot know peace, his heart is tortured with fear and doubt, and the scent of danger. We cannot be happy as long as our hands are cluttered with weapons."

The young man put the gun in his pocket, obedient as a child. He raised his hands in the *wai* salute to Nai Phan, who was famous for his fried rice and coffee and his generosity.

"I ought to shoot myself instead of shooting you," he said.

"Don't speak like a crazy man," said the shopkeeper, handing the young man the money. "This is all there is. Take it, it is yours. It is not a gift made in anger. I know that the prisons are full, but not of criminals. You are a man like myself, like any other man; any man, even a minister, would do the same if he were desperate."

The young gunman sat down. "I have never met you, and I have never met anyone who speaks like you. I will not take your money, but I have put away my gun. Now I'll go home to my mother like you said." He coughed a few times and continued: "I am a bad son. All the money my mother gave me I spent on the horses; the little I had left I spent on drink—"

"Everyone makes mistakes. What is life but a mixture of experiments, mistakes, and failures?" said Nai Phan.

"I'm not strong, you know," the young man went on. "Did you hear my cough? I'm afraid I've got T.B. I deserve it, I suppose, because I've done bad things—I ought really to die as soon as possible. I should not live on, burdening the earth. Thank you, and goodbye."

"You don't have to go right away. Stay on for a bit and let's talk. I'd like to get to know you. Where do you live? What are your interests? I mean, what do you believe in?"

The young man shook his head hopelessly. "I don't know where to go now. Where can I go? What do I believe in? I don't know. There seems to be nothing in this world worth believing in. I have been a miserable wretch since the day I was born; no wonder I don't like my fellow man. Sometimes I think everyone must be responsible for my bad luck. I don't want to be around people. I don't trust anyone. I hate the way men talk to each other, the way they spend their lives, the way they love and praise each other, the way they laugh and smile."

Nai Phan nodded understandingly. "Everyone feels like that sometimes."

"Can you believe me? I'm not interested in anything any more. I'm tired of everything. The whole world seems empty. There's no substance, nothing a man can hold on to or respect. If I really wanted to work I suppose I could always look for a job. But I hate the sight of human kind, I don't want any favours from them. I stay one week in one job, two weeks in another—I never stay long anywhere."

"Do you read books?"

"I used to. But I've given up. I don't even read newspapers now. Why should I? I know too well what's in them. Only shooting, robbery, murder! They change the places and the names, but the stories are always the same."

The young man rubbed his chin and squinted thoughtfully at Nai Phan. "Lucky for you you did not show any fear or anger when I threatened you with the gun. I would have killed you for sure. This world is full of men who like to show anger, mean-spirited men who are always crying out that civilization and morality are deteriorating. I don't believe it. I don't believe that because hundreds or thousands have gone bad all men must do the same. I know now that I did not come here for money but to prove to myself that my own belief is right. I used to think that although the world is losing hope and is sinking into an abyss, dirty and soiled by the sins of men, there would remain at least one man who is not a man just because he looks like one, but a real human being. He must know how to love others, how to win the respect of other men. But I could not quite believe it because I had never met anyone like that. For years I have been thinking, 'Let me meet a man who has not grown evil with the world's evil, so that I can believe that there is still goodness, so that I can have the strength to go on living.' Now I have met such a man. You have given me everything I wanted. There is nothing more to give. I am going home now. Certainly in my mind, I shall never hate the world again. I have discovered at last the sort of life I want to lead."

The stranger seemed more cheerful. He got up to leave and then, remembering, he brought out his gun. He handed it to the shopkeeper.

"Please take this. I no longer need it. It is the brand of the savage. Any man who carries a gun has no compassion or respect for others, he only respects the gun. Bandits may live by their guns, but their lives will be troubled always by the fact that their enemies may come upon them unawares. They have no time to look at the sunset or to sing. When a man has no time to sing, it is better to be a cricket or a mynah bird."

The gunman smiled happily, and waving in farewell, he added: "I'll come back to see you again, but don't let me see the gun again. It is the enemy of the pure life. Goodbye."

The stranger vanished in the darkness. Nai Phan, the shopkeeper, bent his head to inspect his newest acquisition. He was thinking that tomorrow he would sell it. He badly needed a new coffee strainer.

III EUROPE

The Vampire

BY JAN NERUDA

he excursion steamer brought us from Constantinople to the shore of the island of Prinkipo and we disembarked. The number of passengers was not large. There was one Polish family, a father, a mother, a daughter and her bridegroom, and then we two. Oh, yes, I must not forget that when we were already on the wooden bridge which crosses the Golden Horn to Constantinople, a Greek, a rather youthful man, joined us. He was probably an artist, judging by the portfolio he carried under his arm. Long black locks floated to his shoulders, his face was pale, and his black eyes were deeply set in their sockets. In the first moment he interested me, especially for his obligingness and for his knowledge of local conditions. But he talked too much, and I then turned away from him.

All the more agreeable was the Polish family. The father and mother were good-natured, fine people, the lover a handsome young fellow, of direct and refined manners. They had come to Prinkipo to spend the summer months for the sake of the daughter, who was slightly ailing. The beautiful pale girl was either just recovering from a severe illness or else a serious disease was just fastening its hold upon her. She leaned upon her lover when she walked and very often sat down to rest, while a frequent dry little cough interrupted her whispers. Whenever she coughed, her escort would considerately pause in their walk. He always cast upon her a glance of sympathetic suffering and she would look back at him as if she would say: "It is nothing. I am happy!" They believed in health and happiness.

On the recommendation of the Greek, who departed from us immediately at the pier, the family secured quarters in the hotel on the hill. The hotelkeeper was a Frenchman and his entire building was equipped comfortably and artistically, according to the French style.

We breakfasted together and when the noon heat had abated somewhat we all betook ourselves to the heights, where in the grove of Siberian stone pines we could refresh ourselves with the view. Hardly had we found a suitable spot and settled ourselves when the Greek appeared again. He greeted us lightly, looked about, and seated himself only a few steps from us. He opened his portfolio and began to sketch.

"I think he purposely sits with his back to the rocks so that we can't look at his sketch," I said.

"We don't have to," said the young Pole. "We have enough before us to look at." After a while he added, "It seems to me he's sketching us in as a sort of background. Well—let him!"

We truly did have enough to gaze at. There is not a more beautiful or more happy corner in the world than that very Prinkipo! The political martyr, Irene, contemporary of Charles the Great, lived there for a month as an exile. If I could live a month of my life there I would be happy for the memory of it for the rest of my days! I shall never forget even that one day spent at Prinkipo.

The air was as clear as a diamond, so soft, so caressing, that one's whole soul swung out upon it into the distance. At the right beyond the sea projected the brown Asiatic summits; to the left in the distance purpled the steep coasts of Europe. The neighbouring Chalki, one of the nine islands of the "Prince's Archipelago," rose with its cyprus forests into the peaceful heights like a sorrowful dream, crowned by a great structure—an asylum for those whose minds are sick.

The Sea of Marmara was but slightly ruffled and played in all colours like a sparkling opal. In the distance the sea was as white as milk, then rosy, between the two islands a glowing orange, and below us it was beautifully greenish blue, like a transparent sapphire. It was resplendent in its own beauty. Nowhere were there any large ships—only two small craft flying the English flag sped along the shore. One was a steamboat as big as a watchman's booth, the second had about twelve oarsmen, and when their oars rose simultaneously molten silver dripped from them. Trustful dolphins darted in and out among them and dove with long, arching flights above the surface of the water. Through the blue heavens now and then calm eagles winged their way, measuring the space between two continents.

The entire slope below us was covered with blossoming roses whose fragrance filled the air. From the coffeehouse near the sea music was carried up to us through the clear air, hushed somewhat by the distance.

The effect was enchanting. We all sat silent and steeped our souls completely in the picture of paradise. The young Polish girl lay on the grass with her head supported on the bosom of her lover. The pale oval of her delicate face was slightly tinged with soft colour, and from her blue eyes tears suddenly gushed forth. The lover understood, bent down and kissed tear after tear. Her mother also was moved to tears, and I—even I—felt a strange twinge.

"Here mind and body both must get well," whispered the girl. "How happy a land this is!"

"God knows I haven't any enemies, but if I had I would forgive them here!" said the father in a trembling voice.

And again we became silent. We were all in such a wonderful mood— so unspeakably sweet it all was! Each felt for himself a whole world of happiness and each one would have shared his happiness with the whole world. All felt the same—and so no one disturbed another. We had scarcely even noticed that the Greek, after an hour or so, had arisen, folded his portfolio, and with a slight nod had taken his departure. We remained.

Finally after several hours, when the distance was becoming over-spread with a darker violet, so magically beautiful in the south, the mother reminded us it was time to depart. We arose and walked down towards the hotel with the easy, elastic steps that characterize carefree children. We sat down in the hotel under the handsome veranda.

Hardly had we been seated when we heard below the sounds of quarreling and oaths. Our Greek was wrangling with the hotelkeeper, and for the entertainment of it we listened.

The amusement did not last long. "If I didn't have other guests," growled the hotelkeeper, and ascended the steps towards us.

"I beg you to tell me, sir," asked the young Pole of the approaching hotelkeeper, "who is that gentleman? What's his name?"

"Eh—who knows what the fellow's name is?" grumbled the hotelkeeper, and he gazed venomously downwards. "We call him the Vampire."

"An artist?"

"Fine trade! He sketches only corpses. Just as soon as someone in Constantinople or here in the neighbourhood dies, that very day he has a picture of the dead one completed. That fellow paints them beforehand— and he never makes a mistake—just like a vulture!"

The old Polish woman shrieked affrightedly. In her arms lay her daughter pale as chalk. She had fainted.

In one bound the lover had leaped down the steps. With one hand he seized the Greek and with the other reached for the portfolio.

We ran down after him. Both men were rolling in the sand. The contents of the portfolio were scattered all about. On one sheet, sketched with a crayon, was the head of the young Polish girl, her eyes closed and a wreath of myrtle on her brow.

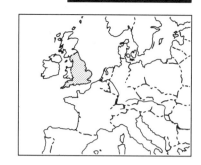

The First Death of Her Life

BY ELIZABETH TAYLOR

Suddenly tears poured from her eyes. She rested her forehead against her mother's hand and let the tears soak into the counterpane.

Dear Mr. Wilcox, she began; for her mind was always composing letters. I shall not be at the shop for the next four days, as my mother has passed away and I shall not be available until after the funeral. My mother passed away very peacefully....

The nurse came in. She took her patient's wrist for a moment, replaced it, removed a jar of forced lilac from beside the bed as if this were no longer necessary, and went out again.

The girl kneeling by the bed had looked up.

Dear Mr. Wilcox, she resumed, her face returning to the counterpane. My mother has died. I shall come back to work the day after tomorrow. Yours sincerely, Lucy Mayhew.

Her father was late. She imagined him hurrying from work, bicycling through the darkening streets, dogged, hunched up, slush thrown up by his wheels. Her mother did not move. She stroked her hand with its loose gold ring, the callused palms, the fine long fingers. Then she stood up stiffly, her knees bruised from the waxed floor, and went to the window.

Snowflakes turned idly, drifting down over the hospital gardens. It was four o'clock in the afternoon, and already the day seemed over. So few sounds came from this muffled and discoloured world. In the hospital itself there was a deep silence.

Her thoughts came to her in words, as if her mind spoke them first, understood them later. She tried to think of her childhood: little scenes she selected to prove how they loved each other. Other scenes, especially last week's quarrel, she chose to forget, not knowing that in this moment she sent them away forever. Only loving kindness remained.

But all the same, intolerable pictures broke through—her mother at the sink; her mother ironing; her mother standing between the lace curtains, staring out at the dreary street with a wounded look in her eyes; her mother tying the same lace curtains with yellow ribbons; attempts at lightness, gaiety, which came to nothing; her mother gathering her huge black cat to her, burying her face in its fur, and a great shivering sigh—of despair, boredom—escaping her.

She no longer sighed. She lay very still and sometimes took a little sip of air. Her arms were neatly at her sides. Her eyes, which all day long had been turned to the white lilac, were closed. Her cheekbones rose sharply from her bruised, exhausted face. She smelled faintly of wine.

A small lilac flower floated on a glass of champagne, now discarded on the table at her side.

The champagne, with which they hoped to stretch out the thread of her life minute by minute; the lilac; the room of her own, coming to her at the end of a life of drabness and denial, just as, all along the mean street where they lived, the dying and the dead might claim a lifetime's savings from the bereaved.

She is no longer there, Lucy thought, standing beside the bed.

All day her mother had stared at the white lilac; now she had sunk away. Outside, beyond the hospital gardens, mist settled over the town, blurred the street lamps.

The nurse returned with the matron. Ready to be on her best behaviour, Lucy tautened. In her heart she trusted her mother to die without frightening her, and when the matron, deftly drawing Lucy's head to rest on her own shoulder, said in her calm voice, "She has gone," she felt she had met this happening halfway.

A little bustle began, quick footsteps along the empty passages, and for a moment she was left alone with her dead mother. She laid her hand timidly on her soft dark hair, so often touched, played with when she was a little girl, standing on a stool behind her mother's chair while she sewed.

There was still the smell of wine and the hospital smell. It was growing dark in the room. She went to the dressing table and took her mother's handbag, very worn and shiny, and a book, a library book which she had chosen carefully for her, believing she would read it.

Then she had a quick sip from the glass on the table, a mouthful of champagne, which she had never tasted before, and, looking wounded and aloof, walked down the middle of the corridor, feeling the nurses falling away to the left and right.

Opening the glass doors onto the snowy gardens, she thought that it was like the end of a film. But no music rose up and engulfed her. Instead there was her father turning in at the gates. He propped his bicycle up against the wall and began to run clumsily across the wet gravel.

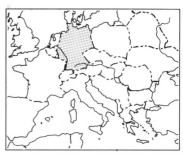

Going to Jerusalem

BY MARIE LUISE KASCHNITZ

TRANSLATED BY CLAUDIA STOEFFLER

Last year in May a mysterious disease spread throughout our town. In the months to follow it attacked the greater part of the population. The doctors knew nothing about the causes and the nature of this disease. They treated the symptoms—the patients' general debility and unusual restlessness—with the standard fortifying or subduing remedies. It was said they were waiting for the first patient to die so that they could dissect him and use the findings to continue their research. In the meantime, though they themselves were sick by now, they tried to reassure their patients who were not bedridden. In fact, most of the patients came to their waiting rooms almost daily for fear of missing a newly discovered cure or any other new development. They assured them that in spite of their extreme weakness and nervous trembling, their vital organs were not affected and that there was no cause for alarm. And as long as the doctors kept seeing them, the patients were completely convinced that they were right. Their dispositions improved and they were even able to make jokes. But this cheerfulness was short-lived. As soon as they went out into the street and saw all the frightened faces nervously twitching they fell back into their former gloom and fear.

In the last few days of summer the morale in our town was already quite low. No one had been allowed to leave the city during those summer months because of the very real possibility of contagion and this had left us all in an extremely depressed state. Many of us had imagined that we need only have left the city for a vacation in order to get well—just as a termi-nally ill patient desperately wants to leave his bed because he believes that he will be truly tormented there and only there. The first death, which was generally regarded as the last form of salvation, had not occurred yet, and we were beginning to watch each other closely, on the lookout for the shadow of death in the faces of even our most beloved friends.

The strange events I am about to relate took place on three consecu-tive days in the month of October, in the waiting room of my doctor, who was widely reputed for his extreme patience and whose waiting room was always crowded. On the first day all of the chairs had already been taken by nine o'clock, and there were many people standing between them. It was cold and damp outside. A light was burning in the vestibule which served as an additional waiting room; winter coats were clinging to each other on the coat racks while their owners were crouched down next to each other in morose silence. All of a sudden a man began to tell a story. No one wanted to listen to him—after all, we weren't in the Orient—and how could people in our situation still care about stories anyway? The man was leaning against the wall way in the back of the room and took no notice of our angry coughing; his voice, which had sounded just as dull and weak as ours at first, grew increasingly stronger as he continued to talk. This aroused astonishment and then anger. I turned around to look at him; he was pale just as we all were, of medium height, middle-aged, and shabbily dressed. He had bright, inquisitive eyes like those of a child. The story he was telling was repulsive. It was the story of a man who had been eaten alive by rats in a prison and who was thinking about all sorts of equally horrible experiences while this was happening. However, the defiant perseverance with which the storyteller presented these atrocities had us all listening to him in the end—attentively, no, even eagerly.

The following day at about the same time most of the same people as the day before were in the waiting room, since the doctor had closed his office early. The stranger was there as well and was leaning against the same place on the panelled wall as he had the day before. When it looked as if he were about to begin another story, he immediately had an attentive audi-ence—an audience that angrily hissed at each newcomer entering the room as if they were in the theatre or in a concert hall. However, it soon turned out that the stranger had no intention of telling a story this time, either because he was too tired or too listless. He said one word, was silent for a long time, said another word and stopped again, and so on and so forth. It was not particularly entertaining since these words had no connection with each other and were not even special words; in short, it was a sort of hodge-podge. It seems incomprehensible why we listened to him so attentively and why every patient called into the doctor's office only went hesitatingly, almost against his will. It was probably because each individually spoken word evoked certain memories or hopes within us. Somehow each word seemed to hang in empty space, large and heavy.

On the following day the mood in the waiting room was cheerful, one could almost say it was gay. The stranger had come up with a game for us to play and had already begun to give us instructions. Many chairs were needed for the game and some were taken out of the doctor's dining room. I suddenly remembered, wasn't there supposed to be a piano, too, with some-one playing "I'm Going to Jerusalem;" then the player suddenly stops and everyone has to find a seat, but there aren't enough for everyone; one chair is missing. Crazy, I thought, a game like this in a doctor's waiting room. What are we anyway, children? But I said nothing; I got in line and began circling the chairs along with everyone else. There was no piano. The stranger was drumming out a beat on a gong with his fingers. The gong was probably part of the doctor's dining room set. The stranger was beating out an entrancing but terrifying rhythm. We moved forward, giggling, whisper-ing and then becoming silent, faster and faster, tripping, shuffling along, always expecting the drumming to stop. When it finally did, we rushed for the chairs, no longer playfully, but filled with fear and anger as if it were of the utmost importance—a matter of life and death—to get a seat. And then we were suddenly all sitting; no one was standing. There was no chair miss-ing after all—but why? Because the stranger had fallen down, because he was lying sprawled out on the floor next to the door, dead.

Almost a year has passed since the day we played that childish game in the doctor's waiting room. The disease is as good as cured; even the most difficult cases have shown signs of improvement. It's possible, but no one knows for sure, that our town was saved by the death of the first victim, that very same storyteller and word-sayer. It's also possible that at precisely that time a cure for the mysterious disease had been discovered somewhere else, in a completely different country, in America or in Australia; in any case, a lot of research has been done on it. But even if that is true, I shall continue to think of that peculiar stranger for a long time to come. I will try to reconstruct his unpleasant story; sometimes I catch myself beating out the fascinating rhythm of his drumming with my fingers on a table. I will try to recall and write down the words he had said between the long periods of silence. Blackberry—bush—rain—ice flower—midnight ... is it possible that it really wasn't anything else?

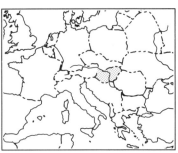

Mr. Selfsame

OR, PSYCHOPHYSICS OF THE FRICTION
BETWEEN THE UPPER STRATA OF
SOCIETY AND THE COMMON PEOPLE
(BEING A COMPREHENSIVE STUDY OF THE CAUSES OF SOCIAL STRUGGLES,
IN TWO VOLUMES)

BY FRIGYES KARINTHY

TRANSLATED BY ISTVÁN FARKAS

Volume One

Mr. Selfsame (clutching the handles of the door of a tramcar, his feet planted against a notice saying "Full up," which means that not more than another twenty-five persons may now board the tram, pressing his forehead against the pile of crushed corpses on the platform): What d'you mean, there's no more room? There certainly is—if you'll just move up a little! It's an outrage not to let a chap get in. Why, I've just as much right to get in as you people who are inside already! Awfully sorry I've stepped on your hand, sir, there's a war on, you know. Now if there's no other way, we shall have to use force to assert our rights! If the management sits back, twiddling their thumbs, while some can get in and others can't—well, then it's we who'll set things right. D'you think I'm not in a hurry just as you are? What d'you mean, you got on the car at the last stop? A fat lot I care! You've been on it long enough! Get out! Jabber as much as you like—the issue isn't who's been waiting longer and who hasn't, thanks to God knows what corrupt favouritism, but rather who is clever enough and tough enough to deserve getting on. Out of my way! Down with the car-driver! Down with fat-bellies! Up the revolution! Cha-aarge—! (In a sweeping attack, he pushes his way on to the platform. The car moves off.)

Volume Two

Mr. Selfsame (at next stop, pressing forward to the edge of the platform, harangues the crowd surging up the steps): Now, now, gentlemen! Please! For heaven's sake, don't you see there's no more room in here? Why, this platform's on the point of breaking down! So stop pushing and jostling like so many dumb sheep!! Where's your human dignity, gentlemen? After all, we are human beings! Why, even brute beasts know better than to try and get on a tram that's full up! For goodness' sake, gentlemen, let's maintain law and order or we face the annihilation of all that a wise government has created for the benefit of the Hungary of tomorrow and for constitutional development within the bounds of law! Patience, gentlemen, patience! Wait for the next tram. Patience exercised with competence and prudence is sure to bear fruit in good time, is sure to bring us a better future—always, of course, within the confines of legality. Think of the civilized West, gentlemen. In the name of society I call upon each of you, gentlemen, peaceably to disengage his solar plexus from that of his neighbour and to wait for the next tram! Long live our conductor! Long live our beloved driver, who has shown such commendable wisdom in guiding our car in these days of hardship! Long live the Government!

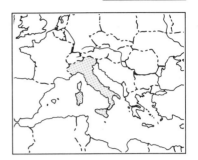

The Giraffe

BY MAURO SENESI

The giraffe entered our town in the morning and looked at us all from high above. It had been brought along to attract a crowd by one of those men who set themselves up in the squares to sell razor blades. It was taller than the steeple, seen in perspective, but its eyes seemed close to us just the same, and rosy and good like stars at dawn.

Not only the children fell under a spell watching it, but we boys too, even the men and the women at first. It was the most extraordinary thing that had ever been in our square. Slowly it would lower its head and then raise it again to a dizzying height. It must have seen over the houses the clotted red of the roofs and the horizon, who knows how far.

We boys made faces at it from below and shouted dirty words as if it were a girl with a long neck; it was only a way of distinguishing ourselves from the children, who admired it with their mouths wide open, but inside we felt still more joy and excitement than they did. By now we had discovered everything in our world, we knew the alleys, the houses of the town one by one, and the people, the words, the seasons, the days always the same: a reality full of limits that now the giraffe extended easily. We felt we were in Africa just to see it.

Every minute we had free—Flavio, Agostino, Boddo, the others, and I—there we were in the square, making a circle around it. The peddler said, "Will you come, come and buy my blades?" But our beards hadn't grown yet enough for us to need them.

All at once we saw the man's face turn red and then white, we saw him fall to the ground and lie there, still. The giraffe swung its head down slowly and kept it low, immobile over him. Soon after, the doctor arrived and said, "He's dead, just like that."

When they had taken him away, the giraffe raised its head again in the middle of the square. It moved its jaws, and its eyes had suddenly become attentive. The people standing around said, "Poor animal, what will we do with it?"

No one knew, not even the policeman, and it was then that Rolandino jumped out and said, "I'll keep it, until someone comes to get it."

What will you do with it, Rolandino, with a giraffe?

Rolandino was a stubby boy, couldn't even reach high enough to touch its belly, so of course the people standing there had to laugh, but we boys told him, "We'll help you, or else it'll eat you alive."

Rolandino took it by the halter and we pushed it from behind, because at first it didn't want to budge. The people asked us, "Where will you take it? What will you do with it?"

What will we do with it, boys, with a giraffe?

At last it moved and from then on gently followed us. It was lovely and new, leading it through our narrow streets. The roofs couldn't imprison that high head, and it seemed they took on another aspect and we ourselves had another look about us too. It was as if the giraffe were our periscope, to see from up above who knows what, who knows where.

Meanwhile we studied every spot on its skin, every movement of its delicate muscles, its every expression. By the time we were done, it seemed we had built it with our own hands.

A thing pure and agile amid the stumpy, blackened shapes of the houses; even the girls seemed homely in comparison, standing still at their doors, and you could tell by their eyes how much they would have liked to come along after us. Whereas the old women crossed themselves as if it were a wild beast, our giraffe.

We didn't know what to give it to eat, but it took care of that itself, denuding the trees the Mayor had had planted in a little square to camouflage it as a public park. A giraffe, certainly, is more important than leaves (anyway the winter would have eaten them), and yet everyone put up a fuss, even to going and calling the policeman, who came and said, "If you don't take it away I'll kill it with my revolver."

Then it began to get dark and the eyes of our giraffe grew little by little larger and almost bloody, and we led it close to other people on purpose to give them a fright. Even most of the men, besides the old women, didn't know, right then and there, whether giraffes are fierce or not.

Rolandino especially was happy when the giraffe—letting its head droop low—made someone go running. It was a kind of revenge for him, so tiny and used to having to run away from everyone else. He felt tall and free, escaped from reality, when he had that absurd wonderful animal close by, as for that matter all of us did, even though we kept pretending we had taken it up as a game.

The darkness became so thick it swallowed up the giraffe's head, which was taller still than the street lamps; there remained only its grey and slender legs dancing among us, over the stones. For a while, we continued wandering through the town, by now deserted. Our town went to bed early nights. We took the giraffe in front of the windows, so that its head looked in from outside. No one had been expecting it, that glance, in the privacy of their homes, and cries of fear or of shame were heard. Who knows what our giraffe had discovered?

When all the shutters had been closed with a bang, a tremor seemed to pass down the animal's long legs. Rolandino said, "He's cold, he's used to the sun of Africa, where can we find a place for him to sleep?"

There wasn't a house or a stall high enough for it and we didn't know what to do. The cold came from every part of the horizon, squeezing us together into a tight circle. The giraffe's skin was icy as a stone and all at once we seemed to have a monument before us.

A funny giraffe monument, boys, pierces slender and long into the sky. What shall we do with it?

Rolandino had an idea and said, "It'd fit into the church."

We felt dismayed for a second, but then one of us said, "I'll go and rob the key from the sexton." Another said, "God will certainly be happy to have it as a guest."

It took some doing to make it lower its head enough—and it wasn't much—to enter the church. Then we had to light a candle or two and the giraffe looked smaller to us but its shadow immense over the nave. Motionless it remained all night in front of the altar while we dozed here and there among the pews and the confessionals. By morning however it had eaten the roses, the carnations, the lilies, the chrysanthemums, and the candles, too.

It was then that the little old women dressed in black arrived for the first Mass and they began to shout, to cry, to pray. The giraffe, frightened, withdrew to the front of the church, placing its head right next to that of Jesus.

The Priest arrived from the sacristy and at first buried his hands in his red hair but then we thought we saw him smile, even though he charged us to take that beast immediately out of the house of God.

The town had awakened early that morning; we found the square full of people who were angry with us and our giraffe, the women on account of the profaned church and the men perhaps on account of its glances at them through their windows the night before, sudden, merciless, and divine. But there must have been other reasons too for the hatred of the people: like the defence of an equilibrium, of a reality that we wanted to subvert with our giraffe. So many reasons there must have been, but we boys couldn't understand, we knew only that they had matured in a single night, like poisonous mushrooms.

Even the Mayor was there and furious because of his lovely little trees, now bare. He said, "We'll have to kill the giraffe." Everyone agreed. If they kill it, boys, shall we start the revolution?

Luckily Rolandino had another idea. He began to run all of a sudden, pulling the giraffe behind him, the Mayor and the people moved aside. We other boys slipped into the gap he had opened, without giving heed to our mothers and our bosses who were calling us, because it was time to return to everyday life.

Out of the square and beyond the town we ran, behind the sinuous giraffe, to look for hayfields. Soon we were moving in harmony with it, a magical lightness in our limbs, until panting we stopped in a field on the side of a hill and Rolandino said happily, "We've made it."

Among ourselves we pretended it was a game, whereas it wasn't. We set to work pulling hay from the earth with our hands and the farmers looked at us grimly from the threshing floor but they didn't have the courage to come out. Who knows whether they're fierce, those giraffes?

Meanwhile we made plans for getting it back in the town, thinking of ways to force it on the Mayor and the people. Livio said, "We could build it a house next to the town walls and put a fence around it, make a zoo."

Rolandino said the giraffe had to stay free.

But our talk was useless, and it was slow, for we knew we were defeated. And the giraffe knew it, too; we held the hay up but it didn't want any. It kept its head high and immobile on its stiffened neck, its eyes had an opaque, anemic red in them, like the stars when they're on the point of dying out.

Rolandino said, "It's the cold, or maybe those leaves it ate have hurt it somehow." There were tears in his voice.

Our giraffe stood still, its head piercing the sky. We called it in vain, we punched it with sticks and climbed on one another's shoulders to carry the sweet-smelling hay to its mouth, which it didn't open.

Slowly, then, it folded its legs. Its neck alone remained erect for an instant, before flowing to the ground with a long desperate sob. Its eyes were at our feet and we saw that they were spent, solid, and smooth, like those of marble statues.

Our giraffe has died by itself, boys, there was no need for them to kill it. Damn this town anyway, where giraffes can't live, because there's room only for the things that are already here.

A Son's Return

BY ANDRIS JAKUBĀNS

TRANSLATED BY DUDLEY HEGER

On the outskirts of Riga, in a little street called Linden, in a tiny, tumble-down house with a rusty roof and creaky steps, Kalniņš lay on her death bed. She lay seriously, solemnly, with her hands folded across her breast. She gazed out the window at the white lilac bushes, the black smoke-stacks of the factory. She listened to the bleating of her goat and the rumble of the electric trains travelling endlessly from Torņakalns to Zasulauks, from Zasulauks to Torņakalns.

"How are you feeling, Mamma?" her daughter asked.

"No word from Arnolds?" she asked, instead of answering.

"Would you like something to drink? I'll make you some linden tea. It will help your chest pains."

"Could it be that he has sent a telegram, and you are keeping it from me?"

"No, Mamma, nothing has come. You get some rest now. Take a little nap."

"All right, I'll try. Maybe I'll see Arnolds in a dream."

The doctor came. He took the patient's pulse, measured her blood pressure.

"I must say, you look much better today. That's a good girl."

"Doctor, please, would you peek into the mailbox for me? Isn't there anything from my son? The postman was just here. I don't trust my daughter. Just take a look, please, doctor."

The doctor put his instruments back into his bag and went out the door. He looked into the mailbox by the gate. It was empty.

"Is he your youngest son?"

"Youngest, only, and good-for-nothing," answered Kalniņš. And once again she listened to the trains rumbling from Torņakalns to Zasulauks, from Zasulauks to Torņakalns.

In the hall, while he was washing his hands in a white-enamelled basin, the doctor asked Kalniņš's daughter what had become of Arnolds. Zelma pulled her mother's door closed.

"He ran off. He just took and ran off! And nobody knows where. He never writes; he never comes to visit. He didn't even say goodbye to mother. And he didn't even finish school. He's a hooligan and a trouble-maker. Did you see that mangy goat in the yard? He used to paint it up like a zebra, like a giraffe, like heaven knows what! That's why she started to lose her coat. She used to look like the devil; now she's getting to look like a pig with horns. Her milk has dried up, and all she's good for is making a racket night and day. But mamma doesn't want to part with her. You know how old people are. They get queer notions.

"And you know what else he used to do? Put bullets on the train tracks. When the trains would come by, the bullets would go off. It didn't hurt the trains any, of course, but we couldn't sleep nights. Every time, we thought the end had come for us all. He was an empty-headed fellow, I tell you: nothing on his mind but pranks and stupidities. Who knows where he is now; his kind doesn't come to any good. I think that if mamma ever sees him again, it will only be in the next world."

"You know your mother is very ill. The only reason she hasn't gone, as you say, to the next world, is that she is hoping to see her son again in this one."

The doctor wiped his hands on a white linen towel, and left without saying goodbye. There was a scent of lilacs in the yard, and the doctor reflected how hard it is to die sometimes. Much harder than being born... The end had come for this woman. Her daughter and son-in-law had made preparations for the funeral. Yesterday the daughter's husband had started a conversation about their plans to sell the tumble-down old house and buy a co-operative apartment in a new building. And the goat, which used to look like the devil, and now had come to resemble a horned pig, was also to be sold. It should have been done long ago. Why keep a laughingstock for the boys of Linden Street and the rest of the neighbourhood? But the mother is waiting, waiting, for her son.

The shutters creak; the goat bleats. Zelma came out onto the porch and threw water from the basin in which the doctor had washed his hands onto the goat. The goat shook the water off, fell silent, and began to eat the white blossoms of the lilac bush.

A taxi appeared in the narrow street. The doctor squeezed up against the fence to let it pass. The taxi stopped at the house of Kalniņš.

"My boy has come," the mother whispered. "Daughter, run out into the yard, bring your brother into the house."

Zelma ran out onto the porch and saw a man laughing in the middle of the yard.

"How do you like that, she's still alive. Just look at her eating those lilacs! A goat in the role of a gardener!"

"Get away, you pest!" Zelma threw a basket at the goat. The basket caught on the goat's horn and the goat, trying to shake it off, began to turn somersaults around the yard. The man laughed, and tried without success to free the animal from the basket.

"Mother is dying," his sister said, and repeated: "Mother is dying."

The mother looked at him with dry, time-faded eyes.

"How short your hair is, son. Such a big man, and such short hair. You've grown good-looking, but you still have your freckles."

"Mamma!"

"Son, you naughty boy, you scamp, how could you ..." Tears stood in the mother's eyes, then started to roll down along her deep wrinkles.

Her son suddenly saw how old she had become.

"Son, how could you? You didn't finish school; you didn't even say goodbye to your mother. You could at least have done that much. Are you married?"

"Yes."

"Did you finish school?"

"No."

"Is your wife a good girl?"

"Yes, she's all right."

"Do you have any children?"

"No children."

"Bring me something to drink. Zelma has brewed some linden tea."

His sister handed him the cup. He wanted to give it to his mother, but she asked him to hold it to her lips himself.

"Why did you come without your wife?"

"I'll bring her soon, Mamma."

"And you didn't bring a present for me."

"Please forgive me; I thought that the old house had probably been torn down long ago, and that I wouldn't find anyone here."

"Yes, that's the way you are."

"That's the way I am."

"You're the same as always."

"Almost."

"Do you still play tricks?"

"Yes, there's that."

"You didn't shave today?"

"No."

"Like your father; he didn't like to go to the barber either. He was always going around unshaven. He died last year. In the fall. He sawed the firewood for the winter. He brought the potatoes from the market. And he died. He had just got the potatoes home when he died. If I die now, you will say: 'I had just got home, and Mamma died.' "

Kalniņš fell silent and looked at her son, then at the lilacs in the yard.

"You probably don't have much time? You're in a hurry? At least tell me where you work. What you do."

Her son was silent. You could hear the goat thrashing around with the basket. Some boys, sitting on the fence, were shouting: "Pig! Hey, pig with horns! Where are you going with that basket?"

"So you had to start teasing the goat right away?"

"Mamma, could you wait an hour or so? I'll be quick."

Her son stood up.

"Don't go! Don't go away! Zelma, give him something to eat. He's hungry."

"Mamma, I'll be back in forty minutes."

"Don't go!"

"I'll be back. Wait, Mamma."

"Why get upset; that's the way he always was. You know that better than I do." The daughter straightened the blanket on her mother's bed.

"He said he would be back, didn't he?"

"He said. He said," she mimicked. She was glad that her husband was not here; otherwise, she would have had to tell him all over again how ashamed she was of her brother, would have had once more to express her amazement that no one had as yet finished off a bandit like him, would have had to repeat that it was as plain as day that his place in the next world was not in heaven, but in the Other Place.

"Daughter, you have no kindness in your heart. And you don't understand what it is to wait."

"Mamma, try to get some rest."

"Zelma, go out into the yard; maybe he hasn't really left at all."

And her mother once again listened to the electric trains rumble from Torņakalns to Zasulauks, from Zasulauks to Torņakalns.

And in forty minutes there occurred an event that became the subject of endless discussion on Linden Street, and in the whole district. Because of this event, the death of old Kalniņš, that same old Kalniņš who had the goat that looked like a pig, and who had the rascal son, became a legend. It is told and retold, and every teller adds a little something of his own. In a word, old Kalniņš died on the day when ...

A bus stopped at the end of Linden Street. From it emerged strangely dressed people with comical makeup. They mustered up into a long line. In front was a band. They moved off along the street. The band played loud enough to scare the devil. The whole procession turned in to Kalniņš's yard. This was all seen by the Bērziņi, and the Ozoliņi, and the Kļaviņi, and the Liepiņi, and the Vītoliņi, and the Priedīši, and the Englīši, and the Apsīši, and the Osīši[1]... all of Linden Street saw the circus enter Kalniņš's yard. An honest-to-goodness, real-life circus. There was a lady with dogs, a man with a bear, two huge strongmen with weights, three beautiful girls (dressed like ballerinas), and clowns, and also one long, tall fellow in a tailcoat. The one in the tails went into the house and carried Kalniņš out onto the porch. He set her down in a rocking chair and bowed to the ground before her. Everyone understood that it was her long-lost son, Arnolds. Then Arnolds waved his hand, and out of nowhere appeared—a huge bouquet of white lilacs. He handed it to his mother. Then another bouquet appeared, this time of purple lilacs. After that appeared an orange bouquet, and so on and on. Kalniņš sat amid the flowers and cried. Then Arnolds brought out something that looked like a suitcase and opened it. Out came the man with the bear. And they started to dance and bow down to his mother. He opened the thing like a suitcase again, and out came the three beautiful girls (dressed like ballerinas). They also bowed down to his mother, as if asking her pardon for something.

"Which one of them is your wife?" asked Kalniņš.

"My wife will be here in just a minute."

Arnolds once again opened the thing like a suitcase, and out came the lady with the dogs. The dogs turned somersaults and bowed. The lady went up to his mother, kissed her, and threw a huge shawl, with silver ornaments, around the old woman's shoulders. She said that she loved Kalniņš's son very much, and that soon they would have a baby.

All this was so wonderful that Kalniņš began to cry. All this was so astonishing that Bērziņiete and Vītoliņiete, Kļaviņiete and Liepiņiete, Apsiņiene and Priedītiete, Eglitiene, Apsītiene and Ošiņiete[2], together with all their daughters, cried along with her. Arnolds cried, and so did his sister Zelma. And, as is well known, when people cry from joy their tears are not salty.

Only the hairless goat failed to understand any of it. She just watched the clowns as they swung through the trees and threw swords from up there to Arnolds. He caught the swords in his bare hands and threw them back to the clowns, meanwhile tossing around thirty-kilogram weights.

"Alas, son, life hasn't taught you anything. You were a trickster before, and a trickster you have remained," said old Kalniņš, and died.

Immediately the swords fell to the ground. Everyone hung their heads, even the bear and the dogs. The band fell silent. It grew still, very still. You could hear the lilac bushes swaying in the wind, it was so still.

They buried old Kalniņš at the Martinovsky cemetery, right beside her husband.

Arnolds and his wife rove around the whole world; Zelma and her husband now live in a big co-operative apartment building.

---

[1] Common Latvian family names formed from the names of trees, respectively: birch, oak, maple, linden, willow, pine, fir, aspen, ash.

[2] The same names, but in the feminine form.

The Elephant

BY SLAWOMIR MROŻEK

TRANSLATED BY KONRAD SYROP

The director of the Zoological Gardens had shown himself to be an upstart. He regarded his animals simply as stepping stones on the road of his own career. He was indifferent to the educational importance of his establishment. In his zoo the giraffe had a short neck, the badger had no burrow, and the whistlers, having lost all interest, whistled rarely and with some reluctance. These shortcomings should not have been allowed, especially as the zoo was often visited by parties of schoolchildren.

The zoo was in a provincial town, and it was short of some of the most important animals, among them the elephant. Three thousand rabbits were a poor substitute for the noble giant. However, as our country developed, the gaps were being filled in a well-planned manner. On the occasion of the anniversary of the Liberation, on 22nd July, the zoo was notified that it had at long last been allocated an elephant. All the staff, who were devoted to their work, rejoiced at this news. All the greater was their surprise when they learned that the director had sent a letter to Warsaw, renouncing the allocation and putting forward a plan for obtaining an elephant by more economic means.

"I, and all the staff," he had written, "are fully aware how heavy a burden falls upon the shoulders of Polish miners and foundry men because of the elephant. Desirous of reducing our costs, I suggest that the elephant mentioned in your communication should be replaced by one of our own procurement. We can make an elephant out of rubber, of the correct size, fill it with air, and place it behind railings. It will be carefully painted the correct colour and even on close inspection will be indistinguishable from the real animal. It is well known that the elephant is a sluggish animal and it does not run and jump about. In the notice on the railings we can state that this particular elephant is particularly sluggish. The money saved in this way can be turned to the purchase of a jet plane or the conservation of some church monument.

"Kindly note that both the idea and its execution are my modest contribution to the common task and struggle.

"I am, etc."

This communication must have reached a soulless official, who regarded his duties in a purely bureaucratic manner and did not examine the heart of the matter but, following only the directive about reduction of expenditure, accepted the director's plan. On hearing the Ministry's approval, the director issued instructions for the making of the rubber elephant.

The carcass was to have been filled with air by two keepers blowing into it from opposite ends. To keep the operation secret the work was to be completed during the night because the people of the town, having heard that an elephant was joining the zoo, were anxious to see it. The director insisted on haste also because he expected a bonus, should his idea turn out to be a success.

The two keepers locked themselves in a shed normally housing a workshop, and began to blow. After two hours of hard blowing they discovered that the rubber skin had risen only a few centimetres above the floor and its bulge in no way resembled an elephant. The night progressed. Outside, human voices were stilled and only the cry of the jackass interrupted the silence. Exhausted, the keepers stopped blowing and made sure that the air already inside the elephant should not escape. They were not young and were unaccustomed to this kind of work.

"If we go on at this rate," said one of them, "we shan't finish by morning. And what am I to tell my missus? She'll never believe me if I say that I spent the night blowing up an elephant."

"Quite right," agreed the second keeper. "Blowing up an elephant is not an everyday job. And it's all because our director is a leftist."

They resumed their blowing, but after another half-hour they felt too tired to continue. The bulge on the floor was larger but still nothing like the shape of an elephant.

"It's getting harder all the time," said the first keeper.

"It's an uphill job, all right," agreed the second. "Let's have a little rest."

While they were resting, one of them noticed a gas pipe ending in a valve. Could they not fill the elephant with gas? He suggested it to his mate.

They decided to try. They connected the elephant to the gas pipe, turned the valve, and to their joy in a few minutes there was a full-sized beast standing in the shed. It looked real: the enormous body, legs like columns, huge ears, and the inevitable trunk. Driven by ambition the director had made sure of having in his zoo a very large elephant indeed.

"First class," declared the keeper who had the idea of using gas. "Now we can go home."

In the morning the elephant was moved to a special run in a central position, next to the monkey cage. Placed in front of a large real rock it looked fierce and magnificent. A big notice proclaimed: "Particularly sluggish. Hardly moves."

Among the first visitors that morning was a party of children from the local school. The teacher in charge of them was planning to give them an object-lesson about the elephant. He halted the group in front of the animal and began:

"The elephant is a herbivorous mammal. By means of its trunk it pulls out young trees and eats their leaves."

The children were looking at the elephant with enraptured admiration. They were waiting for it to pull out a young tree, but the beast stood still behind its railings.

"... The elephant is a direct descendant of the now-extinct mammoth. It's not surprising, therefore, that it's the largest living land animal."

The more conscientious pupils were making notes.

"... Only the whale is heavier than the elephant, but then the whale lives in the sea. We can safely say that on land the elephant reigns supreme."

A slight breeze moved the branches of the trees in the zoo.

"... The weight of a fully grown elephant is between four thousand and six thousand kilograms."

At that moment the elephant shuddered and rose in the air. For a few seconds it swayed just above the ground, but a gust of wind blew it upward until its mighty silhouette was against the sky. For a short while people on the ground could see the four circles of its feet, its bulging belly, and the trunk, but soon, propelled by the wind, the elephant sailed above the fence and disappeared above the treetops. Astonished monkeys in the cage continued staring into the sky.

They found the elephant in the neighbouring botanical gardens. It had landed on a cactus and punctured its rubber hide.

The schoolchildren who had witnessed the scene in the zoo soon started neglecting their studies and turned into hooligans. It is reported that they drink liquor and break windows. And they no longer believe in elephants.

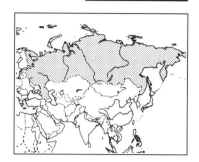

The Ninny

BY ANTON CHEKHOV

TRANSLATED BY ROBERT PAYNE

Just a few days ago I invited Yulia Vassilyevna, the governess of my children, to come to my study. I wanted to settle my account with her.

"Sit down, Yulia Vassilyevna," I said to her. "Let's get our accounts settled. I'm sure you need some money, but you keep standing on ceremony and never ask for it. Let me see. We agreed to give you thirty rubles a month, didn't we?"

"Forty."

"No, thirty. I made a note of it. I always pay the governess thirty. Now, let me see. You have been with us for two months?"

"Two months and five days."

"Two months exactly. I made a note of it. So you have sixty rubles coming to you. Subtract nine Sundays. You know you don't tutor Kolya on Sundays, you just go out for a walk. And then the three holidays ... "

Yulia Vassilyevna blushed and picked at the trimmings of her dress, but said not a word.

"Three holidays. So we take off twelve rubles. Kolya was sick for four days—those days you didn't look after him. You looked after Vanya, only Vanya. Then there were the three days you had toothache, when my wife gave you permission to stay away from the children after dinner. Twelve and seven makes nineteen. Subtract.... That leaves ... hm ... forty-one rubles. Correct?"

Yulia Vassilyevna's left eye reddened and filled with tears. Her chin trembled. She began to cough nervously, blew her nose, and said nothing.

"Then around New Year's Day you broke a cup and saucer. Subtract two rubles. The cup cost more than that—it was a heirloom, but we won't bother about that. We're the ones who pay. Another matter. Due to your carelessness Kolya climbed a tree and tore his coat. Subtract ten. Also, due to your carelessness the chambermaid ran off with Vanya's boots. You ought to have kept your eyes open. You get a good salary. So we dock off five more.... On the tenth of January you took ten rubles from me."

"I didn't," Yulia Vassilyevna whispered.

"But I made a note of it."

"Well, yes—perhaps ... "

"From forty-one we take twenty-seven. That leaves fourteen."

Her eyes filled with tears, and her thin, pretty little nose was shining with perspiration. Poor little child!

"I only took money once," she said in a trembling voice. "I took three rubles from your wife ... never anything more."

"Did you now? You see, I never made a note of it. Take three from fourteen. That leaves eleven. Here's your money, my dear. Three, three, three ... one and one. Take it, my dear."

I gave her the eleven rubles. With trembling fingers she took them and slipped them into her pocket.

"*Merci*," she whispered.

I jumped up, and began pacing up and down the room. I was in a furious temper.

"Why did you say '*merci*'?" I asked.

"For the money."

"Dammit, don't you realize I've been cheating you? I steal your money, and all you can say is '*merci*'!"

"In my other places they gave me nothing."

"They gave you nothing! Well, no wonder! I was playing a trick on you—a dirty trick.... I'll give you your eighty rubles, they are all here in an envelope made out for you. Is it possible for anyone to be such a nitwit? Why didn't you protest? Why did you keep your mouth shut? Is it possible that there is anyone in this world who is so spineless? Why are you such a ninny?"

She gave me a bitter little smile. On her face I read the words: "Yes, it is possible."

I apologized for having played this cruel trick on her, and to her great surprise gave her the eighty rubles. And then she said *"merci"* again several times, always timidly, and went out. I gazed after her, thinking how very easy it is in this world to be strong.

Father and I

BY PÄR LAGERKVIST

I remember one Sunday afternoon when I was about ten years old, Daddy took my hand and we went for a walk in the woods to hear the birds sing. We waved goodbye to mother, who was staying at home to prepare supper, and so couldn't go with us. The sun was bright and warm as we set out briskly on our way. We didn't take this bird singing too seriously, as though it was something special or unusual. We were sensible people, Daddy and I. We were used to the woods and the creatures in them, so we didn't make any fuss about it. It was just because it was Sunday afternoon and Daddy was free. We went along the railway line where other people aren't allowed to go, but Daddy belonged to the railway and had a right to. And in this way we came direct into the woods and did not need to take a roundabout way. Then the bird song and all the rest began at once. They chirped in the bushes; hedge sparrows, thrushes, and warblers; and we heard all the noises of the little creatures as we came into the woods. The ground was thick with anemones, the birches were dressed in their new leaves, and the pines had young, green shoots. There was such a pleasant smell everywhere. The mossy ground was steaming a little, because the sun was shining upon it. Everywhere there was life and noise; bumblebees flew out of their holes, midges circled where it was damp. The birds shot out of the bushes to catch them and then dived back again. All of a sudden a train came rushing along and we had to go down the embankment. Daddy hailed the driver with two fingers to his Sunday hat: the driver saluted and waved his hand. Everything seemed on the move. As we went on our way along the sleepers which lay and oozed tar in the sunshine, there was a smell of everything, machine oil and almond blossom, tar and heather, all mixed. We took big steps from sleeper to sleeper so as not to step among the stones, which were rough to walk on, and wore your shoes out. The rails shone in the sunshine. On both sides of the line stood the telephone poles that sang as we went by them. Yes! That was a fine day! The sky was absolutely clear. There wasn't a single cloud to be seen: there just couldn't be any on a day like this, according to what Daddy said. After a while we came to a field of oats on the right side of the line, where a farmer, whom we knew, had a clearing. The oats had grown thick and even; Daddy looked at it knowingly, and I could feel that he was satisfied. I didn't understand that sort of thing much, because I was born in town. Then we came to the bridge over the brook that mostly hadn't much water in it, but now there was plenty. We took hands so that we shouldn't fall down between the sleepers. From there it wasn't far to the railway gatekeeper's little place, which was quite buried in green. There were apple trees and gooseberry bushes right close to the house. We went in there, to pay a visit, and they offered us milk. We looked at the pigs, the hens, and the fruit trees, which were in full blossom, and then we went on again. We wanted to go to the river, because there it was prettier than anywhere else. There was something special about the river, because higher upstream it flowed past Daddy's old home. We never liked going back before we got to it, and, as usual, this time we got there after a fair walk. It wasn't far to the next station; but we didn't go on there. Daddy just looked to see whether the signals were right. He thought of everything. We stopped by the river, where it flowed broad and friendly in the sunshine, and the thick leafy trees on the banks mirrored themselves in the calm water. It was all so fresh and bright. A breeze came from the little lakes higher up. We climbed down the bank, went a little way along the very edge. Daddy showed me the fishing spots. When he was a boy he used to sit there on the stones and wait for perch all day long. Often he didn't get a single bite, but it was a delightful way to spend the day. Now he never had time. We played about for some time by the side of the river, and threw in pieces of bark that the current carried away, and we threw stones to see who could throw farthest. We were, by nature, very merry and cheerful, Daddy and I. After a while we felt a bit tired. We thought we had played enough, so we started off home again.

Then it began to get dark. The woods were changed. It wasn't quite dark yet, but almost. We made haste. Maybe mother was getting anxious, and waiting supper. She was always afraid that something might happen, though nothing had. This had been a splendid day. Everything had been just as it should, and we were satisfied with it all. It was getting darker and darker, and the trees were so queer. They stood and listened for the sound of footsteps, as though they didn't know who we were. There was a glow-worm under one of them. It lay down there in the dark and stared at us. I held Daddy's hand tight, but he didn't seem to notice the strange light: he just went on. It was quite dark when we came to the bridge over the stream. It was roaring down underneath us as if it wanted to swallow us up, as the ground seemed to open under us. We went along the sleepers carefully, holding hands tight so that we shouldn't fall in. I thought Daddy would carry me over, but he didn't say anything about it. I suppose he wanted me to be like him, and not think anything of it. We went on. Daddy was so calm in the darkness, walking with even steps without speaking. He was thinking his own thoughts. I couldn't understand how he could be so calm when everything was so ghostly. I looked round scared. It was nothing but darkness everywhere. I hardly dared to breathe deeply, because then the darkness comes into one, and that was dangerous, I thought. One must die soon. I remember quite well thinking so then. The railway embankment was very steep. It finished in black night. The telephone posts stood up ghostlike against the sky, mumbling deep inside as though someone were speaking, way down in the earth. The white china hats sat there scared, cowering with fear, listening. It was all so creepy. Nothing was real, nothing was natural, all seemed a mystery. I went closer to Daddy, and whispered: "Why is it so creepy when it's dark?"

"No, child, it isn't creepy," he said, and took my hand.

"Oh, yes, but it is, Daddy."

"No, you mustn't think that. We know there is a God don't we?" I felt so lonely, so abandoned. It was queer that it was only me that was frightened, and not Daddy. It was queer that we didn't feel the same about it. And it was queerer still that what he said didn't help, didn't stop me being frightened. Not even what he said about God helped. The thought of God made one feel creepy too. It was creepy to think that He was everywhere here in the darkness, down there under the trees, and in the telephone posts that mumbled so—probably that was Him everywhere. But all the same one could never see Him.

We went along silently, each of us thinking his own thoughts. My heart felt cramped as though the darkness had come in and was squeezing it.

Then, when we were in a bend, we suddenly heard a great noise behind us. We were startled out of our thoughts. Daddy pulled me down the embankment and held me tight, and a train rushed by; a black train. The lights were out in all the carriages, as it whizzed past us. What could it be? There shouldn't be any train now. We looked at it, frightened. The furnace roared in the big engine, where they shovelled in coal, and the sparks flew out into the night. It was terrible. The driver stood so pale and immovable, with such a stony look in the glare. Daddy didn't recognize him—didn't know who he was. He was just looking ahead as though he was driving straight into darkness, far into darkness, which had no end.

Startled and panting with fear I looked after the wild thing. It was swallowed up in the night. Daddy helped me up onto the line, and we hurried home. He said, "That was strange! What train was that I wonder? And I didn't know the driver either." Then he didn't say any more.

I was shaking all over. That had been for me—for my sake. I guessed what it meant. It was all the fear which would come to me, all the unknown; all that Daddy didn't know about, and couldn't save me from. That was how the world would be for me, and the strange life I should live; not like Daddy's, where everyone was known and sure. It wasn't a real world, or a real life—it just rushed burning into the darkness which had no end.

IV LATIN AMERICA

The Stolen Party

BY LILIANA HEKER

TRANSLATED BY ALBERTO MANGUEL

As soon as she arrived she went straight to the kitchen to see if the monkey was there. It was: what a relief! She wouldn't have liked to admit that her mother had been right. *Monkeys at a birthday?* her mother had sneered. *Get away with you, believing any nonsense you're told!* She was cross, but not because of the monkey, the girl thought; it's just because of the party.

"I don't like you going," she told her. "It's a rich people's party."

"Rich people go to Heaven too," said the girl, who studied religion at school.

"Get away with Heaven," said the mother. "The problem with you, young lady, is that you like to fart higher than your ass."

The girl didn't approve of the way her mother spoke. She was barely nine, and one of the best in her class.

"I'm going because I've been invited," she said. "And I've been invited because Luciana is my friend. So there."

"Ah yes, your friend," her mother grumbled. She paused. "Listen, Rosaura," she said at last. "That one's not your friend. You know what you are to them? The maid's daughter, that's what."

Rosaura blinked hard: she wasn't going to cry. Then she yelled: "Shut up! You know nothing about being friends!"

Every afternoon she used to go to Luciana's house and they would both finish their homework while Rosaura's mother did the cleaning. They had their tea in the kitchen and they told each other secrets. Rosaura loved everything in the big house, and she also loved the people who lived there.

"I'm going because it will be the most lovely party in the whole world, Luciana told me it would. There will be a magician, and he will bring a monkey and everything."

The mother swung around to take a good look at her child, and pompously put her hands on her hips.

"Monkeys at a birthday?" she said. "Get away with you, believing any nonsense you're told!"

Rosaura was deeply offended. She thought it unfair of her mother to accuse other people of being liars simply because they were rich. Rosaura too wanted to be rich, of course. If one day she managed to live in a beautiful palace, would her mother stop loving her? She felt very sad. She wanted to go to that party more than anything else in the world.

"I'll die if I don't go," she whispered, almost without moving her lips.

And she wasn't sure whether she had been heard, but on the morning of the party she discovered that her mother had starched her Christmas dress. And in the afternoon, after washing her hair, her mother rinsed it in apple vinegar so that it would be all nice and shiny. Before going out, Rosaura admired herself in the mirror, with her white dress and glossy hair, and thought she looked terribly pretty.

Señora Ines also seemed to notice. As soon as she saw her, she said:

"How lovely you look today, Rosaura."

Rosaura gave her starched skirt a slight toss with her hands and walked into the party with a firm step. She said hello to Luciana and asked about the monkey. Luciana put on a secretive look and whispered into Rosaura's ear: "He's in the kitchen. But don't tell anyone, because it's a surprise."

Rosaura wanted to make sure. Carefully she entered the kitchen and there she saw it: deep in thought, inside its cage. It looked so funny that the girl stood there for a while, watching it, and later, every so often, she would slip out of the party unseen and go and admire it. Rosaura was the only one allowed into the kitchen. Señora Ines had said: "You yes, but not the others, they're much too boisterous, they might break something." Rosaura had never broken anything. She even managed the jug of orange juice, carrying it from the kitchen into the dining room. She held it carefully and didn't spill a single drop. And Señora Ines had said: "Are you sure you can manage a jug as big as that?" Of course she could manage. She wasn't a butterfingers, like the others. Like that blonde girl with the bow in her hair. As soon as she saw Rosaura, the girl with the bow had said:

"And you? Who are you?"

"I'm a friend of Luciana," said Rosaura.

"No," said the girl with the bow, "you are not a friend of Luciana because I'm her cousin and I know all her friends. And I don't know you."

"So what," said Rosaura. "I come here every afternoon with my mother and we do our homework together."

"You and your mother do your homework together?" asked the girl, laughing.

"I and Luciana do our homework together," said Rosaura, very seriously.

The girl with the bow shrugged her shoulders.

"That's not being friends," she said. "Do you go to school together?"

"No."

"So where do you know her from?" said the girl, getting impatient.

Rosaura remembered her mother's words perfectly. She took a deep breath.

"I'm the daughter of the employee," she said.

Her mother had said very clearly: "If someone asks, you say you're the daughter of the employee; that's all." She also told her to add: "And proud of it." But Rosaura thought that never in her life would she dare say something of the sort.

"What employee?" said the girl with the bow. "Employee in a shop?"

"No," said Rosaura angrily. "My mother doesn't sell anything in any shop, so there."

"So how come she's an employee?" said the girl with the bow.

Just then Señora Ines arrived saying *shh shh*, and asked Rosaura if she wouldn't mind helping serve out the hot dogs, as she knew the house so much better than the others.

"See?" said Rosaura to the girl with the bow, and when no one was looking she kicked her in the shin.

Apart from the girl with the bow, all the others were delightful. The one she liked best was Luciana, with her golden birthday crown; and then the boys. Rosaura won the sack race, and nobody managed to catch her when they played tag. When they split into two teams to play charades, all the boys wanted her for their side. Rosaura felt she had never been so happy in all her life.

But the best was still to come. The best came after Luciana blew out the candles. First the cake. Señora Ines had asked her to help pass the cake around, and Rosaura had enjoyed the task immensely, because everyone called out to her, shouting "Me, me!" Rosaura remembered a story in which there was a queen who had the power of life or death over her subjects. She had always loved that, having the power of life or death. To Luciana and the boys she gave the largest pieces, and to the girl with the bow she gave a slice so thin one could see through it.

After the cake came the magician, tall and bony, with a fine red cape. A true magician: he could untie handkerchiefs by blowing on them and make a chain with links that had no openings. He could guess what cards were pulled out from a pack, and the monkey was his assistant. He called the monkey "partner." "Let's see here, partner," he would say, "Turn over a card." And, "Don't run away, partner: time to work now."

The final trick was wonderful. One of the children had to hold the monkey in his arms and the magician said he would make him disappear.

"What, the boy?" they all shouted.

"No, the monkey!" shouted back the magician.

Rosaura thought that this was truly the most amusing party in the whole world.

The magician asked a small fat boy to come and help, but the small fat boy got frightened almost at once and dropped the monkey on the floor. The magician picked him up carefully, whispered something in his ear, and the monkey nodded almost as if he understood.

"You mustn't be so unmanly, my friend," the magician said to the fat boy.

"What's unmanly?" said the fat boy.

The magician turned around as if to look for spies.

"A sissy," said the magician. "Go sit down."

Then he stared at all the faces, one by one. Rosaura felt her heart tremble.

"You, with the Spanish eyes," said the magician. And everyone saw that he was pointing at her.

She wasn't afraid. Neither holding the monkey, nor when the magician made him vanish; not even when, at the end, the magician flung his red cape over Rosaura's head and uttered a few magic words … and the monkey reappeared, chattering happily, in her arms. The children clapped furiously. And before Rosaura returned to her seat, the magician said:

"Thank you very much, my little countess."

She was so pleased with the compliment that a while later, when her mother came to fetch her, that was the first thing she told her.

"I helped the magician and he said to me, 'Thank you very much, my little countess.' "

It was strange because up to then Rosaura had thought that she was angry with her mother. All along Rosaura had imagined that she would say to her: "See that the monkey wasn't a lie?" But instead she was so thrilled that she told her mother all about the wonderful magician.

Her mother tapped her on the head and said: "So now we're a countess!"

But one could see that she was beaming.

And now they both stood in the entrance, because a moment ago Señora Ines, smiling, had said: "Please wait here a second."

Her mother suddenly seemed worried.

"What is it?" she asked Rosaura.

"What is what?" said Rosaura. "It's nothing; she just wants to get the presents for those who are leaving, see?"

She pointed at the fat boy and at a girl with pigtails who were also waiting there, next to their mothers. And she explained about the presents. She knew, because she had been watching those who left before her. When one of the girls was about to leave, Señora Ines would give her a bracelet. When a boy left, Señora Ines gave him a yo-yo. Rosaura preferred the yo-yo because it sparkled, but she didn't mention that to her mother. Her mother might have said: "So why don't you ask for one, you blockhead?" That's what her mother was like. Rosaura didn't feel like explaining that she'd be horribly ashamed to be the odd one out. Instead she said:

"I was the best-behaved at the party."

And she said no more because Señora Ines came out into the hall with two bags, one pink and one blue.

First she went up to the fat boy, gave him a yo-yo out of the blue bag, and the fat boy left with his mother. Then she went up to the girl and gave her a bracelet out of the pink bag, and the girl with the pigtails left as well.

Finally she came up to Rosaura and her mother. She had a big smile on her face and Rosaura liked that. Señora Ines looked down at her, then looked up at her mother, and then said something that made Rosaura proud:

"What a marvellous daughter you have, Herminia."

For an instant, Rosaura thought that she'd give her two presents: the bracelet and the yo-yo. Señora Ines bent down as if about to look for something. Rosaura also leaned forward, stretching out her arm. But she never completed the movement.

Señora Ines didn't look in the pink bag. Nor did she look in the blue bag. Instead she rummaged in her purse. In her hand appeared two bills.

"You really and truly earned this," she said handing them over. "Thank you for all your help, my pet."

Rosaura felt her arms stiffen, stick close to her body, and then she noticed her mother's hand on her shoulder. Instinctively she pressed herself against her mother's body. That was all. Except her eyes. Rosaura's eyes had a cold, clear look that fixed itself on Señora Ines's face.

Señora Ines, motionless, stood there with her hand outstretched. As if she didn't dare draw it back. As if the slightest change might shatter an infinitely delicate balance.

The Third Bank of the River

BY JOÃO GUIMARÃES ROSA

TRANSLATED BY BARBARA SHELBY

Father was a reliable, law-abiding, practical man, and had been ever since he was a boy, as various people of good sense testified when I asked them about him. I don't remember that he seemed any crazier or even any moodier than anyone else we knew. He just didn't talk much. It was our mother who gave the orders and scolded us every day—my sister, my brother, and me. Then one day my father ordered a canoe for himself.

He took the matter very seriously. He had the canoe made to his specifications of fine *vinhático* wood; a small one, with a narrow board in the stern as though to leave only enough room for the oarsman. Every bit of it was hand-hewn of special strong wood carefully shaped, fit to last in the water for twenty or thirty years. Mother railed at the idea. How could a man who had never fiddled away his time on such tricks propose to go fishing and hunting now, at his time of life? Father said nothing. Our house was closer to the river then than it is now, less than a quarter of a league away: there rolled the river, great, deep, and silent, always silent. It was so wide that you could hardly see the bank on the other side. I can never forget the day the canoe was ready.

Neither happy nor excited nor downcast, Father pulled his hat well down on his head and said one firm goodbye. He spoke not another word, took neither food nor other supplies, gave no parting advice. We thought Mother would have a fit, but she only blanched white, bit her lip, and said bitterly: "Go or stay; but if you go, don't you ever come back!" Father left his answer in suspense. He gave me a mild look and motioned me to go aside with him a few steps. I was afraid of Mother's anger, but I obeyed anyway, that time. The turn things had taken gave me the courage to ask: "Father, will you take me with you in that canoe?" But he just gave me a long look in return: gave me his blessing and motioned me to go back. I pretended to go, but instead turned off into a deep woodsy hollow to watch. Father stepped into the canoe, untied it, and began to paddle off. The canoe slipped away, a straight, even shadow like an alligator, slithery, long.

Our father never came back. He hadn't gone anywhere. He stuck to that stretch of the river, staying halfway across, always in the canoe, never to spring out of it, ever again. The strangeness of that truth was enough to dismay us all. What had never been before, was. Our relatives, the neighbours, and all our acquaintances met and took counsel together.

Mother, though, behaved very reasonably, with the result that everybody believed what no one wanted to put into words about our father: that he was mad. Only a few of them thought he might be keeping a vow, or—who could tell—maybe he was sick with some hideous disease like leprosy, and that was what had made him desert us to live out another life, close to his family and yet far enough away. The news spread by word of mouth, carried by people like travellers and those who lived along the banks of the river, who said of Father that he never landed at spit or cove, by day or by night, but always stuck to the river, lonely and outside human society. Finally, Mother and our relatives realized that the provisions he had hidden in the canoe must be getting low and thought that he would have to either land somewhere and go away from us for good—that seemed the most likely—or repent once and for all and come back home.

But they were wrong. I had made myself responsible for stealing a bit of food for him every day, an idea that had come to me the very first night, when the family had lighted bonfires on the riverbank and in their glare prayed and called out to Father. Every day from then on I went back to the river with a lump of hard brown sugar, some corn bread, or a bunch of bananas. Once, at the end of an hour of waiting that had dragged on and on, I caught sight of Father; he was way off, sitting in the bottom of the canoe as if suspended in the mirror smoothness of the river. He saw me, but he did not paddle over or make any sign. I held up the things to eat and then laid them in a hollowed-out rock in the river bluff, safe from any animals who might nose around and where they would be kept dry in rain or dew. Time after time, day after day, I did the same thing. Much later I had a surprise: Mother knew about my mission but, saying nothing and pretending she didn't, made it easier for me by putting out leftovers where I was sure to find them. Mother almost never showed what she was thinking.

Finally she sent for an uncle of ours, her brother, to help with the farm and with money matters, and she got a tutor for us children. She also arranged for the priest to come in his vestments to the river edge to exorcise Father and call upon him to desist from his sad obsession. Another time, she tried to scare Father by getting two soldiers to come. But none of it was any use. Father passed by at a distance, discernible only dimly through the river haze, going by in the canoe without ever letting anyone go close enough to touch him or even talk to him. The reporters who went out in a launch and tried to take his picture not long ago failed just like everybody else; Father crossed over to the other bank and steered the canoe into the thick swamp that goes on for kilometres, part reeds and part brush. Only he knew every hand's breadth of its blackness.

We just had to try to get used to it. But it was hard, and we never really managed. I'm judging by myself, of course. Whether I wanted to or not, my thoughts kept circling back and I found myself thinking of Father. The hard nub of it was that I couldn't begin to understand how he could hold out. Day and night, in bright sunshine or in rainstorms, in muggy heat or in the terrible cold spells in the middle of the year, without shelter or any protection but the old hat on his head, all through the weeks, and months, and years—he marked in no way the passing of his life. Father never landed, never put in at either shore or stopped at any of the river islands or sand-bars; and he never again stepped onto grass or solid earth. It was true that in order to catch a little sleep he may have tied up the canoe at some concealed islet-spit. But he never lighted a fire on shore, had no lamp or candle, never struck a match again. He did no more than taste food; even the morsels he took from what we left for him along the roots of the fig tree or in the hollow stone at the foot of the cliff could not have been enough to keep him alive. Wasn't he ever sick? And what constant strength he must have had in his arms to maintain himself and the canoe ready for the piling up of the floodwaters where danger rolls on the great current, sweeping the bodies of dead animals and tree trunks downstream—frightening, threatening, crashing into him. And he never spoke another word to a living soul. We never talked about him, either. We only thought of him. Father could never be forgotten; and if, for short periods of time, we pretended to ourselves that we had forgotten, it was only to find ourselves roused suddenly by his memory, startled by it again and again.

My sister married; but Mother would have no festivities. He came into our minds whenever we ate something especially tasty, and when we were wrapped up snugly at night we thought of those bare unsheltered nights of cold, heavy rain, and Father with only his hand and maybe a calabash to bail the storm water out of the canoe. Every so often someone who knew us would remark that I was getting to look more and more like my father. But I knew that now he must be bushy-haired and bearded, his nails long, his body cadaverous and gaunt, burnt black by the sun, hairy as a beast and almost as naked, even with the pieces of clothing we left for him at intervals.

He never felt the need to know anything about us; had he no family affection? But out of love, love and respect, whenever I was praised for something good I had done, I would say: "It was Father who taught me how to do it that way." It wasn't true, exactly, but it was a truthful kind of lie. If he didn't remember us any more and didn't want to know how we were, why didn't he go farther up the river or down it, away to landing places where he would never be found? Only he knew. When my sister had a baby boy, she got it into her head that she must show Father his grandson. All of us went and stood on the bluff. The day was fine and my sister was wearing the white dress she had worn at her wedding. She lifted the baby up in her arms and her husband held a parasol over the two of them. We called and we waited. Our father didn't come. My sister wept; we all cried and hugged one another as we stood there.

After that my sister moved far away with her husband, and my brother decided to go live in the city. Times changed, with the slow swiftness of time. Mother went away too in the end, to live with my sister because she was growing old. I stayed on here, the only one of the family who was left. I could never think of marriage. I stayed where I was, burdened down with all life's cumbrous baggage. I knew Father needed me, as he wandered up and down on the river in the wilderness, even though he never gave a reason for what he had done. When at last I made up my mind that I had to know and finally made a firm attempt to find out, people told me rumour had it that Father might have given some explanation to the man who made the canoe for him. But now the builder was dead; and no one really knew or could recollect any more except that there had been some silly talk in the beginning, when the river was first swollen by such endless torrents of rain that everyone was afraid the world was coming to an end; then they had said that

Father might have received a warning, like Noah, and so prepared the canoe ahead of time. I could half-recall the story. I could not even blame my father. And a few first white hairs began to appear on my head.

I was a man whose words were all sorrowful. Why did I feel so guilty, so guilty? Was it because of my father, who made his absence felt always, and because of the river-river-river, the river—flowing forever? I was suffering the onset of old age—this life of mine only postponed the inevitable. I had bad spells, pains in the belly, dizziness, twinges of rheumatism. And he? Why, oh why must he do what he did? He must suffer terribly. Old as he was, was he not bound to weaken in vigour sooner or later and let the canoe overturn or, when the river rose, let it drift unguided for hours downstream, until it finally went over the brink of the loud rushing fall of the cataract, with its wild boiling and death? My heart shrank. He was out there, with none of my easy security. I was guilty of I knew not what, filled with boundless sorrow in the deepest part of me. If I only knew—if only things were otherwise. And then, little by little, the idea came to me.

I could not even wait until next day. Was I crazy? No. In our house, the word *crazy* was not spoken, had never been spoken again in all those years; no one was condemned as crazy. Either no one is crazy, or everyone is. I just went, taking along a sheet to wave with. I was very much in my right mind. I waited. After a long time he appeared; his indistinct bulk took form. He was there, sitting in the stern. He was there, a shout away. I called out several times. And I said the words which were making me say them, the sworn promise, the declaration. I had to force my voice to say: "Father, you're getting old, you've done your part.... You can come back now, you don't have to stay any longer.... You come back, and I'll do it, right now or whenever you want me to; it's what we both want. I'll take your place in the canoe!" And as I said it my heart beat to the rhythm of what was truest and best in me.

He heard me. He got to his feet. He dipped the paddle in the water, the bow pointed toward me; he had agreed. And suddenly I shuddered deeply, because he had lifted his arm and gestured a greeting—the first, after so many years. And I could not.... Panic-stricken, my hair standing on end, I ran, I fled, I left the place behind me in a mad headlong rush. For he seemed to be coming from the hereafter. And I am pleading, pleading, pleading for forgiveness.

I was struck by the solemn ice of fear, and I fell ill. I knew that no one ever heard of him again. Can I be a man, after having thus failed him? I am what never was—the unspeakable. I know it is too late for salvation now, but I am afraid to cut life short in the shallows of the world. At least, when death comes to the body, let them take me and put me in a wretched little canoe, and on the water that flows forever past its unending banks, let me go—down the river, away from the river, into the river—the river.

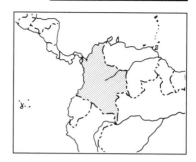

Tuesday Siesta

BY GABRIEL GARCIA MARQUEZ

TRANSLATED BY J. S. BERNSTEIN

The train emerged from the quivering tunnel of sandy rocks, began to cross the symmetrical, interminable banana plantations, and the air became humid and they couldn't feel the sea breeze any more. A stifling blast of smoke came in the car window. On the narrow road parallel to the railway there were oxcarts loaded with green bunches of bananas. Beyond the road, in odd, uncultivated spaces, there were offices with electric fans, red brick buildings, and residences with chairs and little white tables on the terraces among dusty palm trees and rose bushes. It was eleven in the morning, and the heat had not yet begun.

"You'd better close the window," the woman said. "Your hair will get full of soot."

The girl tried to, but the shade wouldn't move because of the rust.

They were the only passengers in the lone third-class car. Since the smoke of the locomotive kept coming through the window, the girl left her seat and put down the only things they had with them: a plastic sack with some things to eat and a bouquet of flowers wrapped in newspaper. She sat on the opposite seat, away from the window, facing her mother. They were both in severe and poor mourning clothes.

The girl was twelve years old, and it was the first time she'd ever been on a train. The woman seemed too old to be her mother, because of the blue veins on her eyelids and her small, soft, and shapeless body, in a dress cut like a cassock. She was riding with her spinal column braced firmly against the back of the seat, and held a peeling patent-leather portfolio in her lap with both hands. She bore the conscientious serenity of someone accustomed to poverty.

By twelve the heat had begun. The train stopped for ten minutes to take on water at a station where there was no town. Outside, in the mysterious silence of the plantations, the shadows seemed clean. But the still air inside the car smelled like untanned leather. The train did not pick up speed. It stopped at two identical towns with wooden houses painted bright colours. The woman's head nodded and she sank into sleep. The girl took off her shoes. Then she went to the washroom to put the bouquet of flowers in some water.

When she came back to her seat, her mother was waiting to eat. She gave her a piece of cheese, half a cornmeal pancake, and a cookie, and took an equal portion out of the plastic sack for herself. While they ate, the train crossed an iron bridge very slowly and passed a town just like the ones before, except that in this one there was a crowd in the plaza. A band was playing a lively tune under the oppressive sun. At the other side of town the plantations ended in a plain which was cracked from the drought.

The woman stopped eating.

"Put on your shoes," she said.

The girl looked outside. She saw nothing but the deserted plain, where the train began to pick up speed again, but she put the last piece of cookie into the sack and quickly put on her shoes. The woman gave her a comb.

"Comb your hair," she said.

The train whistle began to blow while the girl was combing her hair. The woman dried the sweat from her neck and wiped the oil from her face with her fingers. When the girl stopped combing, the train was passing the outlying houses of a town larger but sadder than the earlier ones.

"If you feel like doing anything, do it now," said the woman. "Later, don't take a drink anywhere even if you're dying of thirst. Above all, no crying."

The girl nodded her head. A dry, burning wind came in the window, together with the locomotive's whistle and the clatter of the old cars. The woman wrapped up the pancake with the rest of the food and put it in the portfolio. For a moment a complete picture of the town, on that bright August Tuesday, shone in the window. The girl wrapped the flowers in the soaking-wet newspapers, moved a little farther away from the window, and stared at her mother. She received a pleasant expression in return. The train began to whistle and slowed down. A moment later it stopped.

There was no one at the station. On the other side of the street, on the sidewalk shaded by the almond trees, only the pool hall was open. The town was floating in the heat. The woman and the girl got off the train and crossed the abandoned station—the tiles split apart by the grass growing up between—and the street to the shady sidewalk.

It was almost two. At that hour, weighted down by drowsiness, the town was taking a siesta. The stores, the town offices, the public school were closed at eleven, and didn't reopen until a little before four, when the train went back. Only the hotel across from the station, with its bar and pool hall, and the telegraph office at one side of the plaza stayed open. The houses, most of them built on the banana company's model, had their doors locked from inside and their blinds drawn. In some of them it was so hot that the residents ate lunch in the patio. Others leaned a chair against the wall, in the shade of the almond trees, and took their siesta right out in the street.

Keeping to the protective shade of the almond trees, the woman and the girl entered the town without disturbing the siesta. They went directly to the priest's house. The woman scratched the metal grating on the door with her fingernail, waited a moment, and scratched again. An electric fan was humming inside. They did not hear the steps. They hardly heard the slight creaking of a door, and immediately a cautious voice, right next to the metal grating: "Who is it?" The woman tried to see through the grating.

"I need the Father," she said.

"He's sleeping now."

"It's an emergency," the woman insisted.

Her voice showed a calm determination.

The door was opened a little way, noiselessly, and a plump, older woman appeared, with very pale skin and hair the colour of iron. Her eyes seemed too small behind her thick eyeglasses.

"Come in," she said, and opened the door all the way.

They entered a room permeated with an old smell of flowers. The woman of the house led them to a wooden bench and signalled them to sit down. The girl did so, but her mother remained standing, absent-mindedly, with both hands clutching the portfolio. No noise could be heard above the electric fan.

The woman of the house reappeared at the door at the far end of the room. "He says you should come back after three," she said in a very low voice. "He just lay down five minutes ago."

"The train leaves at three-thirty," said the woman.

It was a brief and self-assured reply, but her voice remained pleasant, full of undertones. The woman of the house smiled for the first time.

"All right," she said.

When the far door closed again, the woman sat down next to her daughter. The narrow waiting room was poor, neat, and clean. On the other side of the wooden railing which divided the room, there was a worktable, a plain one with an oilcloth cover, and on top of the table a primitive typewriter next to a vase of flowers. The parish records were beyond. You could see that it was an office kept in order by a spinster.

The far door opened and this time the priest appeared, cleaning his glasses with a handkerchief. Only when he put them on was it evident that he was the brother of the woman who had opened the door.

"How can I help you?" he asked.

"The keys to the cemetery," said the woman.

The girl was seated with the flowers in her lap and her feet crossed under the bench. The priest looked at her, then looked at the woman, and then through the wire mesh of the window at the bright, cloudless sky.

"In this heat," he said. "You could have waited until the sun went down."

The woman moved her head silently. The priest crossed to the other side of the railing, took out of the cabinet a notebook covered in oilcloth, a wooden penholder, and an inkwell, and sat down at the table. There was more than enough hair on his hands to account for what was missing on his head.

"Which grave are you going to visit?" he asked.

"Carlos Centeno's," said the woman.

"Who?"

"Carlos Centeno," the woman repeated.

The priest still did not understand.

"He's the thief who was killed here last week," said the woman in the same tone of voice. "I am his mother."

The priest scrutinized her. She stared at him with quiet self-control, and the Father blushed. He lowered his head and began to write. As he filled the page, he asked the woman to identify herself, and she replied unhesitatingly, with precise details, as if she were reading them. The Father began to sweat. The girl unhooked the buckle of her left shoe, slipped her heel out of it, and rested it on the bench rail. She did the same with the right one.

It had all started the Monday of the previous week, at three in the morning, a few blocks from there. Rebecca, a lonely widow who lived in a house full of odds and ends, heard above the sound of the drizzling rain someone trying to force the front door from outside. She got up, rummaged around in her closet for an ancient revolver that no one had fired since the days of Colonel Aureliano Buendia, and went into the living room without turning on the lights. Orienting herself not so much by the noise at the lock as by a terror developed in her by twenty-eight years of loneliness, she fixed in her imagination not only the spot where the door was but also the exact height of the lock. She clutched the weapon with both hands, closed her eyes, and squeezed the trigger. It was the first time in her life that she had fired a gun. Immediately after the explosion, she could hear nothing except the murmur of the drizzle on the galvanized roof. Then she heard a little metallic bump on the cement porch, and a very low voice, pleasant but terribly exhausted: "Ah, Mother." The man they found dead in front of the house in the morning, his nose blown to bits, wore a flannel shirt with coloured stripes, everyday pants with a rope for a belt, and was barefoot. No one in town knew him.

"So his name was Carlos Centeno," murmured the Father when he finished writing.

"Centeno Ayala," said the woman. "He was my only boy."

The priest went back to the cabinet. Two big rusty keys hung on the inside of the door; the girl imagined, as her mother had when she was a girl and as the priest himself must have imagined at some time, that they were Saint Peter's keys. He took them down, put them on the open notebook on the railing, and pointed with his forefinger to a place on the page he had just written, looking at the woman.

"Sign here."

The woman scribbled her name, holding the portfolio under her arm. The girl picked up the flowers, came to the railing shuffling her feet, and watched her mother attentively.

The priest sighed.

"Didn't you ever try to get him on the right track?"

The woman answered when she finished signing.

"He was a very good man."

The priest looked first at the woman and then at the girl, and realized with a kind of pious amazement that they were not about to cry. The woman continued in the same tone:

"I told him never to steal anything that anyone needed to eat, and he minded me. On the other hand, before, when he used to box, he used to spend three days in bed, exhausted from being punched."

"All his teeth had to be pulled out," interrupted the girl.

"That's right," the woman agreed. "Every mouthful I ate those days tasted of the beatings my son got on Saturday nights."

"God's will is inscrutable," said the Father.

But he said it without much conviction, partly because experience had made him a little skeptical and partly because of the heat. He suggested that they cover their heads to guard against sunstroke. Yawning, and now almost completely asleep, he gave them instructions about how to find Carlos Centeno's grave. When they came back, they didn't have to knock. They should put the key under the door; and in the same place, if they could, they should put an offering for the Church. The woman listened to his directions with great attention, but thanked him without smiling.

The Father had noticed that there was someone looking inside, his nose pressed against the metal grating, even before he opened the door to the street. Outside was a group of children. When the door was opened wide, the children scattered. Ordinarily, at that hour there was no one in the street. Now there were not only children. There were groups of people under the almond trees. The Father scanned the street swimming in the heat and then he understood. Softly, he closed the door again.

"Wait a moment," he said without looking at the woman.

His sister appeared at the far door with a black jacket over her nightshirt and her hair down over her shoulders. She looked silently at the Father.

"What was it?" he asked.

"The people have noticed," murmured his sister.

"You'd better go out by the door to the patio," said the Father.

"It's the same there," said his sister. "Everybody is at the windows."

The woman seemed not to have understood until then. She tried to look into the street through the metal grating. Then she took the bouquet of flowers from the girl and began to move toward the door. The girl followed her.

"Wait until the sun goes down," said the Father.

"You'll melt," said his sister, motionless at the back of the room. "Wait and I'll lend you a parasol."

"Thank you," replied the woman. "We're all right this way."

She took the girl by the hand and went into the street.

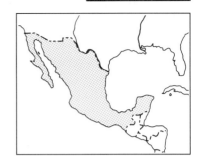

The Blue Bouquet

BY OCTAVIO PAZ

TRANSLATED BY ELIOT WEINBERGER

I woke covered with sweat. Hot steam rose from the newly sprayed, red-brick pavement. A grey-winged butterfly, dazzled, circled the yellow light. I jumped from my hammock and crossed the room barefoot, careful not to step on some scorpion leaving his hideout for a bit of fresh air. I went to the little window and inhaled the country air. One could hear the breathing of the night, feminine, enormous. I returned to the centre of the room, emptied water from a jar into a pewter basin, and wet my towel. I rubbed my chest and legs with the soaked cloth, dried myself a little, and, making sure that no bugs were hidden in the folds of my clothes, got dressed. I ran down the green stairway. At the door of the boardinghouse I bumped into the owner, a one-eyed taciturn fellow. Sitting on a wicker stool, he smoked, his eye half-closed. In a hoarse voice, he asked:

"Where are you going?"

"To take a walk. It's too hot."

"Hmmm—everything's closed. And no streetlights around here. You'd better stay put."

I shrugged my shoulders, muttered "back soon," and plunged into the darkness. At first I couldn't see anything. I fumbled along the cobblestone street. I lit a cigarette. Suddenly the moon appeared from behind a black cloud, lighting a white wall that was crumbled in places. I stopped, blinded by such whiteness. Wind whistled slightly. I breathed the air of the tamarinds. The night hummed, full of leaves and insects. Crickets bivouacked in the tall grass. I raised my head: up there the stars too had set up camp. I thought that the universe was a vast system of signs, a conversation between giant beings. My actions, the cricket's saw, the star's blink, were nothing but pauses and syllables, scattered phrases from that dialogue. What word could it be, of which I was only a syllable? Who speaks the word? To whom is it spoken? I threw my cigarette down on the sidewalk. Falling, it drew a shining curve, shooting out brief sparks like a tiny comet.

I walked a long time, slowly. I felt free, secure between the lips that were at that moment speaking me with such happiness. The night was a garden of eyes. As I crossed the street, I heard someone come out of a doorway. I turned around, but could not distinguish anything. I hurried on. A few moments later I heard the dull shuffle of sandals on the hot stone. I didn't want to turn around, although I felt the shadow getting closer with every step. I tried to run. I couldn't. Suddenly I stopped short. Before I could defend myself, I felt the point of a knife in my back, and a sweet voice:

"Don't move, mister, or I'll stick it in."

Without turning, I asked:

"What do you want?"

"Your eyes, mister," answered the soft, almost painful voice.

"My eyes? What do you want with my eyes? Look, I've got some money. Not much, but it's something. I'll give you everything I have if you let me go. Don't kill me."

"Don't be afraid, mister. I won't kill you. I'm only going to take your eyes."

"But why do you want my eyes?" I asked again.

"My girlfriend has this whim. She wants a bouquet of blue eyes. And around here they're hard to find."

"My eyes won't help you. They're brown, not blue."

"Don't try to fool me, mister. I know very well that yours are blue."

"Don't take the eyes of a fellow man. I'll give you something else."

"Don't play saint with me," he said harshly. "Turn around."

I turned. He was small and fragile. His palm sombrero covered half his face. In his right hand he held a country machete that shone in the moonlight.

"Let me see your face."

I struck a match and put it close to my face. The brightness made me squint. He opened my eyelids with a firm hand. He couldn't see very well.

Standing on tiptoe, he stared at me intensely. The flame burned my fingers. I dropped it. A silent moment passed.

"Are you convinced now? They're not blue."

"Pretty clever, aren't you?" he answered. "Let's see. Light another one."

I struck another match, and put it near my eyes. Grabbing my sleeve, he ordered:

"Kneel down."

I knelt. With one hand he grabbed me by the hair, pulling my head back. He bent over me, curious and tense, while his machete slowly dropped until it grazed my eyelids. I closed my eyes.

"Keep them open," he ordered.

I opened my eyes. The flame burned my lashes. All of a sudden he let me go.

"All right, they're not blue. Beat it."

He vanished. I leaned against the wall, my head in my hands. I pulled myself together. Stumbling, falling, trying to get up again. I ran for an hour through the deserted town. When I got to the plaza, I saw the owner of the boardinghouse, still sitting in the front of the door. I went in without saying a word. The next day I left town.

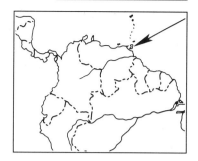

B. Wordsworth

BY V. S. NAIPAUL

Three beggars called punctually every day at the hospitable houses in Miguel Street. At about ten an Indian came in his dhoti and white jacket, and we poured a tin of rice into the sack he carried on his back. At twelve an old woman smoking a clay pipe came and she got a cent. At two a blind man led by a boy called for his penny.

Sometimes we had a rogue. One day a man called and said he was hungry. We gave him a meal. He asked for a cigarette and wouldn't go until we had lit it for him. That man never came again.

The strangest caller came one afternoon at about four o'clock. I had come back from school and was in my home-clothes. The man said to me, "Sonny, may I come inside your yard?"

He was a small man and he was tidily dressed. He wore a hat, a white shirt, and black trousers.

I asked, "What you want?"

He said, "I want to watch your bees."

We had four small gru-gru palm trees and they were full of uninvited bees.

I ran up the steps and shouted, "Ma, it have a man outside here. He say he want to watch the bees."

My mother came out, looked at the man, and asked in an unfriendly way, "What you want?"

The man said, "I want to watch your bees."

His English was so good, it didn't sound natural, and I could see my mother was worried.

She said to me, "Stay here and watch him while he watch the bees."

The man said, "Thank you, madam. You have done a good deed today."

He spoke very slowly and very correctly as though every word was costing him money.

We watched the bees, this man and I, for about an hour, squatting near the palm trees.

The man said, "I like watching bees. Sonny, do you like watching bees?"

I said, "I ain't have the time."

He shook his head sadly. He said, "That's what I do, I just watch. I can watch ants for days. Have you ever watched ants? And scorpions, and centipedes, and *congorees*—have you watched those?"

I shook my head.

I said, "What you does do, mister?"

He got up and said, "I am a poet."

I said, "A good poet?"

He said, "The greatest in the world."

"What your name, mister?"

"B. Wordsworth."

"B for Bill?"

"Black. Black Wordsworth. White Wordsworth was my brother. We share one heart. I can watch a small flower like the morning glory and cry."

I said, "Why you does cry?"

"Why, boy? Why? You will know when you grow up. You're a poet, too, you know. And when you're a poet you can cry for everything."

I couldn't laugh.

He said, "You like your mother?"

"When she not beating me."

He pulled out a printed sheet from his hip pocket and said, "On this paper is the greatest poem about mothers and I'm going to sell it to you at a bargain price. For four cents."

I went inside and I said, "Ma, you want to buy a poetry for four cents?"

My mother said, "Tell that blasted man to haul his tail away from my yard, you hear."

I said to B. Wordsworth, "My mother say she ain't have four cents."

B. Wordsworth said, "It is the poet's tragedy."

And he put the paper back in his pocket. He didn't seem to mind.

I said, "Is a funny way to go round selling poetry like that. Only calypsonians do that sort of thing. A lot of people does buy?"

He said, "No one has yet bought a single copy."

"But why you does keep on going round, then?"

He said, "In this way I watch many things, and I always hope to meet poets."

I said, "You really think I is a poet?"

"You're as good as me," he said.

And when B. Wordsworth left, I prayed I would see him again.

About a week later, coming back from school one afternoon, I met him at the corner of Miguel Street.

He said, "I have been waiting for you for a long time."

I said, "You sell any poetry yet?"

He shook his head.

He said, "In my yard I have the best mango tree in Port of Spain. And now the mangoes are ripe and red and very sweet and juicy. I have waited here for you to tell you this and to invite you to come and eat some of my mangoes."

He lived in Alberto Street in a one-roomed hut placed right in the centre of the lot. The yard seemed all green. There was the big mango tree. There was a coconut tree and there was a plum tree. The place looked wild, as though it wasn't in the city at all. You couldn't see all the big concrete houses in the street.

He was right. The mangoes were sweet and juicy. I ate about six, and the yellow mango juice ran down my arms to my elbows and down my mouth to my chin and my shirt was stained.

My mother said when I got home, "Where was you? You think you is a man now and could go all over the place? Go cut a whip for me."

She beat me rather badly, and I ran out of the house swearing that I would never come back. I went to B. Wordsworth's house. I was so angry, my nose was bleeding.

B. Wordsworth said, "Stop crying, and we will go for a walk."

I stopped crying, but I was breathing short. We went for a walk. We walked down St. Clair Avenue to the Savannah and we walked to the racecourse.

B. Wordsworth said, "Now, let us lie on the grass and look up at the sky, and I want you to think how far those stars are from us."

I did as he told me, and I saw what he meant. I felt like nothing, and at the same time I had never felt so big and great in all my life. I forgot all my anger and all my tears and all the blows.

When I said I was better, he began telling me the names of the stars, and I particularly remembered the constellation of Orion the Hunter, though I don't really know why. I can spot Orion even today, but I have forgotten the rest.

Then a light was flashed into our faces, and we saw a policeman. We got up from the grass.

The policeman said, "What you doing here?"

B. Wordsworth said, "I have been asking myself the same question for forty years."

We became friends, B. Wordsworth and I. He told me, "You must never tell anybody about me and about the mango tree and the coconut tree and the plum tree. You must keep that a secret. If you tell anybody, I will know, because I am a poet."

I gave him my word and I kept it.

I liked his little room. It had no more furniture than George's front room, but it looked cleaner and healthier. But it also looked lonely.

One day I asked him, "Mister Wordsworth, why you does keep all this bush in your yard? Ain't it does make the place damp?"

He said, "Listen, and I will tell you a story. Once upon a time a boy and girl met each other and they fell in love. They loved each other so much they got married. They were both poets. He loved words. She loved grass and flowers and trees. They lived happily in a single room, and then one day, the girl poet said to the boy poet, 'We are going to have another poet in the family.' But this poet was never born, because the girl died, and the young poet died with her, inside her. And the girl's husband was very sad, and he said he would never touch a thing in the girl's garden. And so the garden remained, and grew high and wild."

I looked at B. Wordsworth, and as he told me this lovely story, he seemed to grow older. I understood his story.

We went for long walks together. We went to the Botanical Gardens and the Rock Gardens. We climbed Chancellor Hill in the late afternoon and watched the darkness fall on Port of Spain, and watched the lights go on in the city and on the ships in the harbour.

He did everything as though he were doing it for the first time in his life. He did everything as though he were doing some church rite.

He would say to me, "Now, how about having some ice cream?"

And when I said yes, he would grow very serious and say, "Now, which café shall we patronize?" As though it were a very important thing. He would think for some time about it, and finally say, "I think I will go and negotiate the purchase with that shop."

The world became a most exciting place.

One day, when I was in his yard, he said to me, "I have a great secret which I am now going to tell you."

I said, "It really secret?"

"At the moment, yes."

I looked at him, and he looked at me. He said, "This is just between you and me, remember. I am writing a poem."

"Oh." I was disappointed.

He said, "But this is a different sort of poem. This is the greatest poem in the world."

I whistled.

He said, "I have been working on it for more than five years now. I will finish it in about twenty-two years from now, that is, if I keep on writing at the present rate."

"You does write a lot, then?"

He said, "Not any more. I just write one line a month. But I make sure it is a good line."

I asked, "What was last month's good line?"

He looked up at the sky, and said, *"The past is deep."*

I said, "It is a beautiful line."

B. Wordsworth said, "I hope to distil the experiences of a whole month into that single line of poetry. So, in twenty-two years, I shall have written a poem that will sing to all humanity."

I was filled with wonder.

Our walks continued. We walked along the sea wall at Docksite one day, and I said, "Mr. Wordsworth, if I drop this pin in the water, you think it will float?"

He said, "This is a strange world. Drop your pin, and let us see what will happen."

The pin sank.

I said, "How is the poem this month?"

But he never told me any other line. He merely said, "Oh, it comes, you know. It comes."

Or we would sit on the sea wall and watch the liners come into the harbour.

But of the greatest poem in the world I heard no more.

I felt he was growing older.

"How you does live, Mr. Wordsworth?" I asked him one day.

He said, "You mean how I get money?"

When I nodded, he laughed in a crooked way.

He said, "'I sing calypsoes in the calypso season."

"And that last you the rest of the year?"

"It is enough."

"But you will be the richest man in the world when you write the greatest poem?"

He didn't reply.

One day when I went to see him in his little house, I found him lying on his little bed. He looked so old and so weak, that I found myself wanting to cry.

He said, "The poem is not going well."

He wasn't looking at me. He was looking through the window at the coconut tree, and he was speaking as though I wasn't there. He said, "When I was twenty I felt the power within myself." Then, almost in front of my eyes, I could see his face growing older and more tired. He said, "But that— that was a long time ago."

And then—I felt it so keenly, it was as though I had been slapped by my mother. I could see it clearly on his face. It was there for everyone to see. Death on the shrinking face.

He looked at me, and saw my tears and sat up.

He said, "Come." I went and sat on his knees.

He looked into my eyes, and he said, "Oh, you can see it, too. I always knew you had the poet's eye."

He didn't even look sad, and that made me burst out crying loudly.

He pulled me to his thin chest, and said, "Do you want me to tell you a funny story?" and he smiled encouragingly at me.

But I couldn't reply.

He said, "When I have finished this story, I want you to promise that you will go away and never come back to see me. Do you promise?"

I nodded.

He said, "Good. Well, listen. That story I told you about the boy poet and the girl poet, do you remember that? That wasn't true. It was something I just made up. All this talk about poetry and the greatest poem in the world, that wasn't true, either. Isn't that the funniest thing you have heard?"

But his voice broke.

I left the house, and ran home crying, like a poet, for everything I saw.

I walked along Alberto Street a year later, but I could find no sign of the poet's house. It hadn't vanished, just like that. It had been pulled down, and a big, two-storeyed building had taken its place. The mango tree and the plum tree and the coconut tree had all been cut down, and there was brick and concrete everywhere.

It was just as though B. Wordsworth had never existed.

V THE MIDDLE EAST

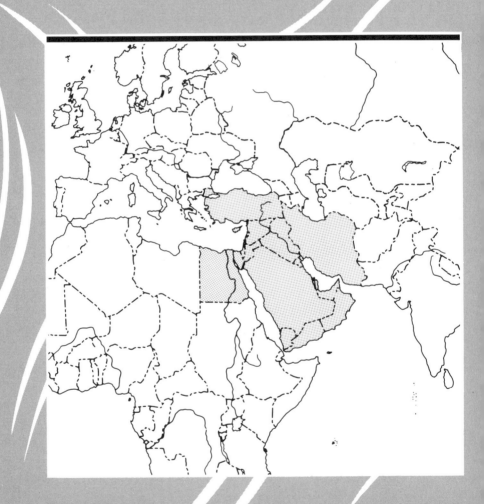

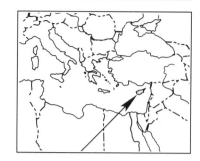

Gregory

BY PANOS IOANNIDES

TRANSLATED BY MARION BYRON RAIZIS AND CATHERINE RAIZIS

My hand was sweating as I held the pistol. The curve of the trigger was biting against my finger.

Facing me, Gregory trembled.

His whole being was beseeching me, "Don't!"

Only his mouth did not make a sound. His lips were squeezed tight. If it had been me, I would have screamed, shouted, cursed.

The soldiers were watching ...

The day before, during a brief meeting, they had each given their opinions: "It's tough luck, but it has to be done. We've got no choice."

The order from Headquarters was clear: "As soon as Lieutenant Rafel's execution is announced, the hostage Gregory is to be shot and his body must be hanged from a telegraph pole in the main street as an exemplary punishment."

It was not the first time that I had to execute a hostage in this war. I had acquired experience, thanks to Headquarters which had kept entrusting me with these delicate assignments. Gregory's case was precisely the sixth.

The first time, I remember, I vomited. The second time I got sick and had a headache for days. The third time I drank a bottle of rum. The fourth, just two glasses of beer. The fifth time I joked about it: "This little guy, with the big pop-eyes, won't be much of a ghost!"

But why, dammit, when the day came did I have to start thinking that I'm not so tough, after all? The thought had come at exactly the wrong time and spoiled all my disposition to do my duty.

You see, this Gregory was such a miserable little creature, such a puny thing, such a nobody, damn him.

That very morning, although he had heard over the loudspeakers that Rafel had been executed, he believed that we would spare his life because we had been eating together so long.

"Those who eat from the same mess tins and drink from the same water canteen," he said, "remain good friends no matter what."

And a lot more of the same sort of nonsense.

He was a silly fool—we had smelled that out the very first day Headquarters gave him to us. The sentry guarding him had got dead drunk and had dozed off. The rest of us with exit permits had gone from the barracks. When we came back, there was Gregory sitting by the sleeping sentry and thumbing through a magazine.

"Why didn't you run away, Gregory?" we asked, laughing at him, several days later.

And he answered, "Where would I go in this freezing weather? I'm O.K. here."

So we started teasing him.

"You're dead right. The accommodations here are splendid ..."

"It's not bad here," he replied. "The barracks where I used to be are like a sieve. The wind blows in from every side ..."

We asked him about his girl. He smiled.

"Maria is a wonderful person," he told us. "Before I met her she was engaged to a no-good fellow, a pig. He gave her up for another girl. Then nobody in the village wanted to marry Maria. I didn't miss my chance. So what if she is second-hand. Nonsense. Peasant ideas, my friend. She's beautiful and good-hearted. What more could I want? And didn't she load me with watermelons and cucumbers every time I passed by her vegetable garden? Well, one day I stole some cucumbers and melons and watermelons and I took them to her. 'Maria,' I said, 'from now on I'm going to take care of you.' She started crying and then me, too. But ever since that day she has given me lots of trouble—jealousy. She wouldn't let me go even to my mother's. Until the day I was recruited, she wouldn't let me go far from her apron strings. But that was just what I wanted ..."

He used to tell this story over and over, always with the same words, the same commonplace gestures. At the end he would have a good laugh and start gulping from his water jug.

His tongue was always wagging! When he started talking, nothing could stop him. We used to listen and nod our heads, not saying a word. But sometimes, as he was telling us about his mother and family problems, we couldn't help wondering, "Eh, well, these people have the same headaches in their country as we've got."

Strange, isn't it!

Except for his talking too much, Gregory wasn't a bad fellow. He was a marvellous cook. Once he made us some apple tarts, so delicious we licked the platter clean. And he could sew, too. He used to sew on all our buttons, patch our clothes, darn our socks, iron our ties, wash our clothes …

How the devil could you kill such a friend?

Even though his name was Gregory and some people on his side had killed one of ours, even though we had left wives and children to go to war against him and his kind—but how can I explain? He was our friend. He actually liked us! A few days before, hadn't he killed with his own bare hands a scorpion that was climbing up my leg? He could have let it send me to hell!

"Thanks, Gregory!" I said then, "Thank God who made you …"

When the order came, it was like a thunderbolt. Gregory was to be shot, it said, and hanged from a telegraph pole as an exemplary punishment.

We got together inside the barracks. We sent Gregory to wash some underwear for us.

"It ain't right."

"What is right?"

"Our duty!"

"Shit!"

"If you dare, don't do it! They'll drag you to court-martial and then bang-bang …"

Well, of course. The right thing is to save your skin. That's only logical. It's either your skin or his. His, of course, even if it was Gregory, the fellow you've been sharing the same plate with, eating with your fingers, and who was washing your clothes that very minute.

What could I do? That's war. We had seen worse things.

So we set the hour.

We didn't tell him anything when he came back from the washing. He slept peacefully. He snored for the last time. In the morning, he heard the news over the loudspeaker and he saw that we looked gloomy and he began to suspect that something was up. He tried talking to us, but he got no answers and then he stopped talking.

He just stood there and looked at us, stunned and lost ...

Now, I'll squeeze the trigger. A tiny bullet will rip through his chest. Maybe I'll lose my sleep tonight but in the morning I'll wake up alive.

Gregory seems to guess my thoughts. He puts out his hand and asks, "You're kidding, friend! Aren't you kidding?"

What a jackass! Doesn't he deserve to be cut to pieces? What a thing to ask at such a time. Your heart is about to burst and he's asking if you're kidding. How can a body be kidding about such a thing? Idiot! This is no time for jokes. And you, if you're such a fine friend, why don't you make things easier for us? Help us kill you with fewer qualms? If you would get angry—curse our Virgin, our God—if you'd try to escape it would be much easier for us and for you.

So it is now.

Now, Mr. Gregory, you are going to pay for your stupidities wholesale. Because you didn't escape the day the sentry fell asleep; because you didn't escape yesterday when we sent you all alone to the laundry—we did it on purpose, you idiot! Why didn't you let me die from the sting of the scorpion?

So now don't complain. It's all your fault, nitwit.

Eh? What's happening to him now?

Gregory is crying. Tears flood his eyes and trickle down over his clean-shaven cheeks. He is turning his face and pressing his forehead against the wall. His back is shaking as he sobs. His hands cling, rigid and helpless, to the wall.

Now is my best chance, now that he knows there is no other solution and turns his face from us.

I squeeze the trigger.

Gregory jerks. His back stops shaking up and down.

I think I've finished him! How easy it is ... But suddenly he starts crying out loud, his hands claw at the wall and try to pull it down. He screams, "No, no ..."

I turn to the others. I expect them to nod, "That's enough."

They nod, "What are you waiting for?"

I squeeze the trigger again.

The bullet smashed into his neck. A thick spray of blood spurts out.

Gregory turns. His eyes are all red. He lunges at me and starts punching me with his fists.

"I hate you, hate you ..." he screams.

I emptied the barrel. He fell and grabbed my leg as if he wanted to hold on.

He died with a terrible spasm. His mouth was full of blood and so were my boots and socks.

We stood quietly, looking at him.

When we came to, we stooped and picked him up. His hands were frozen and wouldn't let my legs go.

I still have their imprints, red and deep, as if made by a hot knife.

"We will hang him tonight," the men said.

"Tonight or now?" they said.

I turned and looked at them one by one.

"Is that what you all want?" I asked.

They gave me no answer.

"Dig a grave," I said.

Headquarters did not ask for a report the next day or the day after. The top brass were sure that we had obeyed them and had left him swinging from a pole.

They didn't care to know what happened to that Gregory, alive or dead.

An Incident in the Ghobashi Household

BY ALIFA RIFAAT

TRANSLATED BY DENYS JOHNSON-DAVIES

Zeinat woke to the strident call of the red cockerel from the rooftop above where she was sleeping. The Ghobashi house stood on the outskirts of the village and in front of it the fields stretched out to the river and the railway track.

The call of the red cockerel released answering calls from neighbouring rooftops. Then they were silenced by the voice of the muezzin from the lofty minaret among the mulberry trees calling: "Prayer is better than sleep."

She stretched out her arm to the pile of children sleeping alongside her and tucked the end of the old rag-woven kilim round their bodies, then shook her eldest daughter's shoulder.

"It's morning, another of the Lord's mornings. Get up, Ni'ma—today's market day."

Ni'ma rolled onto her back and lazily stretched herself. Like someone alerted by the sudden slap of a gust of wind, Zeinat stared down at the body spread out before her. Ni'ma sat up and pulled her djellaba over her thighs, rubbing at her sleep-heavy eyes in the rounded face with the prominent cheekbones.

"Are you going to be able to carry the grain to the market, daughter, or will it be too heavy for you?"

"Of course, mother. After all, who else is there to go?"

Zeinat rose to her feet and went out with sluggish steps to the court-yard, where she made her ablutions. Having finished the ritual prayer, she remained in the seated position as she counted off on her fingers her glorifications of Allah. Sensing that Ni'ma was standing behind her, she turned round to her:

"What are you standing there for? Why don't you go off and get the tea ready?"

Zeinat walked towards the corner where Ghobashi had stored the maize crop in sacks; he had left them as a provision for them after he had taken his air ticket from the office that had found him work in Libya and which would be bringing him back in a year's time.

"May the Lord keep you safe while you're away, Ghobashi," she muttered.

Squatting in front of a sack, the grain measure between her thighs, she scooped up the grain with both hands till the measure was full, then poured it into a basket. Coughing, she waved away the dust that rose up into her face, then returned to her work.

The girl went to the large clay jar, removed the wooden covering and dipped the mug into it and sprinkled water on her face; she wetted the tips of her fingers and parted her plaits, then tied her handkerchief over her head. She turned to her mother:

"Isn't that enough, mother? What do we want the money for?"

Zeinat struck her knees with the palms of her hands and tossed her head back.

"Don't we have to pay off Hamdan's wage?—or was he cultivating the beans for us for nothing, just for the fun of hard work?"

Ni'ma turned away and brought the stove from the window shelf, arranging the dried corn-cobs in a pyramid and lighting them. She put it alongside her mother, then filled the teapot with water from the jar and thrust it into the embers. She squatted down and the two sat in silence. Suddenly Zeinat said:

"Since when has the buffalo been with young?"

"From after my father went away."

"That's to say, right after the Great Feast, daughter?"

Ni'ma nodded her head in assent, then lowered it and began drawing lines in the dust.

"Why don't you go off and see how many eggs have been laid while the tea's getting ready."

Zeinat gazed into the glow of the embers. She had a sense of peace as she stared into the dancing flames. Ghobashi had gone and left the whole load on her shoulders: the children, the two kirats of land, and the buffalo. "Take care of Ni'ma," he had said the night before he left. "The girl's body has ripened." He had then spread out his palms and said, "O Lord, for the sake of the Prophet's honour, let me bring back with me a marriage dress for her of pure silk." She had said to him, "May your words go straight from your lips to Heaven's gate, Ghobashi." He wouldn't be returning before the following Great Feast. What would happen when he returned and found out the state of affairs? She put her head between the palms of her hands and leaned over the fire, blowing away the ashes. "How strange," she thought, "are the girls of today! The cunning little thing was hanging out her towels at the time of her period every month just as though nothing had happened, and here she is in her fourth month and there's nothing show-ing."

Ni'ma returned and untied the cloth from round the eggs, put two of them in the fire and the rest in a dish. She then brought two glasses and the tin of sugar and sat down next to her mother, who was still immersed in her thoughts.

"Didn't you try to find some way out?"

Ni'ma hunched her shoulders in a gesture of helplessness.

"Your father's been gone four months. Isn't there still time?"

"What's the use? If only the Lord were to spare you the trouble of me. Wouldn't it be for the best, mother, if my foot were to slip as I was filling the water jar from the canal and we'd be done with it?"

Zeinat struck herself on the breast and drew her daughter to her.

"Don't say such a wicked thing. Don't listen to such promptings of the Devil. Calm down and let's find some solution before your father returns."

Zeinat poured out the tea. In silence she took quick sips at it, then put the glass in front of her and shelled the egg and bit into it. Ni'ma sat watch-ing her, her fingers held round the hot glass. From outside came the raised voices of women discussing the prospects at the day's market, while men exchanged greetings as they made their way to the fields. Amidst the voices could be heard Hamdan's laughter as he led the buffalo to the two kirats of land surrounding the house.

"His account is with Allah," muttered Zeinat. "He's fine and doesn't have a worry in the world."

Ni'ma got up and began winding round the end of her headcloth so as to form a pad on her head. Zeinat turned round and saw her preparing herself to go off to the market. She pulled her by her djellaba and the young girl sat down again. At this moment they heard a knocking at the door and the voice of their neighbour, Umm al-Khair, calling:

"Good health to you, folk. Isn't Ni'ma coming with me to market as usual, Auntie Zeinat? Or isn't she up yet?"

"Sister, she's just going off to stay with our relatives."

"May Allah bring her back safely."

Ni'ma looked at her mother enquiringly, while Zeinat placed her finger to her mouth. When the sound of Umm al-Khair's footsteps died away, Ni'ma whispered:

"What are you intending to do, mother? What relatives are you talking about?"

Zeinat got up and rummaged in her clothes box and took out a handkerchief tied round some money, also old clothes. She placed the handkerchief in Ni'ma's palm and closed her fingers over it.

"Take it—they're my life savings."

Ni'ma remained silent as her mother went on:

"Get together your clothes and go straight away to the station and take a ticket to Cairo. Cairo's a big place, daughter, where you'll find protection and a way to make a living till Allah brings you safely to your time. Then bring it back with you at dead of night without anyone seeing you or hearing you."

Zeinat raised the end of her djellaba and put it between her teeth. Taking hold of the old clothes, she began winding them round her waist. Then she let fall the djellaba. Ni'ma regarded her in astonishment:

"And what will we say to my father?"

"It's not time for talking. Before you go off to the station, help me with the basket so that I can go to the market for people to see me like this. Isn't it better, when he returns, for your father to find himself with a legitimate son than an illegitimate grandson?"

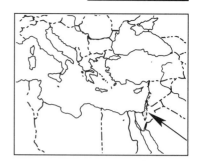

Twilight

BY SHULAMITH HAREVEN

TRANSLATED BY MIRIAM ARAD

Last night I spent a year in the city where I was born. I had long known the password for getting there: Dante's line, "I am the way to the city of sorrow." In a clear voice I said, "*Per me si va nella città dolente*," and time split open and I was there. In that one night's year I met a man, married, became pregnant, and gave birth to a murky child who grew fast, all without light.

The city of my birth was very dark, extinguished, because the sun had left it and gone away a long, long time ago, and people in the street walked swiftly through the gloom, warming hands and lighting up faces with candles or matches. Here and there someone moved about with an oil lamp. The streets were wide, as I remembered them, but many windows were boarded up, the planks hammered in crosswise. Other windows were stuffed with rags and old newspapers against the cold. As there was no light, not a single tree was left in the streets, only black fenced-in staves. Not one plant showed on windowsills.

I saw no one I recognized at first, yet everyone seemed very familiar, smiling faintly. They never went so far as to break into laughter. They already knew they would live without sun from now and forever more. There was an air of humility and resignation about them. They were as kind to each other as they could be. Two acquaintances meeting in the street would warm one another's hands with a shy smile.

They wore the clothes I remembered from childhood: You could always tell a man's calling by his dress. Policemen wore policemen's uniforms, of course; the judge went about as a judge, alighting from his carriage in wig and gown; the chimney sweep was invariably in his work clothes, and so was the coachman, and so was the Count. The children were dressed as children: sailor collars and lace, and the girls with knees frozen in dresses of stiff scalloped taffeta. Many wore school uniforms: dark blue or brown, high-school badges embroidered on their caps. Everyone knew where he belonged.

No one had died in the city of my birth since the sun had gone beyond recall, and no one had had new garments made. Their uniform-like clothes were not quite tattered yet, not by any means; but they reminded one of the costumes of a theatre wardrobe worn over and over for many performances; somewhat greying at the seams, somewhat fraying at the cuffs, stale smells buried in each fold. And yet, such clean people, clean as smoke.

I seemed to require no sleep or food in the city of my birth, but only speech. Now I have slept, I told myself, now I have eaten, and it would be as though I had slept and eaten and could go on. And on and on I went, through the dark streets, only some of which I remembered, and some of which were ruined and not repaired but closed.

One night I drove to the opera in a carriage. The horse defecated as it went, but the odour of the dung did not reach me. I realized all of a sudden there were no smells in this city. The coachman wore an old battered top hat, and when I paid my fare he raised his hat in greeting and cracked his whip in a special way, an expert crack in the air. He knew me for a visitor, but he did not know that I came from the land of the sun. Perhaps he did not know about that land at all, though it was so near, right beyond the wall, only a password between the twilight and it. Most people do not know.

At the opera I met the man I married that night, that year. They were singing Mozart on stage, and the audience was so pleased, so responsive, that at times it seemed audience and singers might be interchangeable. I myself, I imagine, could have gone up there and joined the singer in *"Voi che sapete."* There was a festive mood about it all, an air of goodwill, bravo, bravo, rows of women's hats bobbing joyously.—How can one live without Mozart?

The man sitting by my side at the opera leaned over and said, "We must leave at the intermission, quickly, because the opera will be surrounded by soldiers after the performance and this whole audience taken away to freight trains."

I consented, though wondering how come all these people knew it and none escaped. In the intermission the man took my hand and we left quickly by a side door. Trucks with bored soldiers were already posted in the square, the soldiers preparing to get off and surround the building. Their sergeants, papers in hand, were checking the order of deployment. A young soldier was whistling *"Voi che sapete"* and said to his fellow, "How can one live without Mozart?"

In the dark light, the no-light, I asked the man holding my hand without my feeling its touch how come people weren't escaping, and he said, "Why, this whole thing repeats itself each night."

He drew me over to a door, narrow as a servants' entrance, and beyond it a slippery, winding staircase, mounting to a roof. The roof was very peculiar: We were standing at the altitude of an airplane's flight, perhaps thirty-five hundred metres, perhaps more, very high. Yet I could see every single detail in the opera square below.

The floodlights of the soldiers' trucks came on suddenly, tearing the darkness, glaring and terrible, and with this evil light came the wails, the shouts and curses. Now everything happened fast. The people in their festive clothes piled up on the trucks, and there was no more telling them apart, batch after driven batch. Only the soldiers stood out clearly, because they had light, harsh and frightful, and because they were shouting so.

"Operation Cauldron," said the man by my side. "Every night it repeats itself. Every night they are driven in trucks like that to the trains and do not return. Next evening they are back, going to the opera, and it all starts over again. The only difference is that the people are a little less alive each time. They fade, like pictures in an album. But the process is so slow it is barely noticeable."

"And you—don't they take you in Operation Cauldron?" I asked.

"No," he said, "I'm already ..." and stopped with a wave of the hand. Then he added, "You don't have to go either. Of course, if you want to ..."

The moment he said that I was seized by a whirlwind. I wanted, wanted mortally to leap from this tall roof into the dark courtyard now filled with shouting soldiers, go out to the opera square. Together with all the children. Together with all the neighbours, whom now I suddenly recognized one by one, Mrs. Paula and Mr. Arkin and his wife, and Moshe of the haberdashery who used to give me pictures of angels and cherubs to stick in my copybooks, and Bolek the druggist's son. They were all being herded onto the trucks here before my eyes, fearful and apprehensive, the soldiers shouting over their heads. And I wished to leap and be with them. To be taken.

"I did not leap, either," said the man, very sad, as though confessing a sin. The whirlwind began to abate. I held on to the parapet and breathed hard. A fierce desire had come and gone and left me reeling.

One by one the trucks moved off with a terrible jarring noise. In the square lay a child's ballet slipper, a gilt-knobbed walking stick, and an ostrich feather from the hat of a lady in the opera audience. Then they *are* somewhat diminished each night, I thought to myself, and my anxiety found no relief. The emptiness that remained in the square had left my body drained to the core.

"Tomorrow it will all happen again," said the man by my side. Grief was everywhere. It was all over.

"Could we get married?" I asked, like someone asking permission to take a vacant chair in a café. And he nodded and said, "We could, yes."

We did not know where we should live. All that night we wandered through the streets, as there was no telling day from night except for a shade of difference in the depth of darkness; everything was shrouded in the same no-light of the extinguished city. That night we also crossed a park, which since the sun had gone had long ceased being a park; many marble statues were strewn over the ground now, statues of people, some of them smashed. One small statue was very like my grandfather. I wanted to take it away with me, but I had no place to put it. Once or twice I also saw a white marble statue of a horse, its thigh wrenched off, and something like frozen blood on the marble. There had not been so many statues in my childhood days, not just in the park but all over town. They had apparently turned this into a dump, maybe for all the world. The presence of the kind people from the streets was missing here, and we returned to the city that never slept, that always had men and women walking about, huddled against the cold— till we got to a smoky alehouse. A few people, their breath misty in the cold air, their spirits high, were crowded in the doorway but did not go in.

The man with me briefly considered entering the place, then as quickly dismissed the idea. There was a space behind the alehouse, a kind of small courtyard paved with concrete, and in it a tiny shed that I took for an outhouse. He opened its door and we went in; but there was no end to the shed, and its far side had another door, behind which lay, suddenly, a vast deserted residence. It had heavy, very rich furniture, a sideboard and carpets and enormous armchairs, and crystal chandeliers thick with dust and cobwebs. I had always known that this house existed behind some wall or other, and that one day I would inherit it. Generations of my forefathers must have lived here, they and their wives, my grandmothers in their handsome kerchiefs. I went in, unamazed. The furniture was too large and unwieldy, and we decided we would use only one of the rooms, a plain and all but empty one with a kind of stove on the floor to be stoked with paper or wood. The man crouched and lit a fire, the heat of which I did not feel, and his shadow fell across me. I accepted what was to be. He blew on the fire a little, and when it was going somehow he checked the window locks, then stood before me and said, "The wedding took place this afternoon."

I knew these words to be our wedding rites and I was very still, the way one is on solemn occasions. This will be my life from now on, I told myself, in a city without light, perhaps never once leaving this apartment, never entering its large chambers, just this one room, and perhaps one day the soldiers will come for me too, take me to the trucks, the trains, along with all of them, with all of them, with all of them. I shall say to all the children: Wait for me. I shall say: I am coming with you, of course I am coming with you.

All at once the room filled with people, women in shawls, neighbours. They came beaming, bearing gifts, cases, cartons. They all stood squeezed in the doorway, in the room, filling it, joyously offering their blessings in identical words: "The wedding took place this afternoon," they said and kissed me, "The wedding took place this afternoon." The room overflowed with people and with parcels. I opened one, and it held all the toys I had lost as a child and never found. The neighbour who had brought them stood over me, smiling, angelic, and repeated excitedly, "The wedding took place this afternoon." She knew that her present was apt.

Afterward the neighbour women left, their thin voices, fluttery with a small, birdlike gladness, trailing down the staircase, and all the parcels remained: cases and cartons and beribboned boxes. I saw no need to shift them, though they hardly left us space to move about the room.

"This is where we shall live," I told the man in the room with me, and he nodded his head in assent.

So a year went by. We lived like lizards, in crevices, among the empty cases in the room. I do not remember anyone buying food, but every day I crossed the long corridor, past the large, imposing, unheated and unlived-in rooms, to cook something in a kitchen that was like a large cave. Once we even went on an outing. Behind our apartment, not on the alehouse side but on the other, lay a desert stretching for many kilometres, and beyond the desert, in the distant haze, a range of mountain peaks, very far away. We stood at the edge of the house, a few dozen others with us, and looked at those faraway hills.

"Where is that?" I asked the people with us. They grinned good-naturedly and would not tell me, as though I should have known. One of them said, "Los Angeles," but that was a joke. I went in, back to our room, took off my shoes, my feet weary as after a long walk.

Now and then we would hear shouts from one of the nearby houses: The soldiers come for the kill. They never got to us. We would lie numb, waiting for the night's Operation Cauldron to end, the leaden silence to return, the hollow grief.

Toward the end of the year I gave birth. The child tore away from me at one stroke; and I remembered dimly that once, long ago, in my other life, I had loved a man very much, and it was just this way I had felt when he tore away from my body: as though a part of me had suddenly been separated for all time. Then I wept many tears.

The child stood up and walked within a day or two. Next he began talking to me, demanding something, in an incoherent speech I failed to understand; he grew angry and I knew he would not stay with me long. One day he left and did not return. When the man came home he removed his coat wordlessly and we both knew: The child had run off to the opera square. And it had been impossible to prevent.

The days went by, day running into night without any real difference between them. Sometimes kind-hearted neighbours called. Once one of them came with scraps of material, a dressmaker's leftovers; we spent a whole morning sewing children's frocks, except that at the end of the day we had to unravel them all.

One day I knew that time had come full circle: My year in the city without light was over and I was to go back. I said to the man with me, "I'm going."

He nodded. He did not offer to come with me. I would have to fall asleep in order to wake up in the other country anyway, and he could not accompany me into sleep. I think we never slept once in all that year, neither he nor I. Our eyelids were always open, day and night.

I lay down on my bed, which only now turned out to have wheels like a hospital bed, and the man I was with set it going with one hard shove along the corridor, which turned into a steep incline, and the bed rolled into the kitchen. The kitchen, where all that year I had gone to cook, had changed: It had been set up as an operating room. I was not surprised. I lay there waiting, unafraid. All the instruments were apparently ready; only the big lamp above me was still unlit. A stern-faced surgeon in a green coat and cap bent over me, examined me at a glance, and said, "Turn on the light."

The big lamp blazed over my head, and I fell into a heavy sleep, and woke up in my other house.

It was morning. A great sun shone straight into my eyes. Ailanthus branches gently swayed on the veranda, drawing curtains of light whisper-soft across my face. A rich smell of coffee hung in the air, but as yet I could not take deep breaths of it. My soul did not return to me at once.

Through the door came the murmur of my husband's and children's voices, speaking softly so as not to wake me. I cherished them, but could not understand them from within yet, as though they were a translation that had come off well. I lay still, waiting for my soul to flow full in me again, and I knew it was all over and completed: I would no more go back to the city of my birth, to the lightless city. Dante's verse dimmed, faded, returned to the pages of the book, a line like any other: its power exhausted. In a day or two I might even be able to read it without a pang. And sleep too, I told myself wonderingly, be able really to sleep. My past was commuted. From now on I would find nothing there but the stones of Jerusalem, and plants growing with mighty vigour, and a vast light.

I got up to make breakfast, my heart beating hard.

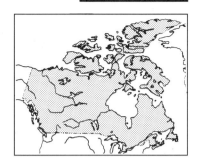

The Czech Dog

BY W. G. HARDY

She had been noticing him sitting in the corner, half hidden by a fern. Because she had been told that he was a Czech newly come to New York, and because he seemed alone and out of place and somewhat tense, she went over and tried to make conversation.

But the room was noisy with well-fed, charitable people, come together in this Red Cross rally, and now that she was near him she sensed emanating from him an unpredictable violence of protest. Trying to view the gathering as she supposed it must appear to him—the cocktails, the gay chatter, the complaints about gasoline rationing, and the dearth of steaks— she thought she understood. So on impulse she said, keeping her voice even:

"Look, I ought to be home early. Will you be an excuse for me to go?"

He was well-bred. He picked up the cue without visible surprise. At her own door she hesitated, and then, stirred by sympathy, and at the same time interested in what kept this man taut and withdrawn, she asked him in.

It was no easier to talk when they were in her living room. She dragged out of him that a month ago he had been flown out of Czechoslovakia to England, and that he was in America on something to do with supplies for the Underground in his country. But he would not enlarge on either point. So she said the obvious thing, hoping that it might get him started:

"It must be terrible in Czechoslovakia."

He nodded—and let it go at that. She looked at his mobile intellectual face, realizing that it was closed against her and wondering why. Just then her dog came into the room. It was a collie, a beautiful animal. She leaned forward and spoke to it, expecting it to come to her. But after a leisurely look around it ignored her, and, ears flat and half laughing with its mouth in the way dogs have, it walked deliberately over to the man, put its head on his knees, and looked up at him. He reached down and scratched behind the silky ears. She remarked with a certain measure of annoyance:

"You seem to be a person dogs like."

He glanced at her quickly. "Yes," he said. He thought a moment. Then, stroking the dog's head gently, he went on: "I know what you have been trying to do. It is kind of you. But it is of no use. Each of us has his own circle of experience into which no one else can enter."

She leaned back in her comfortable chair. "I am not sure that that is always true."

"I think so." He looked away from her and round at the room—the soft light, the pictures, the deep rugs, the graceful vases. The collie, perceiving that the man's attention was diverted, placed itself with dignity at his feet, and putting its head on its forepaws, watched him. "If I tell you that I, who was once a physician—well-to-do, respected, secure—lay on a floor, helpless, and was kicked and beaten, and then revived, and then beaten and kicked—hour after hour—it will only be words to you, because you cannot imagine that ever happening to your brother or your husband, or to anyone you know. Or if I say to you that my sister, as educated and delicately brought up as you, is now in a German concentration camp, you will exclaim 'How terrible!' It will not be actuality—a living actuality—because never in your life have you been, or will you be, in danger of that."

"I suppose we, here in America, must seem—untouched," she murmured, thinking of the meeting they had left and noticing how alive his face was now. "Yet some of us would like to understand."

He shrugged his shoulders. "To you, Freedom is still a careless dress. Forgive me, if I am rhetorical. If you had ever known what it is to cringe in your own country before an alien, to starve, to be helpless. As it is ..." He stopped and looked around him again, as if searching. His eyes chanced on the collie at his feet. It stirred and made a whimpering, inquiring sound in its throat. He reached down to touch it, soothing it. Then he looked across at her hesitantly, almost shyly. "You have a dog, a dog that you love," he said. " If I were, perhaps, to tell you of another dog, a dog in Czechoslovakia ...?"

"Do."

"It was not much of a dog," he explained, sitting up. "It was only a little one, half—no, almost wholly—starved. But its manners were good. At one time it had been, I am sure, someone's pet, sleek, fat, probably impertinent. When I saw it, its coat was ragged and its ears were torn and its ribs were there to count.

"It was on the first morning that it found me. I was, you must understand, carrying a message for the Underground, and it was imperative that that message reach one man, the right man. At the very outset of my journey I was stopped by a patrol. They knocked me about. But I was disguised as a crippled peasant—and as you see, that was good, because I am crippled. Nor did I, who used to walk down the street and give way to no man—even as you in America—forget to be as cringing and as animal-like as the Nazis think a Czech in his own country should be. I begged on my knees. I wept. I went slobbering after my bit of bread when they flung it into the mud. One of them put a hob-nailed boot on my hand—this hand—when I had got hold of it, and laughed, and they all laughed and they let me go. I laughed, too, within myself. I had won, this time.

"But about the dog. I was travelling, you comprehend, between dusk and dawn. It was in the early morning, in a wooded part of my country where I had made myself a hiding-place, that it smelled me out. I cursed it. I flung sticks at it. But dogs know. It came crawling back to me, its tail between its legs, its eyes pleading. I ought to have kicked it away. We Czechs, you must understand, have been left only one possession—the will not to give in. We dare not have any other—except hate. So I ought to have kicked it, brutally, so that it would not come back. But it was lost and homeless and starving and did not comprehend why. It had done no wrong. I could not kick it. I said, to myself: 'Cannot a Czech peasant have a dog with him?'

"I gave it the bit of bread. I let it curl up against me. That night, and the next night, I let it come with me. What food I got I shared with it. It was a good dog. It was so grateful to belong to someone again. And then during the third night I was crawling along a ditch. I was there, you understand, because I was in an area of Czechoslovakia where a Czech is shot at sight. But I was tired of the ditch and of the mud and water in it, I had seen no Germans. I had heard none. I said to myself that I would get out of the ditch. At that instant the dog growled, deep in its throat. I waited. A patrol came tramping by.

"When it had passed I patted the dog and praised it, and it wagged its tail and its whole body, and licked my hand. It was when it licked my hand that I realized how alone I had been, and for how long. I had been kicked and beaten. I had had other things done to me—things that leave you no—no dignity. I, who had once been prosperous and secure and free, had been compelled to stand by helpless in my own home while what was done to my wife was done. Something had died in me. But now it began to stir again. I, who for so long had had no part in any emotion but hate, felt that dog lick my hand. I hugged it. I hugged it to myself."

He paused, and she could see that his mind was a long way off. Sitting here in this secure, comfortable room, she tried to visualize the ditch and the darkness and this man, so quiet, so proud, so impeccably-mannered, down in the mud, hugging a half-starved dog. Yes, she could see the dog—poor thing. She glanced at her own collie. It was continuing to watch the man in complete oblivion of herself.

"And then?" she asked, more sharply than she realized.

The man roused himself. "Then? Oh, then we went on. Two nights later we came at last almost to the end of my journey, to the most crucial part of it, to a place where there was a cordon of sentries through which I must pass. In my other life I would have pronounced it impossible. But those Germans—so methodical that we of the Underground had been able to plot the exact time each sentry passed each post! I waited for the sentry to go by because I knew that then I would have exactly seven and one-half minutes before he returned, and that would be time enough, if I were quick.

"I crouched there in the darkness in a hollow, waiting. There was a certain triumph in me. For I felt now that I would get my message through, and then certain Nazis who had exercised lust and cruelty on helpless ones, and had laughed and thought there would be no reckoning, would find out that they were wrong.

"That was how I felt. I had my arm around the dog and it was warm against me, and we waited.

"But then the dog growled.

"It meant that the sentry was coming. But I was afraid that he might hear. I could not take chances. In that place, at the slightest hint of anything unusual, the orders of the sentries are not to investigate, but to call out the guard. If it were called and a search were made, I would be discovered and my message would not get through. I spoke quickly under my breath to the dog, bidding it be quiet.

"But it kept on growling.

"It was imperative, you must comprehend, that I get through with my message. But I had come to love this dog. I had no wife any longer, and no home and no sister. But I had this dog. And the dog had me. It was all either of us had left to us. So I took a chance. I whispered to it again, begging it to understand and to be still. How could it understand? This was one of the enemy coming—and I had praised it before. It growled louder, deep in its throat.

"I could hear the sentry now. My message had to get through. I leaped on that little, half-starved dog, gripping its body between my knees so that it could not move. I seized its throat with my fingers—these fingers. They are strong, these fingers. They have to be, because if we have no weapons and a man has to be killed . . . . So I squeezed—savagely.

"If only the sentry had gone right by. I prayed that he would go right by. But he took his time. He stopped. He lit a cigarette and took a puff or two and looked about him. Then he put out the cigarette and went on. I unloosed my fingers. If only the dog had been well-fed, strong—like this one here. It wasn't. And I—I had no time. I left it there. I went on."

He stopped speaking. She stirred in her chair. Her mind comprehended what the man was trying to tell her. But she kept seeing that dog, the dog which had trusted him. Her own dog, troubled by the sense of things about him, shifted its head and made that whimpering, questioning sound again. The man leaned down, and smiling in understanding, passed his fingers gently over the collie's head. She looked at those fingers. It was not this man's fault that in his fight for his country he had had to sacrifice everything—even pity. But—those fingers—

"Here, Drake," she said to the collie, getting abruptly to her feet. "Come here!"

The man rose, looked around for his hat and cane, and started for the door.

"Of course, it was a Czech dog," he said, as if to himself.

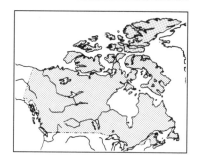

The Loons

BY MARGARET LAURENCE

Just below Manawaka, where the Wachakwa River ran brown and noisy over the pebbles, the scrub oak and grey-green willow and choke-cherry bushes grew in a dense thicket. In a clearing at the centre of the thicket stood the Tonnerre family's shack. The basis of this dwelling was a small square cabin made of poplar poles and chinked with mud, which had been built by Jules Tonnerre some fifty years before, when he came back from Batoche with a bullet in his thigh, the year that Riel was hung and the voices of the Métis entered their long silence. Jules had only intended to stay the winter in the Wachakwa Valley, but the family was still there in the thirties, when I was a child. As the Tonnerres had increased, their settlement had been added to, until the clearing at the foot of the town hill was a chaos of lean-tos, wooden packing cases, warped lumber, discarded car tires, ramshackle chicken coops, tangled strands of barbed wire and rusty tin cans.

The Tonnerres were French half-breeds, and among themselves they spoke a *patois* that was neither Cree nor French. Their English was broken and full of obscenities. They did not belong among the Cree of the Galloping Mountain reservation, further north, and they did not belong among the Scots-Irish and Ukrainians of Manawaka, either. They were, as my Grandmother MacLeod would have put it, neither flesh, fowl, nor good salt herring. When their men were not working at odd jobs or as section hands on the C.P.R., they lived on relief. In the summers, one of the Tonnerre youngsters, with a face that seemed totally unfamiliar with laughter, would knock at the doors of the town's brick houses and offer for sale a lard-pail full of bruised wild strawberries, and if he got as much as a quarter he would grab the coin and run before the customer had time to change her mind. Sometimes old Jules, or his son Lazarus, would get mixed up in a Saturday-night brawl, and would hit out at whoever was nearest, or howl drunkenly among the offended shoppers on Main Street, and then the Mountie would put them for the night in the barred cell underneath the Court House, and the next morning they would be quiet again.

Piquette Tonnerre, the daughter of Lazarus, was in my class at school. She was older than I, but she had failed several grades, perhaps because her attendance had always been sporadic and her interest in schoolwork negligible. Part of the reason she had missed a lot of school was that she had had tuberculosis of the bone, and had once spent many months in hospital. I knew this because my father was the doctor who had looked after her. Her sickness was almost the only thing I knew about her, however. Otherwise, she existed for me only as a vaguely embarrassing presence, with her hoarse voice and her clumsy limping walk and her grimy cotton dresses that were always miles too long. I was neither friendly nor unfriendly towards her. She dwelt and moved somewhere within my scope of vision, but I did not actually notice her very much until that peculiar summer when I was eleven.

"I don't know what to do about that kid," my father said at dinner one evening. "Piquette Tonnerre, I mean. The damn bone's flared up again. I've had her in hospital for quite a while now, and it's under control all right, but I hate like the dickens to send her home again."

"Couldn't you explain to her mother that she has to rest a lot?" my mother said.

"The mother's not there," my father replied. "She took off a few years back. Can't say I blame her. Piquette cooks for them, and she says Lazarus would never do anything for himself as long as she's there. Anyway, I don't think she'd take much care of herself, once she got back. She's only thirteen, after all. Beth, I was thinking—what about taking her up to Diamond Lake with us this summer? A couple of months rest would give that bone a much better chance."

My mother looked stunned.

"But Ewen—what about Roddie and Vanessa?"

"She's not contagious," my father said. "And it would be company for Vanessa."

"Oh dear," my mother said in distress, "I'll bet anything she has nits in her hair."

"For Pete's sake," my father said crossly, "do you think Matron would let her stay in the hospital for all this time like that? Don't be silly, Beth."

Grandmother MacLeod, her delicately featured face as rigid as a cameo, now brought her mauve-veined hands together as though she were about to begin a prayer.

"Ewen, if that half-breed youngster comes along to Diamond Lake, I'm not going," she announced. "I'll go to Morag's for the summer."

I had trouble in stifling my urge to laugh, for my mother brightened visibly and quickly tried to hide it. If it came to a choice between Grandmother MacLeod and Piquette, Piquette would win hands down, nits or not.

"It might be quite nice for you, at that," she mused. "You haven't seen Morag for over a year, and you might enjoy being in the city for a while. Well, Ewen dear, you do what you think best. If you think it would do Piquette some good, then we'll be glad to have her, as long as she behaves herself."

So it happened that several weeks later, when we all piled into my father's old Nash, surrounded by suitcases and boxes of provisions and toys for my ten-month-old brother, Piquette was with us and Grandmother MacLeod, miraculously, was not. My father would only be staying at the cottage for a couple of weeks, for he had to get back to his practice, but the rest of us would stay at Diamond Lake until the end of August.

Our cottage was not named, as many were, "Dew Drop Inn" or "Bide-a-Wee," or "Bonnie Doon." The sign on the roadway bore in austere letters only our name, MacLeod. It was not a large cottage, but it was on the lake-front. You could look out the windows and see, through the filigree of the spruce trees, the water glistening greenly as the sun caught it. All around the cottage were ferns, and sharp-branched raspberry bushes, and moss that had grown over fallen tree trunks. If you looked carefully among the weeds and grass, you could find wild strawberry plants which were in white flower now and in another month would bear fruit, the fragrant globes hanging like miniature scarlet lanterns on the thin hairy stems. The two grey squirrels were still there, gossiping at us from the tall spruce beside the cottage, and by the end of the summer they should again be tame enough to take pieces of crust from my hands. The broad moose antlers that hung above the back door were a little more bleached and fissured after the winter, but otherwise everything was the same. I raced joyfully around my kingdom, greeting all the places I had not seen for a year. My brother, Roderick, who had not been born when we were here last summer, sat on the car rug in the sunshine and examined a brown spruce cone, meticulously turning it round and round in his small and curious hands. My mother and father toted the luggage from car to cottage, exclaiming over how well the place had wintered, no broken windows, thank goodness, no apparent damage from storm-felled branches or snow.

Only after I had finished looking around did I notice Piquette. She was sitting on the swing, her lame leg held stiffly out, and her other foot scuffing the ground as she swung slowly back and forth. Her long hair hung black and straight around her shoulders, and her broad coarse-featured face bore no expression—it was blank, as though she no longer dwelt within her own skull, as though she had gone elsewhere. I approached her very hesitantly.

"Want to come and play?"

Piquette looked at me with a sudden flash of scorn.

"I ain't a kid," she said.

Wounded I stamped angrily away, swearing I would not speak to her for the rest of the summer. In the days that followed, however, Piquette began to interest me, and I began to want to interest her. My reasons did not appear bizarre to me. Unlikely as it may seem, I had only just realized that the Tonnerre family, whom I had always heard called half-breeds, were actually Indians, or as near as made no difference. My acquaintance with Indians was not extensive. I did not remember ever having seen a real Indian, and my new awareness that Piquette sprang from the people of Big Bear and Poundmaker, of Tecumseh, of the Iroquois who had eaten Father Brebeuf's heart—all this gave her an instant attraction in my eyes. I was a devoted reader of Pauline Johnson at this age, and sometimes would orate aloud and in an exalted voice, *West Wind, blow from your prairie nest; Blow from the mountains, blow from the west*—and so on. It seemed to me that Piquette must be in some way a daughter of the forest, a kind of junior prophetess of the wilds, who might impart to me, if I took the right approach, some of the secrets which she undoubtedly knew—where the whippoorwill made her nest, how the coyote reared her young, or whatever it was that it said in Hiawatha.

I set about gaining Piquette's trust. She was not allowed to go swimming, with her bad leg, but I managed to lure her down to the beach—or rather, she came because there was nothing else to do. The water was always icy, for the lake was fed by springs, but I swam like a dog, thrashing my arms and legs around at such speed and with such an output of energy that I never grew cold. Finally, when I had had enough, I came out and sat beside Piquette on the sand. When she saw me approaching, her hand squashed flat the sand castle she had been building, and she looked at me sullenly, without speaking.

"Do you like this place?" I asked, after a while, intending to lead on from there into the question of forest lore.

Piquette shrugged. "It's okay. Good as anywhere."

"I love it," I said. "We come here every summer."

"So what?" Her voice was distant, and I glanced at her uncertainly, wondering what I could have said wrong.

"Do you want to come for a walk?" I asked her. "We wouldn't need to go far. If you walk just around the point there, you come to a bay where great big reeds grow in the water, and all kinds of fish hang around there. Want to? Come on."

She shook her head.

"Your dad said I ain't supposed to do no more walking than I got to."

I tried another line.

"I bet you know a lot about the woods and all that, eh?" I began respectfully.

Piquette looked at me from her large dark unsmiling eyes.

"I don't know what in hell you're talkin' about," she replied. "You nuts or somethin'? If you mean where my old man, and me, and all them live, you better shut up, by Jesus, you hear?"

I was startled and my feelings were hurt, but I had a kind of dogged perseverance. I ignored her rebuff.

"You know something, Piquette? There's loons here, on this lake. You can see their nests just up the shore there, behind those logs. At night, you can hear them even from the cottage, but it's better to listen from the beach. My dad says we should listen and try to remember how they sound, because in a few years when more cottages are built at Diamond Lake and more people come in, the loons will go away."

Piquette was picking up stones and snail shells and then dropping them again.

"Who gives a good goddamn?" she said.

It became increasingly obvious that, as an Indian, Piquette was a dead loss. That evening I went out by myself, scrambling through the bushes that overhung the steep path, my feet slipping on the fallen spruce needles that covered the ground. When I reached the shore, I walked along the firm damp sand to the small pier that my father had built, and sat down there. I heard someone else crashing through the undergrowth and the bracken, and for a moment I thought Piquette had changed her mind, but it turned out to be my father. He sat beside me on the pier and we waited, without speaking.

At night the lake was like black glass with a streak of amber which was the path of the moon. All around, the spruce trees grew tall and close-set, branches blackly sharp against the sky, which was lightened by a cold flickering of stars. Then the loons began their calling. They rose like phantom birds from the nests on the shore, and flew out onto the dark still surface of the water.

No one can ever describe that ululating sound, the crying of the loons, and no one who has heard it can ever forget it. Plaintive, and yet with a quality of chilling mockery, those voices belonged to a world separated by eons from our neat world of summer cottages and the lighted lamps of home.

"They must have sounded just like that," my father remarked, "before any person ever set foot here."

Then he laughed. "You could say the same, of course, about sparrows, or chipmunks, but somehow it only strikes you that way with the loons."

"I know," I said.

Neither of us suspected that this would be the last time we would ever sit here together on the shore, listening. We stayed for perhaps half an hour, and then we went back to the cottage. My mother was reading beside the fireplace. Piquette was looking at the burning birch log, and not doing anything.

"You should have come along," I said, although in fact I was glad she had not.

"Not me," Piquette said. "You wouldn' catch me walkin' way down there jus' for a bunch of squawkin' birds."

Piquette and I remained ill at ease with one another. I felt I had somehow failed my father, but I did not know what was the matter, nor why she would not or could not respond when I suggested exploring the woods or playing house. I thought it was probably her slow and difficult walking that held her back. She stayed most of the time in the cottage with my mother, helping her with the dishes or with Roddie, but hardly ever talking. Then the Duncans arrived at their cottage, and I spent my days with Mavis, who was my best friend. I could not reach Piquette at all, and I soon lost interest in trying. But all that summer she remained as both a reproach and a mystery to me.

That winter my father died of pneumonia, after less than a week's illness. For some time I saw nothing around me, being completely immersed in my own pain and my mother's. When I looked outward once more, I scarcely noticed that Piquette Tonnerre was no longer at school. I do not remember seeing her at all until four years later, one Saturday night when Mavis and I were having Cokes in the Regal Café. The jukebox was booming like tuneful thunder, and beside it, leaning lightly on its chrome and its rainbow glass, was a girl.

Piquette must have been seventeen then, although she looked about twenty. I stared at her, astounded that anyone could have changed so much. Her face, so stolid and expressionless before, was animated now with a gaiety that was almost violent. She laughed and talked very loudly with the boys around her. Her lipstick was bright carmine, and her hair was cut short and frizzily permed. She had not been pretty as a child, and she was not pretty now, for her features were still heavy and blunt. But her dark and slightly slanted eyes were beautiful, and her skin-tight skirt and orange sweater displayed to enviable advantage a soft and slender body.

She saw me, and walked over. She teetered a little, but it was not due to her once-tubercular leg, for her limp was almost gone.

"Hi, Vanessa." Her voice still had the same hoarseness. "Long time no see, eh?"

"Hi," I said. "Where've you been keeping yourself, Piquette?"

"Oh, I been around," she said. "I been away almost two years now. Been all over the place—Winnipeg, Regina, Saskatoon. Jesus, what I could tell you! I come back this summer, but I ain't stayin'. You kids goin' to the dance?"

"No," I said abruptly, for this was a sore point with me. I was fifteen, and thought I was old enough to go to the Saturday-night dances at the Flamingo. My mother, however, thought otherwise.

"Y'oughta come," Piquette said. "I never miss one. It's just about the on'y thing in this jerkwater town that's any fun. Boy, you couldn' catch me stayin' here. I don' give a shit about this place. It stinks."

She sat down beside me, and I caught the harsh over-sweetness of her perfume.

"Listen, you wanna know something, Vanessa?" she confided, her voice only slightly blurred. "Your dad was the only person in Manawaka that ever done anything good to me."

I nodded speechlessly. I was certain she was speaking the truth. I knew a little more than I had that summer at Diamond Lake, but I could not reach her now any more than I had then. I was ashamed, ashamed of my own timidity, the frightened tendency to look the other way. Yet I felt no real warmth towards her—I only felt that I ought to, because of that distant summer and because my father had hoped she would be company for me, or perhaps that I would be for her, but it had not happened that way. At this moment, meeting her again, I had to admit that she repelled and embarrassed me, and I could not help despising the self-pity in her voice. I wished she would go away. I did not want to see her. I did not know what to say to her. It seemed that we had nothing to say to one another.

"I'll tell you something else," Piquette went on. "All the old bitches an' biddies in this town will sure be surprised. I'm gettin' married this fall—my boyfriend, he's an English fella, works in the stockyards in the city there, a very tall guy, got blond wavy hair. Gee, is he ever handsome. Got this real classy name. Alvin Gerald Cummings—some handle, eh? They call him Al."

For the merest instant, then, I saw her. I really did see her, for the first and only time in all the years we had both lived in the same town. Her defiant face, momentarily, became unguarded and unmasked, and in her eyes there was a terrifying hope.

"Gee, Piquette—" I burst out awkwardly, "that's swell. That's really wonderful. Congratulations—good luck—I hope you'll be happy—"

As I mouthed the conventional phrases, I could only guess how great her need must have been, that she had been forced to seek the very things she so bitterly rejected.

When I was eighteen, I left Manawaka and went away to college. At the end of my first year, I came back home for the summer. I spent the first few days in talking non-stop with my mother, as we exchanged all the news that somehow had not found its way into letters—what had happened in my life and what had happened here in Manawaka while I was away. My mother searched her memory for events that concerned people I knew.

"Did I ever write you about Piquette Tonnerre, Vanessa?" she asked one morning.

"No, I don't think so," I replied. "Last I heard of her, she was going to marry some guy in the city. Is she still there?"

My mother looked perturbed, and it was a moment before she spoke, as though she did not know how to express what she had to tell and wished she did not need to try.

"She's dead," she said at last. Then, as I stared at her, "Oh, Vanessa, when it happened, I couldn't help thinking of her as she was that summer—so sullen and gauche and badly dressed. I couldn't help wondering if we could have done something more at that time—but what could we do? She used to be around in the cottage there with me all day, and honestly, it was all I could do to get a word out of her. She didn't even talk to your father very much, although I think she liked him, in her way."

"What happened?" I asked.

"Either her husband left her, or she left him," my mother said, "I don't know which. Anyway, she came back here with two youngsters, both only babies—they must have been born very close together. She kept house, I guess, for Lazarus and her brothers, down in the valley there, in the old Tonnerre place. I used to see her on the street sometimes, but she never spoke to me. She'd put on an awful lot of weight, and she looked a mess, to tell you the truth, a real slattern, dressed any old how. She was up in court a couple of times—drunk and disorderly, of course. One Saturday night last winter, during the coldest weather, Piquette was alone in the shack with the children. The Tonnerres made home brew all the time, so I've heard, and Lazarus said later she'd been drinking most of the day when he and the boys went out that evening. They had an old woodstove there—you know the kind, with exposed pipes. The shack caught fire. Piquette didn't get out, and neither did the children."

I did not say anything. As so often with Piquette, there did not seem to be anything to say. There was a kind of silence around the image in my mind of the fire and the snow, and I wished I could put from my memory the look that I had seen once in Piquette's eyes.

I went up to Diamond Lake for a few days that summer, with Mavis and her family. The MacLeod cottage had been sold after my father's death, and I did not even go to look at it, not wanting to witness my long-ago kingdom possessed now by strangers. But one evening I went down to the shore by myself.

The small pier which my father had built was gone, and in its place there was a large and solid pier built by the government, for Galloping Mountain was now a national park, and Diamond Lake had been renamed Lake Wapakata, for it was felt that an Indian name would have a greater appeal to tourists. The one store had become several dozen, and the settlement had all the attributes of a flourishing resort—hotels, a dance hall, cafés with neon signs, the penetrating odours of potato chips and hot dogs.

I sat on the government pier and looked out across the water. At night the lake at least was the same as it had always been, darkly shining and bearing within its black glass the streak of amber that was the path of the moon. There was no wind that evening, and everything was quiet all around me. It seemed too quiet, and then I realized that the loons were no longer here. I listened for some time, to make sure, but never once did I hear that long-drawn call, half mocking and half plaintive, spearing through the stillness across the lake.

I did not know what had happened to the birds. Perhaps they had gone away to some far place of belonging. Perhaps they had been unable to find such a place, and had simply died out, having ceased to care any longer whether they lived or not.

I remembered how Piquette had scorned to come along, when my father and I sat there and listened to the lake birds. It seemed to me now that in some unconscious and totally unrecognized way, Piquette might have been the only one, after all, who had heard the crying of the loons.

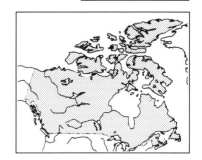

The Dead Child

BY GABRIELLE ROY

TRANSLATED BY JOYCE MARSHALL

Why then did the memory of that dead child seek me out in the very midst of the summer that sang?

When till then no intimation of sorrow had come to me through the dazzling revelations of that season.

I had just arrived in a very small village in Manitoba to finish the school year as replacement for a teacher who had fallen ill or simply, for all I know, become discouraged.

The principal of the Normal School had called me to his office towards the end of my year's study. "Well," he said, "there's a school available for the month of June. It's not much but it's an opportunity. When the time comes for you to apply for a permanent position, you'll be able to say you've had experience. Believe me, it's a help."

And so I found myself at the beginning of June in that very poor village—just a few shacks built on sand, with nothing around it but spindly spruce trees. "A month," I asked myself, "will that be long enough for me to become attached to the children or for the children to become attached to me? Will a month be worth the effort?"

Perhaps the same calculation was in the minds of the children who presented themselves at school that first day of June—"Is this teacher going to stay long enough to be worth the effort?"—for I had never seen children's faces so dejected, so apathetic, or perhaps sorrowful. I had had so little experience. I myself was hardly more than a child.

Nine o'clock came. The room was hot as an oven. Sometimes in Manitoba, especially in the sandy areas, an incredible heat settles in during the first days of June.

Scarcely knowing where or how to begin, I opened the attendance book and called the roll. The names were for the most part very French and today they still return to my memory, like this, for no reason: Madeleine Bérubé, Josephat Brisset, Emilien Dumont, Cécile Lépine....

But most of the children who rose and answered, "Present, mamzelle," when their names were called had the slightly narrowed eyes, warm colouring, and jet black hair that told of métis blood.

They were beautiful and exquisitely polite; there was really nothing to reproach them for except the inconceivable distance they maintained between themselves and me. It crushed me. "Is this what children are like then," I asked myself with anguish, "untouchable, barricaded in some region where you can't reach them?"

I came to the name Yolande Chartrand.

No one answered. It was becoming hotter by the minute. I wiped a bit of perspiration from my forehead. I repeated the name and, when there was still no answer, I looked up at faces that seemed to me completely indifferent.

Then from the back of the classroom, above the buzzing of flies, there arose a voice I at first couldn't place. "She's dead, mamzelle. She died last night."

Perhaps even more distressing than the news was the calm level tone of the child's voice. As I must have seemed unconvinced, all the children nodded gravely as if to say, "It's true."

Suddenly a sense of impotence greater than any I can remember weighed upon me.

"Ah," I said, lost for words.

"She's already laid out," said a boy with eyes like coals. "They're going to bury her for good tomorrow."

"Ah," I repeated.

The children seemed a little more relaxed now and willing to talk, in snatches and at long intervals.

A boy in the middle of the room offered, "She got worse the last two months."

We looked at one another in silence for a long time, the children and I. I now understood that the expression in their eyes that I had taken for indifference was a heavy sadness. Much like this stupefying heat. And we were only at the beginning of the day.

"Since Yolande ... has been laid out," I suggested, "and she was your schoolmate ... and would have been my pupil ... would you like ... after school at four o'clock ... for us to go and visit her?"

On the small, much too serious faces there appeared the trace of a smile, wary, still very sad but a sort of smile just the same.

"It's agreed then, we'll go to visit her, her whole class."

From that moment, despite the enervating heat and the sense that haunted us all, I feel sure, that human efforts are ultimately destined to a sort of failure, the children fixed their attention as much as possible on what I was teaching and I did my best to rouse their interest.

At five past four I found most of them waiting for me at the door, a good twenty children but making no more noise than if they were being kept in after school. Several of them went ahead to show me the way. Others pressed around me so closely I could scarcely move. Five or six of the smaller ones took me by the hand or the shoulder and pulled me forward gently as if they were leading a blind person. They did not talk, merely held me enclosed in their circle.

Together, in this way, we followed a track through the sand. Here and there thin spruce trees formed little clumps. The air was now barely moving. In no time the village was behind us—forgotten, as it were.

We came to a wooden cabin standing in isolation among the little trees. Its door was wide open, so we were able to see the dead child from quite far off. She had been laid out on rough boards suspended between two straight chairs set back to back. There was nothing else in the room. Its usual contents must have been crowded into the only other room in the house for, besides a stove and table and a few pots on the floor, I could see a bed and a mattress piled with clothes. But no chairs. Clearly the two used as supports for the boards on which the dead child lay were the only ones in the house.

The parents had undoubtedly done all they could for their child. They had covered her with a clean sheet. They had given her a room to herself. Her mother, probably, had arranged her hair in the two very tight braids that framed the thin face. But some pressing need had sent them away: perhaps the purchase of a coffin in town or a few more boards to make her one themselves. At any rate, the dead child was alone in the room that had been emptied for her—alone, that is to say, with the flies. A faint odour of death must have attracted them. I saw one with a blue body walk over her forehead. I immediately placed myself near her head and began to move my hand back and forth to drive the flies away.

The child had a delicate little face, very wasted, with the serious expression I had seen on the faces of most of the children here, as if the cares of the adults had crushed them all too early. She might have been ten or eleven years old. If she had lived a little longer, I reminded myself, she would have been one of my pupils. She would have learned something from me. I would have given her something to keep. A bond would have been formed between me and this little stranger—who knows, perhaps even for life.

As I contemplated the dead child, those words "for life"—as if they implied a long existence—seemed to me the most rash and foolish of all the expressions we use so lightly.

In death the child looked as if she were regretting some poor little joy she had never known. I continued at least to prevent the flies from settling upon her. The children were watching me. I realized that they now expected everything from me, though I didn't know much more than they and was just as confused. Still I had a sort of inspiration.

"Don't you think Yolande would like to have someone with her always till the time comes to commit her to the ground?"

The faces of the children told me I had struck the right note.

"We'll take turns then, four or five around her every two hours, until the funeral."

They agreed with a glow in their dark eyes.

"We must be careful not to let the flies touch Yolande's face."

They nodded to show they were in agreement. Standing around me, they now felt a trust in me so complete it terrified me.

In the clearing among the spruce trees a short distance away, I noticed a bright pink stain on the ground whose source I didn't yet know. The sun slanted upon it, making it flame, the one moment in this day that had been touched by a certain grace.

"What sort of girl was she?" I asked.

At first the children didn't understand. Then a boy of about the same age said with tender seriousness, "She was smart, Yolande."

The other children looked as if they agreed.

"And did she do well in school?"

"She didn't come very often this year. She was always being absent."

"Our teacher before last this year said Yolande could have done well."

"How many teachers have you had this year?"

"You're the third, mamzelle. I guess the teachers find it too lonesome here."

"What did Yolande die of?"

"T.B., mamzelle," they replied with a single voice, as if this was the customary way for children to die around here.

They were eager to talk about her now. I had succeeded in opening the poor little doors deep within them that no one perhaps had ever much wanted to see opened. They told me moving facts about her brief life. One day on her way home from school—it was in February; no, said another, in March—she had lost her reader and wept inconsolably for weeks. To study her lesson after that, she had to borrow a book from one of the others—and I saw on the faces of some of them that they'd grudged lending their readers and would always regret this. Not having a dress for her first communion, she entreated till her mother finally made her one from the only curtain in the house: "the one from this room ... a beautiful lace curtain, mamzelle."

"And did Yolande look pretty in her lace curtain dress?" I asked.

They all nodded deeply, in their eyes the memory of a pleasant image.

I studied the silent little face. A child who had loved books, solemnity, and decorous attire. Then I glanced again at that astonishing splash of pink in the melancholy landscape. I realized suddenly that it was a mass of wild roses. In June they open in great sheets all over Manitoba, growing from the poorest soil. I felt some alleviation.

"Let's go and pick some roses for Yolande."

On the children's faces there appeared the same slow smile of gentle sadness I had seen when I suggested visiting the body.

In no time we were gathering roses. The children were not yet cheerful, far from that, but I could hear them at least talking to one another. A sort of rivalry had gripped them. Each vied to see who could pick the most roses or the brightest, those of a deep shade that was almost red.

From time to time one tugged at my sleeve, "Mamzelle, see the lovely one I've found!"

On our return we pulled them gently apart and scattered petals over the dead child. Soon only her face emerged from the pink drift. Then—how could this be?—it looked a little less forlorn.

The children formed a ring around their schoolmate and said of her without the bitter sadness of the morning, "She must have got to heaven by this time."

Or, "She must be happy now."

I listened to them, already consoling themselves as best they could for being alive.

But why, oh why, did the memory of that dead child seek me out today in the very midst of the summer that sang?

Was it brought to me just now by the wind with the scent of roses?

A scent I have not much liked since the long ago June when I went to that poorest of villages—to acquire, as they say, experience.

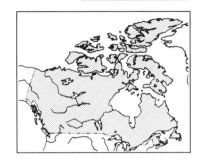

The Whale

BY YVES THÉRIAULT

TRANSLATED BY PATRICIA SILLERS

On every boat and quay from Gaspé to Paspébiac the news spread like wildfire: Ambroise Bourdages claimed that—singlehandedly—he had landed a whale!

The fishermen were all getting a great kick out of it. Now if Ambroise had claimed that he had caught a ninety-kilogram cod that had later managed to get free of the hook, everyone would have made a solemn show of believing it. That would have been an admissible exaggeration, quite in keeping with local instincts, habits, and customs ... But a whale?

Stretching his arms wide Ambroise insisted: "I'm telling you, a whale! Colossal! As big as a boat—bigger even! Ahhh, my friends, my friends ... I spot it sunning itself. Quick as I can I grab a rope, I get a hook on it, I bait it with a herring, I attach a floater, and then I let it out behind the boat ... the whale spies the bait and starts making for it. I let out the line ... thirty, sixty metres. The whale swallows the bait—and it's hooked!"

"This hook of yours, how big is it?" asked Vilmont Babin.

"A big cod hook. Maybe four centimetres ..."

"And it hooked the whale?"

"Yes."

A tremendous burst of laughter shook the whole quay.

About a dozen fishermen were listening as Ambroise related his adventure. A few girls were there too, as there always are when the boats come in. Among them was Gabrielle, who smiled too much at Adélard these days—at least in the opinion of Ambroise, who had eyes only for her.

Unlike the others, who found his story too good—and too funny—to be true, she listened gravely and did not laugh.

There was a look in Gabrielle's eyes that Ambroise could not quite make out. It was a serious expression that suited her natural reserve and good manners—manners very different from those of the rude, obnoxious Adélard.

He was there too, laughing with the others at Ambroise, making fun of him.

"Did you stow your whale in the hold?" he asked Ambroise. "Or weren't you strong enough to haul such a big trophy into your boat?"

This produced a great roar of laughter. Everyone wanted to slap Adélard on the back. Here was a match for Ambroise! Someone with the answer to a tall tale!

"Call me a liar," he said with dignity, "it doesn't bother me. Just remember this: if I were on my deathbed and my mother asked me to repeat every word I've just told you, I'd do it. I didn't lie to you. My men were asleep below. We were heading out towards the Shippegan banks and I was at the tiller. I landed a whale ... and anyone who doesn't believe me can forget it. I know what I did. I hooked a whale with a cod-hook."

He spat on the timbers of the quay, turned on his heel, and left.

Naturally it wasn't long before they were talking about Ambroise Bourdages's alleged miraculous catch in every village on the Coast. As it made the rounds from one quay to another the story was altered and embellished out of all recognition. Ambroise was floored by the version that got back to him.

It was Clovis, the prissy, affected son of the banker in Port-Savoie, where Ambroise lived, who brought back the first of this bizarre gossip.

"Do you know what they're saying at Paspébiac?" he asked Ambroise. "My poor friend, you'd never believe it! It's really terrible!"

"What are they saying?"

"I said it's terrible, but to tell the truth it's mostly funny."

"Let's say it *is* funny. What is it?"

"Good heavens you're tiresome! So impatient ... Well, to hear them talk it seems you caught a whale with your bare hands, held on to it for dear life all by yourself, fought like the devil to haul it by the tail into your boat, and in the end it got away."

Ambroise groaned.

"Ah, no, no! They're all making fun of me!"

Just at that moment Gabrielle came out of the Company store. Her hair floated on the breeze and her smile was as bright as a sunflower.

"How beautiful she is," thought Ambroise, "so tall and graceful. If only she could like me!"

But as she passed close by Ambroise she gave a sarcastic little laugh.

"I have to get proof of my story!" cried Ambroise, when Gabrielle was out of earshot. "Clovis, no one would ever take you for a liar! A banker's son isn't allowed to tell lies!"

"Of course I mustn't tell lies. Lying isn't nice. Besides, I wouldn't want to disgrace my father."

"All right then! Tomorrow you and I are going out to sea. You'll be my witness. We're going to catch another whale, and this time it won't get away!"

Next day they headed out on the water. Despite the sunshine the seas were heavy and sullen. The boat rolled and pitched for eleven long kilometres. But then, just at the end of the run, they saw a jet of spray rising from a whale that was frolicking in the waves—not six metres from the boat.

To summarize the day's adventures we'll say that Ambroise, using all his fisherman's skill, managed to catch the whale with his cod-hook. This was not easily done. The sea monster gave a magnificent display of its strength and agility. On three different occasions, while diving furiously in an effort to get free of the hook, the whale almost capsized the boat. Finally exhausted, it rose calmly to the surface. Ambroise fastened the rope and took the tiller. Slowly he towed his trophy towards the moorings of Port-Savoie.

He was bursting with joy. It had been accomplished despite all the doubt and sarcasm. Even Gabrielle would have to agree that he, Ambroise Bourdages, had not lied about capturing a whale. In fact it was so far from being a lie that a week later he went out and caught another.

This was the way to silence the scandalmongers.

At the same time it ought to establish him as the greatest fisherman and the most respected man on the Coast.

It is not every day that a man catches a whale with such simple tackle. And even if there is an element of luck in it, there is also an element of know-how and gumption that cannot be overlooked.

But just as they were about two kilometres from Port-Savoie the whale suddenly came to life. With one powerful sneeze it spat out the hook—as if to show that it had only been toying with them and could quite easily have escaped earlier, if it had wanted to.

Then it dived and disappeared under the water.

This loss, however, did not bother Ambroise too much.

He had a witness with him. An honest man, a banker's son, a person to corroborate his story who would be believed without question.

As he jumped up onto the quay he let out a great cry.

"Ahoy!"

About fifty people, all aware of the expedition, were waiting when Ambroise and Clovis returned.

Even Gabrielle was there.

Ambroise quickly told what had happened. He described everything in detail. And as the ripples of laughter began to spread: "Listen Ambroise," said Vilmont Babin, "you can get away with it once, but the same lie twice— it won't work!"

With a great sweep of his arm Ambroise pointed to Clovis.

"Clovis was there. He's my witness. An honest witness. He saw it all. He'll tell you that the whale got away just about two kilometres from here."

But Clovis was sporting a smile that looked more like a grin. Then, in his piping voice he declared: "Ambroise is a liar. I never saw him catch a whale!"

The shouts and threats that followed this declaration were so clamorous, and poor Ambroise was so crushed by Clovis's double-dealing, that all he could think of was to run away as fast as possible.

Two hours later he risked going outside again. Clovis was standing by the Post Office. Ambroise hurried over to him. The young man waited for him imperturbably.

"Snake in the grass!" Ambroise yelled at him. "Liar! Worse—you're a perjurer! I'll have you arrested!"

"Just a minute, my friend," said Clovis stiffly. "There's something you don't know. I have my eye on Gabrielle too. Do you really think I'm going to let you impress her with your whale-fishing story? I've decided to fight— with my own weapons! The fortunes of war, old fellow, I'm sorry."

But Ambroise, disconsolate, had already left. He felt trapped, beaten. Farewell dreams! He'd lost Gabrielle forever to wilier men. Clovis, for one. And Adélard. While he, Ambroise, was fighting the shadows.

Once again he raced for home.

But as he was entering the house the sun suddenly reappeared and joy began to revive his hopes. Gabrielle was there, in the kitchen, with Ambroise's mother.

"Ah!" said Ambroise … "Gabrielle?"

She smiled at him.

"Ambroise, I apologize. Forgive me … I misunderstood your lie about the whale!"

"But," said Ambroise, "it wasn't a …"

Gabrielle waved aside his explanation.

"When you tried to tell your story for the second time today, I admit I was disgusted. I knew you were trying to impress me. But after I got home I began to think about it. Do you know what I decided, Ambroise?"

"No … no."

"It's a lucky girl that has a fellow who'll go against everyone just for her, simply to impress her, to win her … "

Ambroise was about to protest strongly again, but suddenly he thought better of it. A sly gleam appeared in his eye. So this was the way the land lay? Well, then.

"Gabrielle," he said softly, "it was the least I could do. A lie like that about a cod would never have been enough—not grand enough! But a whale, an impossible catch… It was a matter of gallantry, of giving it enough weight—you know?"

"Of course. That's why I'm here… "

So Ambroise took her by the hand and led her out into the village and walked with her so that everyone would plainly see that in spite of everything he'd made the best catch of his life … and to hell with the whale!

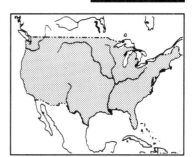

The Story of an Hour

BY KATE CHOPIN

Knowing that Mrs. Mallard was afflicted with a heart trouble, great care was taken to break to her as gently as possible the news of her husband's death.

It was her sister Josephine who told her, in broken sentences; veiled hints that revealed in half concealing. Her husband's friend Richards was there, too, near her. It was he who had been in the newspaper office when intelligence of the railroad disaster was received, with Brently Mallard's name leading the list of "killed." He had only taken the time to assure himself of its truth by a second telegram, and had hastened to forestall any less careful, less tender friend in bearing the sad message.

She did not hear the story as many women have heard the same, with a paralyzed inability to accept its significance. She wept at once, with sudden, wild abandonment, in her sister's arms. When the storm of grief had spent itself she went away to her room alone. She would have no one follow her.

There stood, facing the open window, a comfortable, roomy armchair. Into this she sank, pressed down by a physical exhaustion that haunted her body and seemed to reach into her soul.

She could see in the open square before her house the tops of trees that were all aquiver with the new spring life. The delicious breath of rain was in the air. In the street below a peddler was crying his wares. The notes of a distant song which someone was singing reached her faintly, and countless sparrows were twittering in the eaves.

There were patches of blue sky showing here and there through the clouds that had met and piled one above the other in the west facing her window.

She sat with her head thrown back upon the cushion of the chair, quite motionless, except when a sob came up into her throat and shook her, as a child who has cried itself to sleep continues to sob in its dreams.

She was young, with a fair, calm face, whose lines bespoke repression and even a certain strength. But now there was a dull stare in her eyes, whose gaze was fixed away off yonder on one of those patches of blue sky. It was not a glance of reflection, but rather indicated a suspension of intelligent thought.

There was something coming to her and she was waiting for it, fearfully. What was it? She did not know; it was too subtle and elusive to name. But she felt it, creeping out of the sky, reaching toward her through the sounds, the scents, the colour that filled the air.

Now her bosom rose and fell tumultuously. She was beginning to recognize this thing that was approaching to possess her, and she was striving to beat it back with her will—as powerless as her two white slender hands would have been.

When she abandoned herself a little whispered word escaped her slightly parted lips. She said it over and over under her breath: "free, free, free!" The vacant stare and the look of terror that had followed it went from her eyes. They stayed keen and bright. Her pulses beat fast, and the coursing blood warmed and relaxed every inch of her body.

She did not stop to ask if it were or were not a monstrous joy that held her. A clear and exalted perception enabled her to dismiss the suggestion as trivial.

She knew that she would weep again when she saw the kind, tender hands folded in death; the face that had never looked save with love upon her, fixed and grey and dead. But she saw beyond that bitter moment a long procession of years to come that would belong to her absolutely. And she opened and spread her arms out to them in welcome.

There would be no one to live for during those coming years; she would live for herself. There would be no powerful will bending hers in that blind persistence with which men and women believe they have a right to impose a private will upon a fellow-creature. A kind intention or a cruel intention made the act seem no less a crime as she looked upon it in that brief moment of illumination.

And yet she had loved him—sometimes. Often she had not. What did it matter! What could love, the unsolved mystery, count for in face of this possession of self-assertion which she suddenly recognized as the strongest impulse of her being!

"Free! Body and soul free!" she kept whispering.

Josephine was kneeling before the closed door with her lips to the keyhole, imploring for admission. "Louise, open the door! I beg; open the door—you will make yourself ill. What are you doing, Louise? For heaven's sake open the door."

"Go away. I am not making myself ill." No; she was drinking in a very elixir of life through that open window.

Her fancy was running riot along those days ahead of her. Spring days, and summer days, and all sorts of days that would be her own. She breathed a quick prayer that life might be long. It was only yesterday she had thought with a shudder that life might be long.

She arose at length and opened the door to her sister's importunities. There was a feverish triumph in her eyes, and she carried herself unwittingly like a goddess of Victory. She clasped her sister's waist, and together they descended the stairs. Richards stood waiting for them at the bottom.

Someone was opening the front door with a latchkey. It was Brently Mallard who entered, a little travel-stained, composedly carrying his gripsack and umbrella. He had been far from the scene of accident, and did not even know there had been one. He stood amazed at Josephine's piercing cry; at Richards' quick motion to screen him from the view of his wife.

But Richards was too late.

When the doctors came they said she had died of heart disease—of joy that kills.

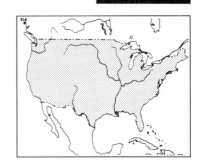

A Clean, Well-Lighted Place

BY ERNEST HEMINGWAY

It was late and every one had left the café except an old man who sat in the shadow the leaves of the tree made against the electric light. In the day time the street was dusty, but at night the dew settled the dust and the old man liked to sit late because he was deaf and now at night it was quiet and he felt the difference. The two waiters inside the café knew that the old man was a little drunk, and while he was a good client they knew that if he became too drunk he would leave without paying, so they kept watch on him.

"Last week he tried to commit suicide," one waiter said.

"Why?"

"He was in despair."

"What about?"

"Nothing."

"How do you know it was nothing?"

"He has plenty of money."

They sat together at a table that was close against the wall near the door of the café and looked at the terrace where the tables were all empty except where the old man sat in the shadow of the leaves of the tree that moved slightly in the wind. A girl and a soldier went by in the street. The street light shone on the brass number on his collar. The girl wore no head covering and hurried beside him.

"The guard will pick him up," one waiter said.

"What does it matter if he gets what he's after?"

"He had better get off the street now. The guard will get him. They went by five minutes ago."

The old man sitting in the shadow rapped on his saucer with his glass. The younger waiter went over to him.

"What do you want?"

The old man looked at him. "Another brandy," he said.

"You'll be drunk," the waiter said. The old man looked at him. The waiter went away.

"He'll stay all night," he said to his colleague. "I'm sleepy now. I never get into bed before three o'clock. He should have killed himself last week."

The waiter took the brandy bottle and another saucer from the counter inside the café and marched out to the old man's table. He put down the saucer and poured the glass full of brandy.

"You should have killed yourself last week," he said to the deaf man. The old man motioned with his finger. "A little more," he said. The waiter poured on into the glass so that the brandy slopped over and ran down the stem into the top saucer of the pile. "Thank you," the old man said. The waiter took the bottle back inside the café. He sat down at the table with his colleague again.

"He's drunk now," he said.

"He's drunk every night."

"What did he want to kill himself for?"

"How should I know."

"How did he do it?"

"He hung himself with a rope."

"Who cut him down?"

"His niece."

"Why did they do it?"

"Fear for his soul."

"How much money has he got?"

"He's got plenty."

"He must be eighty years old."

"Anyway I should say he was eighty."

"I wish he would go home. I never get to bed before three o'clock. What kind of hour is that to go to bed?"

"He stays up because he likes it."

"He's lonely. I'm not lonely. I have a wife waiting in bed for me."

"He had a wife once too."

"A wife would be no good to him now."

"You can't tell. He might be better with a wife."

"His niece looks after him. You said she cut him down."

"I know."

"I wouldn't want to be that old man. An old man is a nasty thing."

"Not always. This old man is clean. He drinks without spilling. Even now, drunk. Look at him."

"I don't want to look at him. I wish he would go home. He has no regard for those who must work."

The old man looked from his glass across the square, then over at the waiters.

"Another brandy," he said, pointing to his glass. The waiter who was in a hurry came over.

"Finished," he said, speaking with that omission of syntax stupid people employ when talking to drunken people or foreigners. "No more tonight. Close now."

"Another," said the old man.

"No. Finished." The waiter wiped the edge of the table with a towel and shook his head.

The old man stood up, slowly counted the saucers, took a leather coin purse from his pocket, and paid for the drinks, leaving half a peseta tip.

The waiter watched him go down the street, a very old man walking unsteadily but with dignity.

"Why didn't you let him stay and drink?" the unhurried waiter asked. They were putting up the shutters. "It is not half-past two."

"I want to go home to bed."

"What is an hour?"

"More to me than to him."

"An hour is the same."

"You talk like an old man yourself. He can buy a bottle and drink at home."

"It's not the same."

"No, it is not," agreed the waiter with a wife. He did not wish to be unjust. He was only in a hurry.

"And you? You have no fear of going home before your usual hour?"

"Are you trying to insult me?"

"No, hombre, only to make a joke."

"No," the waiter who was in a hurry said, rising from pulling down the metal shutters. "I have confidence. I am all confidence."

"You have youth, confidence, and a job," the older waiter said, "You have everything."

"And what do you lack?"

"Everything but work."

"You have everything I have."

"No. I have never had confidence and I am not young."

"Come on. Stop talking nonsense and lock up."

"I am of those who like to stay late at the café," the older waiter said. "With all those who do not want to go to bed. With all those who need a light for the night."

"I want to go home and into bed."

"We are of two different kinds," the older waiter said. He was now dressed to go home. "It is not only a question of youth and confidence although those things are very beautiful. Each night I am reluctant to close up because there may be someone who needs the café."

"Hombre, there are bodegas open all night long."

"You do not understand. This a clean and pleasant café. It is well lighted. The light is very good and also, now, there are shadows of the leaves."

"Good night," said the younger waiter.

"Good night," the other said. Turning off the electric light he continued the conversation with himself. It is the light of course but it is necessary that the place be clean and pleasant. You do not want music. Certainly you do not want music. Nor can you stand before a bar with dignity although that is all that is provided for these hours. What did he fear? It was not fear or dread. It was a nothing that he knew too well. It was all a nothing and a man was nothing too. It was only that and light was all it needed and a certain cleanness and order. Some lived in it and never felt it but he knew it all was nada y pues nada y nada y pues nada[1]. Our nada who art in nada, nada by the name thy kingdom nada thy will be nada in nada as it is in nada. Give us this nada our daily nada and nada us our nada as we nada our nadas and nada us not into nada but deliver us from nada; pues nada. Hail nothing full of nothing, nothing is with thee. He smiled and stood before a bar with a shining steam pressure coffee machine.

"What's yours?" asked the barman.

"Nada."

"Otro loco más[2]," said the barman and turned away.

"A little cup," said the waiter.

The barman poured it for him.

"The light is very bright and pleasant but the bar is unpolished," the waiter said.

The barman looked at him but did not answer. It was too late at night for conversation.

"You want another copita?" the barman asked.

"No, thank you," said the waiter and went out. He disliked bars and bodegas. A clean, well-lighted café was a very different thing. Now, without thinking further, he would go home to his room. He would lie in the bed and finally, with daylight, he would go to sleep. After all, he said to himself, it is probably only insomnia. Many must have it.

[1]nada y pues nada: Spanish for "nothing, and then nothing"

[2]"Another crazy one."

Akhnilo

BY JAMES SALTER

It was late August. In the harbour the boats lay still, not the slightest stirring of their masts, not the softest clink of a sheave. The restaurants had long since closed. An occasional car, headlights glaring, came over the bridge from North Haven or turned down Main Street, past the lighted telephone booths with their smashed receivers. On the highway the discotheques were emptying. It was after three.

In the darkness Fenn awakened. He thought he had heard something, a slight sound, like the creak of a spring, the one on the screen door in the kitchen. He lay there in the heat. His wife was sleeping quietly. He waited. The house was unlocked though there had been many robberies and worse nearer the city. He heard a faint thump. He did not move. Several minutes passed. Without making a sound he got up and went carefully to the narrow doorway where some stairs descended to the kitchen. He stood there. Silence. Another thump and a moan. It was Birdman falling to another place on the floor.

Outside, the trees were like black reflections. The stars were hidden. The only galaxies were the insect voices that filled the night. He stared from the open window. He was still not sure if he had heard anything. The leaves of the immense beech that overhung the rear porch were close enough to touch. For what seemed a long time he examined the shadowy area around the trunk. The stillness of everything made him feel visible but also strangely receptive. His eyes drifted from one thing to another behind the house, the pale Corinthian columns of the arbour next door, the mysterious hedge, the garage with its rotting sills. Nothing.

Eddie Fenn was a carpenter though he'd gone to Dartmouth and majored in history. Most of the time he worked alone. He was thirty-four. He had thinning hair and a shy smile. Not much to say. There was something quenched in him. When he was younger it was believed to be some sort of talent, but he had never really set out in life, he had stayed close to shore. His wife, who was tall and nearsighted, was from Connecticut. Her father had been a banker. *Of Greenwich and Havana* the announcement in the papers had said—he'd managed the branch of a New York bank there when she was a child. That was in the days when Havana was a legend and millionaires committed suicide after smoking a last cigar.

Years had passed. Fenn gazed out at the night. It seemed he was the only listener to an infinite sea of cries. Its vastness awed him. He thought of all that lay concealed behind it, the desperate acts, the longings, the fatal surprises. That afternoon he had seen a robin picking at something near the edge of the grass, seizing it, throwing it in the air, seizing it again: a toad, its small, stunned legs fanned out. The bird threw it again. In ravenous burrows the blind shrews hunted ceaselessly, the pointed tongues of reptiles were testing the air, there was the crunch of abdomens, the passivity of the trapped, the soft throes of mating. We live in slaughter like the ancient kings, he thought. His daughters were asleep down the hall. Nothing is safe except for an hour.

As he stood there the sound seemed to change, he did not know how. It seemed to separate as if permitting something to come forth from it, something glittering and remote. He tried to identify what he was hearing as gradually the cricket, cicada, no, it was something else, something feverish and strange, became more clear. The more intently he listened, the more elusive it was. He was afraid to move for fear of losing it. He heard the soft call of an owl. The darkness of the trees which was absolute seemed to loosen, and through it that single, shrill note.

Unseen the night had opened. The sky was revealing itself, the stars shining faintly. The town was sleeping, abandoned sidewalks, silent lawns. Far off among some pines was the gable of a barn. It was coming from there. He still could not identify it. He needed to be closer, to go downstairs and out the door, but that way he might lose it, it might become silent, aware.

He had a disturbing thought, he was unable to dislodge it: it *was* aware. Quivering there, repeating and repeating itself above the rest, it seemed to be coming only to him. The rhythm was not constant. It hurried, hesitated, went on. It was less and less an instinctive cry and more a kind of signal, a code, not anything he had heard before, not a collection of long and short impulses but something more intricate, in a way almost like speech. The idea frightened him. The words, if that was what they were, were piercing and thin but the awareness of them made him tremble as if they were the combination to a vault.

Beneath the window lay the roof of the porch. It sloped gently. He stood there, perfectly still, as if lost in thought. His heart was rattling. The roof seemed wide as a street. He would have to go out on it hoping he was unseen, moving silently, without abruptness, pausing to see if there was a change in the sound to which he was now acutely sensitive. The darkness would not protect him. He would be entering a night of countless networks, shifting eyes. He was not sure if he should do it, if he dared. A drop of sweat broke free and ran quickly down his bare side. Tirelessly the call continued. His hands were trembling.

Unfastening the screen, he lowered it carefully and leaned it against the house. He was moving quietly, like a serpent, across the faded green roofing. He looked down. The ground seemed distant. He would have to hang from the roof and drop, light as a spider. The peak of the barn was still visible. He was moving toward the lodestar, he could feel it. It was almost as if he were falling. The act was dizzying, irreversible. It was taking him where nothing he possessed would protect him, taking him barefoot, alone.

Fenn felt a thrill go through him. He was going to be redeemed. His life had not turned out as he expected but he still thought of himself as special, as belonging to no one. In fact he thought of failure as romantic. It had almost been his goal. He carved birds, or he had. The tools and partially shaped blocks of wood were on a table in the basement. He had, at one time, almost become a naturalist. Something in him, his silence, his willingness to be apart, was adapted to that. Instead he began to build furniture with a friend who had some money, but the business failed. He was drinking. One morning he woke up lying by the car in the worn ruts of the driveway, the old woman who lived across the street warning away her dog. He went inside before his children saw him. He was very close, the doctor told him frankly, to being an alcoholic. The words astonished him. That was long ago. His family had saved him, but not without cost.

He paused. The earth was firm and dry. He went toward the hedge and across the neighbour's driveway. The tone that was transfixing him was clearer. Following it he passed behind houses he hardly recognized from the back, through neglected yards where cans and rubbish were hidden in dark grass, past empty sheds he had never seen. The ground began to slope gently down, he was nearing the barn. He could hear the voice, *his* voice, pouring overhead. It was coming from somewhere in the ghostly wooden triangle rising like the face of a distant mountain brought unexpectedly close by a turn of the road. He moved towards it slowly, with the fear of an explorer. Above him he could hear the thin stream trilling. Terrified by its closeness he stood still.

At first, he later remembered, it meant nothing, it was too glistening, too pure. It kept pouring out, more and more demonic. He could not identify, he could never repeat, he could not even describe the sound. It had enlarged, it was pushing everything else aside. He stopped trying to comprehend it and instead allowed it to run through him, to invade him like a chant. Slowly, like a pattern that changes its appearance as one stares at it and begins to shift into another dimension, inexplicably the sound altered and exposed its real core. He began to recognize it. It *was* words. They had no meaning, no antecedents, but they were unmistakably a language, the first ever heard from an order vaster and more dense than our own. Above, in the whitish surface, desperate, calling, was the nameless pioneer.

In a kind of ecstasy he stepped closer. Instantly he realized it was wrong. The sound hesitated. He closed his eyes in anguish but too late, it faltered and then stopped. He felt stupid, shamed. He moved back a little, helplessly. All about him the voices clattered. The night was filled with them. He turned this way and that hoping to find it, but the thing he had heard was gone.

It was late. The first pale cast had come to the sky. He was standing near the barn with the fragments of a dream one must struggle to remember: four words, distinct and inimitable, that he had made out. Protecting them, concentrating on them with his strength, he began to carry them back. The cries of the insects seemed louder. He was afraid something would happen, a dog would bark, a light go on in a bedroom and he would be distracted, he would lose his hold. He had to get back without seeing anything, without hearing anything, without thinking. He was repeating the words to himself as he went, his lips moving steadily. He hardly dared breathe. He could see the house. It had turned grey. The windows were dark. He had to get to it. The sound of the night creatures seemed to swell in torment and rage, but he was beyond that. He was escaping. He had gone an immense distance, he was coming to the hedge. The porch was not far away. He stood on the railing, the eave of the roof within reach. The rain gutter was firm, he pulled himself up. The crumbling green asphalt was warm beneath his feet. One leg over the sill, then the other. He was safe. He stepped back from the window instinctively. He had done it. Outside, the light seemed faint and historic. A spectral dawn began to come through the trees.

Suddenly he heard the floor creak. Someone was there, a figure in the soft light drained of colour. It was his wife, he was stunned by the image of her holding a cotton robe about her, her face made plain by sleep. He made a gesture as if to warn her off.

"What is it? What's wrong?" she whispered.

He backed away making vague movements with his hands. His head was sideways, like a horse. He was moving backward. One eye was on her.

"What is it?" she said, alarmed. "What happened?"

No, he pleaded, shaking his head. A word had dropped away. No, no. It was fluttering apart like something in the sea. He was reaching blindly for it.

Her arm went around him. He pulled away abruptly. He closed his eyes.

"Darling, what is it?" He was troubled, she knew. He had never really gotten over his difficulty. He often woke at night, she would find him sitting in the kitchen, his face looking tired and old. "Come to bed," she invited.

His eyes were closed tightly. His hands were over his ears.

"Are you all right?" she said.

Beneath her devotion it was dissolving, the words were spilling away. He began to turn around frantically.

"What is it, what is it?" she cried.

The light was coming everywhere, pouring across the lawn. The sacred whispers were vanishing. He could not spare a moment. Hands clapped to his head he ran into the hall searching for a pencil while she ran after, begging him to tell her what was wrong. They were fading, there was just one left, worthless without the others and yet of infinite value. As he scribbled the table shook. A picture quivered on the wall. His wife, her hair held back with one hand, was peering at what he had written. Her face was close to it.

"What is that?"

Dena, in her nightgown, had appeared in a doorway awakened by the noise.

"What is it?" she asked.

"Help me," her mother cried.

"Daddy, what happened?"

Their hands were reaching for him. In the glass of the picture a brilliant square of blue and green was trembling, the luminous foliage of the trees. The countless voices were receding, turning into silence.

"What is it, what is it?" his wife pleaded.

"Daddy, please!"

He shook his head. He was nearly weeping as he tried to pull away. Suddenly he slumped to the floor and sat there and for Dena they had begun again the phase she remembered from the years she was first in school when unhappiness filled the house and slamming doors and her father clumsy with affection came into their room at night to tell them stories and fell asleep at the foot of her bed.

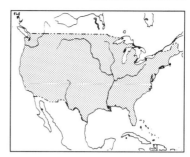

Blue Winds Dancing

BY TOM WHITECLOUD

There is a moon out tonight. Moon and stars and clouds tipped with moonlight. And there is a fall wind blowing in my heart. Ever since this evening, when against a fading sky I saw geese wedge southward. They were going home.... Now I try to study, but against the pages I see them again, driving southward. Going home.

Across the valley there are heavy mountains holding up the night sky, and beyond the mountains there is home. Home, and peace, and the beat of drums, and blue winds dancing over snow fields. The Indian lodge will fill with my people, and our gods will come and sit among them. I should be there then. I should be at home.

But home is beyond the mountains, and I am here. Here where fall hides in the valleys, and winter never comes down from the mountains. Here where all the trees grow in rows; the palms stand stiffly by the road-sides, and in the groves the orange trees line in military rows, and endlessly bear fruit. Beautiful, yes; there is always beauty in order, in rows of growing things! But it is the beauty of captivity. A pine fighting for existence on a windy knoll is much more beautiful.

In my Wisconsin, the leaves change before the snows come. In the air there is the smell of wild rice and venison cooking; and when the winds come whispering through the forests, they carry the smell of rotting leaves. In the evenings, the loon calls, lonely; and birds sing their last songs before leaving. Bears dig roots and eat late fall berries, fattening for their long winter sleep. Later, when the first snows fall, one awakens in the morning to find the world white and beautiful and clean. Then one can look back over his trail and see the tracks following. In the woods there are tracks of deer and snowshoe rabbits, and long streaks where partridges slide to alight. Chipmunks make tiny footprints on the limbs; and one can hear squirrels busy in hollow trees, sorting acorns. Soft lake waves wash the shores, and sunsets burst each evening over the lakes, and make them look as if they were afire.

That land which is my home! Beautiful, calm—where there is no hurry to get anywhere, no driving to keep up in a race that knows no ending and no goal. No classes where men talk and talk, and then stop now and then to hear their own words come back to them from the students. No constant peering into the maelstrom of one's mind; no worries about grades and honours; no hysterical preparing for life until that life is half over; no anxiety about one's place in the thing they call Society.

I hear again the ring of axes in deep woods, the crunch of snow beneath my feet. I feel again the smooth velvet of ghost-birch bark. I hear the rhythm of the drums…. I am tired. I am weary of trying to keep up this bluff of being civilized. Being civilized means trying to do everything you don't want to, never doing anything you want to. It means dancing to the strings of custom and tradition; it means living in houses and never knowing or caring who is next door. These civilized white men want us to be like them—always dissatisfied—getting a hill and wanting a mountain.

Then again, maybe I am not tired. Maybe I'm licked. Maybe I am just not smart enough to grasp these things that go to make up civilization. Maybe I am just too lazy to think hard enough to keep up.

Still, I know my people have many things that civilization has taken from the whites. They know how to give; how to tear one's piece of meat in two and share it with one's brother. They know how to sing—how to make each man his own songs and sing them; for their music they do not have to listen to other men singing over a radio. They know how to make things with their hands, how to shape beads into design and make a thing of beauty from a piece of birch bark.

But we are inferior. It is terrible to have to feel inferior; to have to read reports of intelligence tests, and learn that one's race is behind. It is terrible to sit in classes and hear men tell you that your people worship sticks of wood—that your gods are all false, that the Manitou forgot your people and did not write them a book.

I am tired. I want to walk again among the ghost-birches. I want to see the leaves turn in autumn, the smoke rise from the lodgehouses, and feel the blue winds. I want to hear the drums; I want to hear the drums and feel the blue whispering winds.

There is a train wailing into the night. The trains go across the mountains. It would be easy to catch a freight. They will say he has gone back to the blanket; I don't care. The dance at Christmas....

A bunch of bums warming at a tiny fire talk politics and women and joke about the Relief and the WPA and smoke cigarettes. These men in caps and overcoats and dirty overalls living on the outskirts of civilization are free, but they pay the price of being free in civilization. They are outcasts. I remember a sociology professor lecturing on adjustment to society; hobos and prostitutes and criminals are individuals who never adjusted, he said. He could learn a lot if he came and listened to a bunch of bums talk. He would learn that work and a woman and a place to hang his hat are all the ordinary man wants. These are all he wants, but other men are not content to let him want only these. He must be taught to want radios and automobiles and a new suit every spring. Progress would stop if he did not want these things. I listen to hear if there is any talk of communism or socialism in the hobo jungles. There is none. At best there is a sort of disgusted philosophy about life. They seem to think there should be a better distribution of wealth, or more work, or something. But they are not rabid about it. The radicals live in the cities.

I find a fellow headed for Albuquerque, and talk road-talk with him. "It is hard to ride fruit cars. Bums break in. Better to wait for a cattle car going back to the Middle West, and ride that." We catch the next eastbound and walk the tops until we find a cattle car. Inside, we crouch near the forward wall, huddle, and try to sleep. I feel peaceful and content at last. I am going home. The cattle car rocks. I sleep.

Morning and the desert. Noon and the Salton Sea, lying more lifeless than a mirage under a somber sun in a pale sky. Skeleton mountains rearing on the skyline, thrusting out of the desert floor, all rock and shadow and edges. Desert. Good country for an Indian reservation....

Yuma and the muddy Colorado. Night again, and I wait shivering for the dawn.

Phoenix. Pima country. Mountains that look like cardboard sets on a forgotten stage. Tucson. Papago country. Giant cacti that look like petrified hitchhikers along the highways. Apache country. At El Paso my road-buddy decides to go on to Houston. I leave him, and head north to the mesa country. Las Cruces and the terrible Organ Mountains, jagged peaks that instill fear and wondering. Albuquerque. Pueblos along the Rio Grande. On the boardwalk there are some Indian women in coloured sashes selling bits of pottery. The stone age offering its art to the twentieth century. They hold up a piece and fix the tourists with black eyes until, embarrassed, he buys or turns away. I feel suddenly angry that my people should have to do such things for a living....

Santa Fe trains are fast, and they keep them pretty clean of bums. I decide to hurry and ride passenger coaltenders. Hide in the dark, judge the speed of the train as it leaves, and then dash out, and catch it. I hug the cold steel wall of the tender and think of the roaring fire in the engine ahead, and of the passengers back in the dining car reading their papers over hot coffee. Beneath me there is a blur of rails. Death would come quick if my hands should freeze and I fall. Up over the Sangre De Cristo range, around cliffs and through canyons to Denver. Bitter cold here, and I must watch out for Denver Bob. He is a railroad bull who has thrown bums from fast freights. I miss him. It is too cold, I suppose. On north to the Sioux country.

Small towns lit for the coming Christmas. On the streets of one I see a beam-shouldered young farmer gazing into a window filled with shining silver toasters. He is tall and wears a blue shirt buttoned, with no tie. His young wife by his side looks at him hopefully. He wants decorations for his place to hang his hat to please his woman....

Northward again. Minnesota, and great white fields of snow; frozen lakes, and dawn running into dusk without noon. Long forests wearing white. Bitter cold, and one night the northern lights. I am nearing home.

I reach Woodruff at midnight. Suddenly I am afraid, now that I am but thirty kilometres from home. Afraid of what my father will say, afraid of being looked on as a stranger by my own people. I sit by a fire and think about myself and all the other young Indians. We just don't seem to fit in anywhere—certainly not among the whites, and not among the older people. I think again about the learned sociology professor and his professing. So many things seem to be clear now that I am away from school and do not have to worry about some man's opinion of my ideas. It is easy to think while looking at dancing flames.

Morning. I spend the day cleaning up, and buying some presents for my family with what is left of my money. Nothing much, but a gift is a gift, if a man buys it with his last quarter. I wait until evening, then start up the track toward home.

Christmas Eve comes in on a north wind. Snow clouds hang over the pines, and the night comes early. Walking along the railroad bed, I feel the calm peace of snowbound forests on either side of me. I take my time; I am back in a world where time does not mean so much now. I am alone; alone but not nearly so lonely as I was back on the campus at school. Those are never lonely who love the snow and the pines; never lonely when the pines are wearing white shawls and snow crunches coldly underfoot. In the woods I know there are the tracks of deer and rabbit; I know that if I leave the rails and go into the woods I shall find them. I walk along feeling glad because my legs are light and my feet seem to know that they are home. A deer comes out of the woods just ahead of me, and stands silhouetted on the rails. The North, I feel, has welcomed me home. I watch him and am glad that I do not wish for a gun. He goes into the woods quietly, leaving only the design of his tracks in the snow. I walk on. Now and then I pass a field, white under the night sky, with houses at the far end. Smoke comes from the chimneys of the houses, and I try to tell what sort of wood each is burning by the smoke; some burn pine, others aspen, others tamarack. There is one from which comes black coal smoke that rises lazily and drifts out over the tops of the trees. I like to watch houses and try to imagine what might be happening in them.

Just as a light snow begins to fall I cross the reservation boundary; somehow it seems as though I have stepped into another world. Deep woods in a white-and-black winter night. A faint trail leading to the village.

The railroad on which I stand comes from a city sprawled by a lake—a city with a million people who walk around without seeing one another; a city sucking the life from all the country around; a city with stores and police and intellectuals and criminals and movies and apartment houses; a city with its politics and libraries and zoos.

Laughing, I go into the woods. As I cross a frozen lake I begin to hear the drums. Soft in the night the drums beat. It is like the pulse beat of the world. The white line of the lake ends at a black forest, and above the trees the blue winds are dancing.

I come to the outlying houses of the village. Simple box houses, etched black in the night. From one or two windows soft lamplight falls on the snow. Christmas here, too, but it does not mean much; not much in the way of parties and presents. Joe Sky will get drunk. Alex Bodidash will buy his children red mittens and a new sled. Alex is a Carlisle man, and tries to keep his home up to white standards. White standards. Funny that my people should be ever falling farther behind. The more they try to imitate whites the more tragic the result. Yet they want us to be imitation white men. About all we imitate well are their vices.

The village is not a sight to instil pride, yet I am not ashamed; one can never be ashamed of his own people when he knows they have dreams as beautiful as white snow on a tall pine.

Father and my brother and sister are seated around the table as I walk in. Father stares at me for a moment, then I am in his arms, crying on his shoulder. I give them the presents I have brought, and my throat tightens as I watch my sister save carefully bits of red string from the packages. I hide my feelings by wrestling with my brother when he strikes my shoulder in token of affection. Father looks at me, and I know he has many questions, but he seems to know why I have come. He tells me to go on alone to the lodge, and he will follow.

I walk along the trail to the lodge, watching the northern lights forming in the heavens. White waving ribbons that seem to pulsate with the rhythm of the drums. Clean snow creaks beneath my feet, and a soft wind sighs through the trees, singing to me. Everything seems to say "Be happy! You are home now—you are free. You are among friends—we are your friends; we, the trees, and the snow, and the lights." I follow the trail to the lodge. My feet are light, my heart seems to sing to the music, and I hold my head high. Across white snow fields blue winds are dancing.

Before the lodge door I stop, afraid. I wonder if my people will remember me. I wonder— "Am I Indian, or am I white?" I stand before the door a long time. I hear the ice groan on the lake, and remember the story of the old woman who is under the ice, trying to get out, so she can punish some runaway lovers. I think to myself, "If I am white I will not believe that story; if I am Indian, I will know that there is an old woman under the ice." I listen for a while, and I know that there is an old woman under the ice. I look again at the lights, and go in.

Inside the lodge there are many Indians. Some sit on benches around the walls, others dance in the centre of the floor around a drum. Nobody seems to notice me. It seems as though I were among a people I have never seen before. Heavy women with long black hair. Women with children on their knees—small children that watch with intent black eyes the movements of the dancers, whose small faces are solemn and serene. The faces of the old people are serene too, and their eyes are merry and bright. I look at the old men. Straight, dressed in dark trousers and beaded velvet vests, wearing soft moccasins. Dark, lined faces intent on the music. I wonder if I am at all like them. They dance on, lifting their feet to the rhythm of the drums, swaying lightly, looking upward. I look at their eyes, and am startled at the rapt attention to the rhythm of the music.

The dance stops. The men walk back to the walls, and talk in low tones or with their hands. There is little conversation, yet everyone seems to be sharing some secret. A woman looks at a small boy wandering away, and he comes back to her.

Strange, I think, and then remember. These people are not sharing words—they are sharing a mood. Everyone is happy. I am so used to white people that it seems strange so many people could be together without someone talking. These Indians are happy because they are together, and because the night is beautiful outside, and the music is beautiful. I try hard to forget school and the white people, and be one of these—my people. I try to forget everything but the night, and it is a part of me; that I am one with my people and we are all part of something universal. I watch eyes, and see now that the old people are speaking to me. They nod slightly, imperceptibly, and their eyes laugh into mine. I look around the room. All the eyes are friendly; they all laugh. No one questions my being here. The drums begin to beat again, and I catch the invitation in the eyes of the old men. My feet begin to lift to the rhythm, and I look out beyond the walls into the night and see the lights. I am happy. It is beautiful. I am home.

The Rages of Mrs. Torrens

BY OLGA MASTERS

The rages of Mrs. Torrens kept the town of Tantello constantly in gossip.

Or more accurately in constant entertainment.

It was a town with a sawmill, some clusters of grey unpainted weatherboard cottages, a hall, and the required number of shops for a population of two hundred.

Even while Mrs. Torrens was having a temporary lull from one of her rages the subject was not similarly affected.

"How's the wife these days?" a mill worker would say to Harold while they shovelled a path through the sawdust for a lorry.

The man's eyes would not meet Harold's but slide away.

Remarks like this would be made when life was more than usually dull in Tantello, for example during the long spell between the sports' day in midwinter and the Christmas tree in December.

A mill wife having seen Mrs. Torrens behaving like other mill wives in Tantello that day would suggest while chopping up her meat for stew or melon for jam that Kathleen may never have another of her rages.

It was not said hopefully though just dutifully.

It took some time for Tantello to settle down after the rage that sent Mrs. Torrens and the five little Torrenses flying over the partly-built bridge across Tantello Creek.

The barrier at the finished end was down so Mrs. Torrens one of the few women in Tantello who drove a car ripped across towards the gaping workmen standing with crowbars and other tools.

"Whee-eee-eee!" they called as they flung themselves out of her way clinging to the rails while she flung the old Ford across sending the temporary wooden planks on the gaping floor sliding dangerously and landing the car on the gravel bridge approach.

It paused a second with the workmen expecting it to dive backwards into the creek, then with a groan negotiated the little ridge with the back wheels spitting stones and dust.

A little Torrens screamed in ecstasy (or relief) and standing behind her mother scooped up handfuls of Kathleen's magnificent red hair and laid her face in it.

"Stop that!" cried another little Torrens beside her. "Mumma can't drive the car properly if you do that!"

The little Torrenses told their father this and Harold although not often moved to do so repeated the remark to the mill hands and for weeks afterwards Tantello feasted on it.

"Mumma can't drive the car properly if you do that!" they chuckled over and over above the screams of the machinery cutting timber, not always seeing each other clearly through the smoke from the smouldering sawdust.

"How many stories have you got Dad, on Raging Torrens?" asked a little Cleary one night from the floor where he was doing his homework.

He was Thomas Cleary, aged eleven, and Thomas senior, when there were no fresh stories on the rages of Mrs. Torrens to relate or repeat, boasted to the mill hands on the cleverness of his son and his promising future.

"Head stuck in a book all day long," Thomas senior would say disregarding the predictions of other workers that he would end up in the mill like most other youth of Tantello.

Seated by the stove fire now Thomas senior burst into proud laughter at this fresh evidence of his son's calculating mind and whispered the sentence to have it right to tell at the mill next day.

"How many stories have you got on Raging Torrens?" he whispered into the fire averting his face so that his wife would not see.

Thomas and Evelyn Cleary no longer shared anything. She was a stout plain woman with a lot of hair on her face who pulled her mouth down at most things Thomas said. The day before Thomas had brought home a gift of turnips from a fellow mill hand but Mrs. Cleary threw them to the fowls declaring they gave her wind.

"Now the eggs'll give you wind," said Thomas but the little Clearys did not laugh with him because they sided with the stronger of their parents in the uncanny way children have of defining where their fortunes lie.

As far as the stories on Raging Torrens or Roaring Kathleen went there were too many to list here.

There was the time when she charged out at midnight and flung Harold's pay in the creek.

It was an icy July night with a brilliant moon and when the catastrophe was discovered all the Torrenses went to the creek to try and recover the two pounds in two shilling pieces.

"Oh, Harold I must be mad," moaned Mrs. Torrens thigh deep in water groping around a rock and coming up mostly with flat stones.

(Harold did not tell the mill hands this.)

"My little ones'll die of pneumonia!" she cried, "Oh my little Dollikins, forgive your wicked Mumma!"

Harold had to rise at four o'clock next morning for an early shift so it was he who said they should go home.

"What will we eat now?" murmured a little Torrens old enough to understand the simple economics of life, like passing money across the counter of Bert Herbert's store before goods were passed back.

"Oh, Harold," moaned Mrs. Torrens. "We can't even make a pot of tea. There'll be none for tomorrow if we do!

"O, my poor mannikin! You can't go to work with your innards as dry as the scales on a goanna's back!"

She stood in the glow of the stove fire which Harold had got going among the little Torrenses all crouched over it. Her nightgown slipped from her shoulders showing her white neck threaded with blue veins. Her red hair wet from her wet hands was strewn about and her blue eyes welled with tears. Harold stood staring long at her and the little Torrenses looked from him to their mother and back into the heart of the glowing stove. In a little while without anyone speaking they scurried off to bed.

Kathleen rubbed one icy foot upon the other clutching a threadbare towel about her waist under her nightie to rub dry her icy thighs and buttocks.

"Lie down on the floor close to the fire," whispered Harold. "And afterwards I'll rub you warm again."

"Of course," she whispered back and sinking down reached up both arms to him.

When the pain of the loss of Harold's pay had eased it actually became a subject for discussion. Gathered around the meal table the Torrenses talked about what the two pounds would have bought.

"Pounds and pounds of butter!" cried a little Torrens whose teeth marks were embedded in a slice of bread spread with grey dripping.

"How many pounds then?" asked Harold. "How much is butter? One and threepence? How many pounds in two pounds? Come on, work it out! Thomas Cleary could!"

"What else would it have bought Mumma and Dadda?" cried the seven-year-old Torrens.

"Tinned peaches, jelly, fried sausages!" screeched her sister.

"Blankets! One for each of our beds!" cried Mrs. Torrens unable to contain herself.

Then she dropped her face on her hand and shook her hair down to cover her lowered eyes and dripping tears.

"A new coat with fur on it for Mumma!" said an observing little Torrens.

Kathleen lifted her head and shook back her hair.

"I like my old coat best!" she said.

"See," said Harold clasping his wife's hand. "Mumma doesn't want a new coat. So the money was no use to us after all!"

Although this deduction puzzled some of the little Torrenses they were happy to see their mother smiling and ecstatic when she flung her head towards Harold and fitted it into the curve of his neck and shoulder.

They trooped outside to play soon after.

The creek figured in many of the rages of Mrs. Torrens particularly her milder ones.

When in one of these she took the children to picnic below the bridge on a Sunday afternoon.

The normal Tantello people considered this the height of eccentricity, the place for Sunday picnics being the beach forty kilometres away available to those with reliable cars, and for the others there was the annual outing with the townspeople packed into three timber trucks.

Tantello Creek was a wide bed of sand with only a trickle of water in most parts, but there was a sandbank a few metres upstream from the bridge with a miniature waterfall and a chain of water holes most of them small and shallow petering out as they moved towards the main stream.

This is where Mrs. Torrens took the children for a picnic in full view of Tantello taking Sunday afternoon walks across the bridge.

Mrs. Torrens spread out the bread and jam and watercress gathered by the children and they ate on the green slope below the road with an occasional car passing in line with their heads and the walking Tantello staring from the bridge.

"Go home you little parlingtons and stop staring!" cried Mrs. Torrens waving a thick wedge of bread towards the bridge.

"Are you swearing at us, Mrs. Torrens?" said one of the starers.

"You know swearing when you hear it! Or do you plug your ears after closing times on Saturday when your Pa comes home?"

"Oh, Mumma," breathed an agonized Torrens named Aileen, the eldest of the family.

She shared a seat at school with the group on the bridge.

Aileen left the picnic then and moved with head down towards the water.

"Only mad people make up words," called a daring voice from the bridge.

Aileen lowered her head further in the silence following.

Mrs. Torrens jumped to her feet to herd the little Torrenses to the water to join their sister.

"We'll gather our stones and hold them under the water!" she cried and the little Torrenses with the exception of Aileen dispersed to hunt for flat round stones that changed colour on contact with the running water.

The little Torrenses watched spellbound when the stones emerged wet and glistening and streaked with ochre red, rich browns, soft blues and greys, and sometimes pale gold.

"Oh don't go dull!" screamed the little Torrenses hoping for a miracle to save the colours from merging into a dull stone colour when the water dried.

Aileen some distance away dug her toes into the sand and stared down at them. Her lashes lay soft as broken bracken fern on her apricot cheeks.

"Come on Snobbie Dobbie!" called Mrs. Torrens.

"Come and wash the beautiful stones and see the colours!

"They're brown and beautiful as your eyes, Snobbie Dobbie!"

"Come on, come on!" called the other little Torrenses.

In the end Aileen came and high voices and peals of laughter from the creek bed had the effect of sending the walking Tantello mooching home across the bridge.

Then came the rage that ended all the rages of Mrs. Torrens in Tantello and drove the family from the town.

Harold lost the fingers of his right hand in a mill accident.

Holding a length of timber against a screaming saw, a drift of smoke blew across his eyes and the saw made a raw and ugly stump of his hand and the blood rushed over the saw teeth and down the arm of his old striped shirt and the yelling of the mill hands brought the work to a halt and for a moment all was still except the damaging drift of smoke from a sawdust fire.

A foreman with a knowledge of first aid (for many fingers were lost at the mill although Harold was the first to lose all four) stopped the flow of blood and drove Harold thirty-two kilometres to the nearest hospital.

When the mill was silenced an hour before the midday break the townspeople sensed something was wrong and Mrs. Torrens came running too.

A chain of faces turned and passed the word along that it was Harold. Mrs. Torrens stood still and erect strangely dressed in a black dress with a scarf-like trimming from one shoulder trailing to her waist. On the end she had pinned clusters of red geraniums and on her head she wore a large brimmed black hat with more geraniums tucked into the band of faded ribbon. On her feet she wore old sandshoes with the laces gone.

All the eyes of the watching Tantello were fixed on Mrs. Torrens who stood a little apart. She stared back with a tilted chin and wide and cold blue eyes until they turned away and one by one left the scene. When the last had gone she walked into the mill to the cluster of men around the door of the small detached office.

"We're sorry, Mrs. Torrens," said one of them.

Behind the men was a table with cups on it for the bosses' dinner and a kettle set on a primus stove. Mrs. Torrens looked from the cups to the men's hands and back to the cups and a strange, small smile lit on her face.

Then she stalked to the timber stacked against the fence and climbed with amazing lightness and agility for a big woman onto it stepping up until her waist was level with the top of the fence. The men watched in fascination while she hauled herself onto the fence top and stood there balancing like a great black bird.

Her old sandshoes clinging to the fence top were like scruffy grey birds.

"Come down! We don't want no more accidents," called the mill owner.

But Mrs. Torrens walked one panel with her arms out to balance herself. Then satisfied she was at home she straightened up and walked back coming to a halt at the fence post and standing there looking down on the men whose faces were tipped up like eggs towards her.

She stared long at them.

"What have you done to my mannikin?" she said.

They were silent.

"My beautiful, beautiful mannikin?" she said slightly shaking her head.

"Accidents happen," said a foreman a small and shrivelled man who wet his lips and looked at the boss for approval in making this statement.

Mrs. Torrens walked like a trapeze artist along the fence top to reach the other post.

She swooped once or twice to the left and the right and when she settled herself on the post she lifted her chin and adjusted her hat.

The foreman encouraged by the success of his earlier remark wet his lips again.

"Go home to your kiddies, Mrs. Torrens," he said. "They need you at home."

He considered this well worth repeating in the hotel after work.

Mrs. Torrens stared dreamily down on the men giving her head another little shake.

"My beautiful, beautiful mannikin," she said.

Then she put out both arms and almost ran to the other post laughing a little when she reached there safely.

Someone had lit the primus stove and the shrill whistle of the boiling kettle broke the silence causing everyone except Mrs. Torrens to start.

She merely lowered herself and jumped lightly onto the timber picking her way down until she reached the ground. She shook the sawdust from her old sandshoes as if they were expensive and elegant footwear.

Then she looked about her moving pieces of timber with her foot until she found a shortish piece she could easily grip.

She then walked into the office and swung it back and forth among the things on the table sending the primus like a flaming ball bowling across the floor and pieces of china flying everywhere.

The men were galvanized into action beating at the blaze with bags jumping out of the way of the steam of boiling water and trying vainly to save the cups and avoid contact with the timber wielded by Mrs. Torrens.

After a while she threw her weapon among the debris and stalked off walking lightly casually through the mill gate and up the hill to where the Torrens house was. The little Torrenses home from school for midday dinner stood about with tragic expressions. Mrs. Torrens broke into a brilliant smile.

"All of us will be Dadda's right hand now!" she called. "Dadda will have six right hands!"

She went ahead of them into the house.

"My beautiful, beautiful mannikin," she said.

It may seem strange but that, the most violent of all the rages of Mrs. Torrens, was not generally discussed in Tantello.

Mill wives standing on verandahs and at windows saw her walk the fence and saw she spoke but the husbands evaded the questions on what was said.

Some repeated her words but kept them inside their throats in the darkness of their bedrooms and seizing their wives for love-making held onto the vision of Mrs. Torrens with her still face under her black hat and her strong thighs moving under her black dress as she walked the fence.

Even Thomas Cleary couldn't be persuaded to repeat what Mrs. Torrens said.

Young Thomas tried from the kitchen floor where he was doing his homework.

"What did Rager say, Dad?" said young Thomas. "What was she saying when she walked the fence top?"

"Don't you get ideas about walking the fence top," said Mrs. Cleary from the table where she was sullenly making Thomas senior's lunch for the morrow. "Don't you go copying that crazy woman!"

Thomas senior jerked his head up and opened his mouth but closed it before a denial escaped his lips.

"Go on Dad! You musta heard Rager!" said young Thomas.

But Thomas senior staring into the scarlet stove fire saw only the flaming red of Mrs. Torrens's hair and when a coal broke it seemed like the petals of red geraniums scattering into the ashes. He opened and closed his two good hands on his knees but even that did not ease the hunger inside him.

The Torrenses left Tantello soon after the accident. The townspeople let the family go without ceremony fearful that an appearance of support might jeopardize others' jobs at the mill.

The Torrenses left their furniture to sell for the rent they owed (for they never caught up from the week Kathleen threw Harold's pay into the creek) and took their clothing and what else could be stowed in the car besides the five children.

Mrs. Torrens drove with Harold's useless heavily bandaged hand beside her.

She did in effect become his right hand.

The work they ultimately found in the city was cleaning a factory in two shifts a day, early morning and late afternoon.

Harold learned to wield a broom holding the handle in the crook of his right arm and Kathleen worked beside him picking up the rubbish he missed.

After some practice he was proficient and she could work independently so that they sometimes had time to sit on an upturned box and eat their sandwiches together Harold laying his on his knee between bites and holding his mug of tea with his left hand.

The rages of Mrs. Torrens subsided with the help of medication from a public hospital not far from where they lived.

During these times Mrs. Torrens's blue eyes dulled and her beautiful red hair straightened and she moved slowly and heavily with no life in her step or on her face.

She looked like a lot of the women in Tantello.

The little Torrenses did very well which would have amazed the people of Tantello if they had followed their fortunes in professions and trades.

Mrs. Torrens was in her fifties when she died from a heart attack and Harold made his home with the second daughter Rachel who was a nurse educator in a big hospital with a flat of her own.

It was Aileen who won some modest fame in the rag trade.

She started sweeping floors and picking up pins and scraps of cloth then graduated to more important things.

When she was a beautiful young woman nearing thirty she was designing her own materials and having them made up into styles she created.

Long pursued by a colleague who designed and cut clothes for men she eventually married him and he agreed to her whim to drive through Tantello while on their honeymoon.

"Did you live here?" he said standing with her near the little grey house with the small square verandah now with all the railings missing and the roof on one side dipping dangerously over a tank tilted dangerously too from the half rotted tank stand.

She stood near a clump of red geraniums cold and proud and still as Kathleen stood outside the mill the day Harold lost his fingers.

"I lived here," she said and looked down on Tantello with the mill shut down now and only a few of the houses occupied mostly by Aboriginal families.

"Is that bridge safe to cross?" her husband asked looking at her profile with her lashes lying soft as brown bracken fern on her apricot cheeks.

She stretched her mouth in a smile he didn't understand and began to walk with Kathleen's walk light and casual towards the car.

He was a little ahead and his heart leapt when he heard her speak.

"My beautiful, beautiful mannikin," she said low and passionate.

He turned swiftly to take her hand.

Then he saw her face and felt he shouldn't.

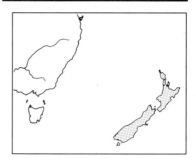

Between Earth and Sky

BY PATRICIA GRACE

I walked out of the house this morning and stretched my arms out wide. Look, I said to myself. Because I was alone except for you. I don't think you heard me.

Look at the sky, I said.

Look at the green earth.

How could it be that I felt so good? So free? So full of the sort of day it was? How?

And at that moment, when I stepped from my house, there was no sound. No sound at all. No bird call, or tractor grind. No fire crackle or twig snap. As though the moment had been held quiet, for me only, as I stepped out into the morning. Why the good feeling, with a lightness in me causing my arms to stretch out and out? How blue, how green, I said into the quiet of the moment. But why, with the sharp nick of bone deep in my back and the band of flesh tightening across my belly?

All alone. Julie and Tamati behind me in the house, asleep, and the others over at the swamp catching eels. Riki two paddocks away cutting up a tree he'd felled last autumn.

I started over the paddocks towards him then, slowly, on these heavy knotted legs. Hugely across the paddocks I went almost singing. Not singing because of needing every breath, but with the feeling of singing. Why, with the deep twist and pull far down in my back and cramping between the legs? Why the feeling of singing?

How strong and well he looked. How alive and strong, stooping over the trunk steadying the saw. I'd hated him for days, and now suddenly I loved him again but didn't know why. The saw cracked through the tree setting little splinters of warm wood hopping. Balls of mauve smoke lifted into the air. When he looked up I put my hands to my back and saw him understand me over the skirl of the saw. He switched off, the sound fluttered away.

I'll get them, he said.

We could see them from there, leaning into the swamp, feeling for eel holes. Three long whistles and they looked up and started towards us, wondering why, walking reluctantly.

Mummy's going, he said.

We nearly got one, Turei said. Ay Jimmy, ay Patsy, ay Reuben?

Yes, they said.

Where? said Danny.

I began to tell him again, but he skipped away after the others. It was good to watch them running and shouting through the grass. Yesterday their activity and noise had angered me, but today I was happy to see them leaping and shouting through the long grass with the swamp mud drying and caking on their legs and arms.

Let Dad get it out, Reuben turned, was calling. He can get the lambs out. Bang! Ay Mum, ay?

Julie and Tamati had woken. They were coming to meet us, dragging a rug.

Not you again, they said taking my bag from his hand.

Not you two again, I said. Rawhiti and Jones.

Don't you have it at two o'clock.

We go off at two.

Your boyfriends can wait.

Our sleep can't.

I put my cheek to his and felt his arm about my shoulders.

Look after my wife, he was grinning at them.

Course, what else.

Go on. Get home and milk your cows, next time you see her she'll be in two pieces.

I kissed all the faces poking from the car windows then stood back on the step waving. Waving till they'd gone. Then turning felt the rush of water.

Quick, I said. The water.

Water my foot; that's piddle.

What you want to piddle in our neat corridor for? Sit down. Have a ride.

Helped into a wheelchair and away, careering over the brown lino.

Stop. I'll be good. Stop I'll tell Sister.

Sister's busy.

No wonder you two are getting smart. Stop …

That's it missus, you'll be back in your bikini by summer. Dr. McIndoe.

And we'll go water-skiing together. Me.

Right you are. Well, see you both in the morning.

The doors bump and swing.

Sister follows.

Finish off girls. Maitland'll be over soon.

All right Sister.

Yes Sister. Reverently.

The doors bump and swing.

You are at the end of the table, wet and grey. Blood stains your pulsing head. Your arms flail in these new dimensions and your mouth is a circle that opens and closes as you scream for air. All head and shoulders and wide mouth screaming. They have clamped the few centimetres of cord which is all that is left of your old life now. They draw mucus and bathe your head.

Leave it alone and give it here, I say.

What for? Haven't you got enough kids already?

Course. Doesn't mean you can boss that one around.

We should let you clean your own kid up?

Think she'd be pleased after that neat ride we gave her. Look at the little hoha. God he can scream.

They wrap you in linen and put you here with me.

Well anyway, here you are. He's all fixed, you're all done. We'll blow. And we'll get them to bring you a cuppa. Be good.

The doors swing open.

She's ready for a cuppa Freeman.

The doors bump shut.

Now. You and I. I'll tell you. I went out this morning. Look, I said, but didn't know why. Why the good feeling. Why, with the nick and press of bone deep inside. But now I know. Now I'll tell you and I don't think you'll mind. It wasn't the thought of knowing you, and having you here close to me that gave me this glad feeling, that made me look upwards and all about as I stepped out this morning. The gladness was because at last I was to be free. Free from that great hump that was you, free from the aching limbs and swelling that was you. That was why this morning each stretching of flesh made me glad.

And freedom from the envy I'd felt, watching him these past days, stepping over the paddocks whole and strong. Unable to match his step. Envying his bright striding. But I could love him again this morning.

These were the reasons each gnarling of flesh made me glad as I came out into that cradled moment. Look at the sky, look at the earth, I said. See how blue, how green. But I gave no thought to you.

And now. You sleep. How quickly you have learned this quiet and rhythmic breathing. Soon they'll come and put a cup in my hand and take you away.

You sleep, and I too am tired, after our work. We worked hard you and I and now we'll sleep. Be close. We'll sleep a little while ay, you and I.

The Doll's House

BY KATHERINE MANSFIELD

When dear old Mrs. Hay went back to town after staying with the Burnells she sent the children a doll's house. It was so big that the carter and Pat carried it into the courtyard, and there it stayed, propped up on two wooden boxes beside the feed-room door. No harm could come to it; it was summer. And perhaps the smell of paint would have gone off by the time it had to be taken in. For, really, the smell of paint coming from that doll's house ("Sweet of old Mrs. Hay, of course; most sweet and generous!")—but the smell of paint was quite enough to make anyone seriously ill, in Aunt Beryl's opinion. Even before the sacking was taken off. And when it was …

There stood the doll's house, a dark, oily, spinach green, picked out with bright yellow. Its two solid little chimneys, glued on to the roof, were painted red and white, and the door, gleaming with yellow varnish, was like a little slab of toffee. Four windows, real windows, were divided into panes by a broad streak of green. There was actually a tiny porch, too, painted yellow, with big lumps of congealed paint hanging along the edge.

But perfect, perfect little house! Who could possibly mind the smell. It was part of the joy, part of the newness.

"Open it quickly, someone!"

The hook at the side was stuck fast. Pat pried it open with his penknife, and the whole house front swung back, and—there you were, gazing at one and the same moment into the drawing room and dining room, the kitchen and two bedrooms. That is the way for a house to open! Why don't all houses open like that? How much more exciting than peering through the slit of a door into a mean little hall with a hat-stand and two umbrellas!

That is—isn't it?—what you long to know about a house when you put your hand on the knocker. Perhaps it is the way God opens houses at the dead of the night when He is taking a quiet turn with an angel....

"Oh-oh!" The Burnell children sounded as though they were in despair. It was too marvellous; it was too much for them. They had never seen anything like it in their lives. All the rooms were papered. There were pictures on the walls, painted on the paper, with gold frames complete. Red carpet covered all the floors except the kitchen; red plush chairs in the drawing room, green in the dining room; tables, beds with real bedclothes, a cradle, a stove, a dresser with tiny plates and one big jug. But what Kezia liked more than anything, what she liked frightfully, was the lamp. It stood in the middle of the dining room table, an exquisite little amber lamp with a white globe. It was even filled all ready for lighting, though, of course, you couldn't light it. But there was something inside that looked like oil and moved when you shook it.

The father and mother dolls, who sprawled very stiff as though they had fainted in the drawing room, and their two little children asleep upstairs, were really too big for the doll's house. They didn't look as though they belonged. But the lamp was perfect. It seemed to smile at Kezia, to say, "I live here." The lamp was real. The Burnell children could hardly walk to school fast enough the next morning. They burned to tell everybody, to describe, to—well—to boast about their doll's house before the school bell rang.

"I'm to tell," said Isabel, "because I'm the eldest. And you can join in after. But I'm to tell first."

There was nothing to answer. Isabel was bossy, but she was always right, and Lottie and Kezia knew too well the powers that went with being eldest. They brushed through the thick buttercups at the road edge and said nothing.

"And I'm to choose who's to come and see it first. Mother said I might."

For it had been arranged that while the doll's house stood in the court-yard they might ask the girls at school, two at a time, to come and look. Not to stay to tea, of course, or to come traipsing through the house. But just to stand quietly in the courtyard while Isabel pointed out the beauties, and Lottie and Kezia looked pleased....

But hurry as they might, by the time they had reached the tarred palings of the boys' playground the bell had begun to jangle. They only just had time to whip off their hats and fall into line before the roll was called. Never mind. Isabel tried to make up for it by looking very important and mysterious and by whispering behind her hand to the girls near her, "Got something to tell you at playtime."

Playtime came and Isabel was surrounded. The girls of her class nearly fought to put their arms round her, to walk away with her, to beam flatteringly, to be her special friend. She held quite a court under the huge pine trees at the side of the playground. Nudging, giggling together, the little girls pressed up close. And the only two who stayed outside the ring were the two who were always outside, the little Kelveys. They knew better than to come anywhere near the Burnells.

For the fact was, the school the Burnell children went to was not at all the kind of place their parents would have chosen if there had been any choice. But there was none. It was the only school for kilometres. And the consequence was all the children of the neighbourhood, the Judge's little girls, the doctor's daughters, the storekeeper's children, the milkman's, were forced to mix together. Not to speak of there being an equal number of rude, rough little boys as well. But the line had to be drawn somewhere. It was drawn at the Kelveys. Many of the children, including the Burnells, were not allowed even to speak to them. They walked past the Kelveys with their heads in the air, and as they set the fashion in all matters of behaviour, the Kelveys were shunned by everybody. Even the teacher had a special voice for them, and a special smile for the other children when Lil Kelvey came up to her desk with a bunch of dreadfully common-looking flowers.

They were the daughters of a spry, hardworking little washerwoman, who went about from house to house by the day. This was awful enough. But where was Mr. Kelvey? Nobody knew for certain. But everybody said he was in prison. So they were the daughters of a washerwoman and a jailbird. Very nice company for other people's children! And they looked it. Why Mrs. Kelvey made them so conspicuous was hard to understand. The truth was they were dressed in "bits" given to her by the people for whom she worked. Lil, for instance, who was a stout, plain child, with big freckles, came to school in a dress made from a green art-serge tablecloth of the Burnells', with red plush sleeves from the Logans' curtains. Her hat, perched on top of her high forehead, was a grown-up woman's hat, once the property of Miss Lecky, the postmistress. It was turned up at the back and trimmed with a large scarlet quill. What a little guy she looked! It was impossible not to laugh. And her little sister, our Else, wore a long white dress, rather like a nightgown, and a pair of little boy's boots. But whatever our Else wore she would have looked strange. She was a tiny wishbone of a child, with cropped hair and enormous solemn eyes—a little white owl. Nobody had ever seen her smile; she scarcely ever spoke. She went through life holding on to Lil, with a piece of Lil's skirt screwed up in her hand. Where Lil went, our Else followed. In the playground, on the road going to and from school, there was Lil marching in front and our Else holding on behind. Only when she wanted anything, or when she was out of breath, our Else gave Lil a tug, a twitch, and Lil stopped and turned round. The Kelveys never failed to understand each other.

Now they hovered at the edge; you couldn't stop them listening. When the little girls turned round and sneered, Lil, as usual, gave her silly, shamefaced smile, but our Else only looked.

And Isabel's voice, so very proud, went on telling. The carpet made a great sensation, but so did the beds with real bedclothes, and the stove with an oven door.

When she finished Kezia broke in. "You've forgotten the lamp, Isabel."

"Oh yes," said Isabel, "and there's a teeny little lamp, all made of yellow glass, with a white globe that stands on the dining room table. You couldn't tell it from a real one."

"The lamp's best of all," cried Kezia. She thought Isabel wasn't making half enough of the little lamp. But nobody paid any attention. Isabel was choosing the two who were to come back with them that afternoon and see it. She chose Emmie Cole and Lena Logan. But when the others knew they were all to have a chance, they couldn't be nice enough to Isabel. One by one they put their arms round Isabel's waist and walked her off. They had something to whisper to her, a secret. "Isabel's *my* friend."

Only the little Kelveys moved away forgotten; there was nothing more for them to hear.

Days passed, and as more children saw the doll's house, the fame of it spread. It became the one subject, the rage. The one question was, "Have you seen Burnell's doll's house? Oh, ain't it lovely!" "Haven't you seen it? Oh, I say!"

Even the dinner hour was given up to talking about it. The little girls sat under the pines eating their thick mutton sandwiches and big slabs of johnny cake spread with butter. While always, as near as they could get, sat the Kelveys, our Else holding on to Lil, listening too, while they chewed their jam sandwiches out of a newspaper soaked with large red blobs.

"Mother," said Kezia, "can't I ask the Kelveys just once?"

"Certainly not, Kezia."

"But why not?"

"Run away, Kezia; you know quite well why not."

At last everybody had seen it except them. On that day the subject rather flagged. It was the dinner hour. The children stood together under the pine trees, and suddenly, as they looked at the Kelveys eating out of their paper, always by themselves, always listening, they wanted to be horrid to them. Emmie Cole started the whisper.

"Lil Kelvey's going to be a servant when she grows up."

"O-oh, how awful!" said Isabel Burnell, and she made eyes at Emmie.

Emmie swallowed in a very meaning way and nodded to Isabel as she'd seen her mother do on those occasions.

"It's true—it's true—it's true," she said.

Then Lena Logan's little eyes snapped. "Shall I ask her?" she whispered.

"Bet you don't," said Jessie May.

"Pooh, I'm not frightened," said Lena. Suddenly she gave a little squeal and danced in front of the other girls. "Watch! Watch me! Watch me now!" said Lena. And sliding, gliding, dragging one foot, giggling behind her hand, Lena went over to the Kelveys.

Lil looked up from her dinner. She wrapped the rest quickly away. Our Else stopped chewing. What was coming now?

"Is it true you're going to be a servant when you grow up, Lil Kelvey?" shrilled Lena.

Dead silence. But instead of answering, Lil only gave her silly, shame-faced smile. She didn't seem to mind the question at all. What a sell for Lena! The girls began to titter.

Lena couldn't stand that. She put her hands on her hips; she shot forward. "Yah, yer father's in prison!" she hissed spitefully.

This was such a marvellous thing to have said that the little girls rushed away in a body, deeply, deeply excited, wild with joy. Someone found a long rope, and they began skipping. And never did they skip so high, run in and out so fast, or do such daring things as on that morning.

In the afternoon Pat called for the Burnell children with the buggy and they drove home. There were visitors. Isabel and Lottie, who liked visitors, went upstairs to change their pinafores. But Kezia thieved out at the back. Nobody was about; she began to swing on the big white gates of the courtyard. Presently, looking along the road, she saw two little dots. They grew bigger, they were coming towards her. Now she could see that one was in front and one close behind. Now she could see that they were the Kelveys. Kezia stopped swinging. She slipped off the gate as if she was going to run away. Then she hesitated. The Kelveys came nearer, and beside them walked their shadows, very long, stretching right across the road with their heads in the buttercups. Kezia clambered back on the gate; she had made up her mind; she swung out.

"Hullo," she said to the passing Kelveys.

They were so astounded that they stopped. Lil gave her silly smile. Our Else stared.

"You can come and see our doll's house if you want to," said Kezia, and she dragged one toe on the ground. But at that Lil turned red and shook her head quickly.

"Why not?" asked Kezia.

Lil gasped, then she said, "Your ma told our ma you wasn't to speak to us."

"Oh well," said Kezia. She didn't know what to reply. "It doesn't matter. You can come and see our doll's house all the same. Come on. Nobody's looking."

But Lil shook her head still harder.

"Don't you want to?" asked Kezia.

Suddenly there was a twitch, a tug at Lil's skirt. She turned round. Our Else was looking at her with big, imploring eyes; she was frowning; she wanted to go. For a moment Lil looked at our Else very doubtfully. But then our Else twitched her skirt again. She started forward. Kezia led the way. Like two little stray cats they followed across the courtyard to where the doll's house stood.

"There it is," said Kezia.

There was a pause. Lil breathed loudly, almost snorted; our Else was still as stone.

"I'll open it for you," said Kezia kindly. She undid the hook and they looked inside.

"There's the drawing room and the dining room, and that's the—"

"Kezia!"

Oh, what a start they gave!

"Kezia!"

It was Aunt Beryl's voice. They turned round. At the back door stood Aunt Beryl, staring as if she couldn't believe what she saw.

"How dare you ask the little Kelveys into the courtyard!" said her cold, furious voice. "You know as well as I do, you're not allowed to talk to them. Run away, children, run away at once. And don't come back again," said Aunt Beryl. And she stepped into the yard and shooed them out as if they were chickens.

"Off you go immediately!" she called, cold and proud.

They did not need telling twice. Burning with shame, shrinking together, Lil huddling along like her mother, our Else dazed, somehow they crossed the big courtyard and squeezed through the white gate.

"Wicked, disobedient little girl!" said Aunt Beryl bitterly to Kezia, and she slammed the doll's house to.

The afternoon had been awful. A letter had come from Willie Brent, a terrifying, threatening letter, saying if she did not meet him that evening in Pulman's Bush, he'd come to the front door and ask the reason why! But now that she had frightened those little rats of Kelveys and given Kezia a good scolding, her heart felt lighter. That ghastly pressure was gone. She went back to the house humming.

When the Kelveys were well out of sight of Burnells', they sat down to rest on a big red drainpipe by the side of the road. Lil's cheeks were still burning; she took off the hat with the quill and held it on her knee. Dreamily they looked over the hay paddocks, past the creek, to the group of wattles where Logan's cows stood waiting to be milked. What were their thoughts?

Presently our Else nudged up close to her sister. But now she had forgotten the cross lady. She put out a finger and stroked her sister's quill; she smiled her rare smile.

"I seen the little lamp," she said softly.

Then both were silent once more.

Albert CAMUS (1913–1960) was born in Moldovi, Algeria. He took a degree in philosophy in Algeria and became a teacher but recurrent tuberculosis ended his teaching career. He then devoted his time to amateur theatre, journalism, and creative writing. He moved to France, where he lived for the rest of his life. In 1957, he won the Nobel Prize in Literature; three years later he was killed in an automobile accident. Camus wrote in French.

"The Guest," set like most of his fiction in Algeria, takes place shortly after World War II during a period of tension between those who wanted an independent Algeria and those who wished it to remain a colony of France. The sensitive schoolteacher Daru is faced with a dilemma when ordered by the authorities to deliver an Algerian murderer to justice. His decision not to follow orders, and to treat his prisoner as a "guest," invites accounting for, and in arriving at an explanation for Daru's decision, the reader must consider all of the story's detail.

Anton CHEKHOV (1860–1904) was born in the small town of Taganrog in southwestern Russia. While working towards a degree in medicine at the University of Moscow, he began writing short stories and sketches. Soon there was a demand for them and his writing became a means of support for himself and his family. Even after he received his medical degree, he continued to devote most of his time to writing. He died of tuberculosis at the age of 44.

In his short stories and plays, Chekhov noted the decline of the Russian aristocracy and predicted the social and political revolutions that later took place. As a writer of over 600 short stories, he perfected techniques of literary realism that have set the standard for the art. Major themes in his stories are the powerlessness of the poor and misfortunate and the lack of understanding between people.

"The Ninny" is typical of many of Chekhov's stories in its brevity, its reliance on dialogue, its ability to expose a problem succinctly, and its irony. The story is told in the first person by a character who is himself part of the action: he records his conversation with the governess as well as his own thoughts during the interview. But in his total absorption with exposing the woman's weakness, he lets down his guard and unwittingly allows the reader to see him for what he is.

Kate CHOPIN (1851–1904) was born into a wealthy family in St. Louis, Missouri. At age 19 she married a Louisiana cotton broker and moved to New Orleans; but after her husband's death in 1884, she returned to St. Louis with her young family and stayed there until her death.

Chopin began writing after her return to St. Louis. During the next 20 years she produced two novels and over 90 short stories, as well as poetry, drama, and critical essays. Her work, which dealt with women's need for personal fulfillment and sexual equality, was not kindly received in an era when these needs were seldom thought about, let alone written down.

The difficulty for a woman to satisfy deep personal needs within marriage is a prevailing theme in much of Chopin's work. It is the major focus in "The Story of an Hour."

Gabriel GARCIA MARQUEZ (1928–) was born in Aractaca, Colombia. He began his writing career as a journalist, working in Latin America, Europe, and the United States. Although he has become a novelist of international stature—he received the Nobel Prize in Literature in 1982—he has insisted that journalism remains his real profession.

Along with some other Latin American writers, Garcia Marquez is known as a "magic realist," placing improbable events against realistic settings. Also, like other Latin American writers, his work often deals with political oppression and conflict. Much of his fiction is set in an imaginary locale called Macondo, modelled on the Colombian town where he grew up.

The town to which mother and daughter travel in "Tuesday Siesta" is Macondo. The mother's son, Carlos, killed a week earlier in a robbery attempt, rests in an unmarked grave at the local cemetery. She and her daughter come to place flowers on his grave. Perhaps it is the townspeople who are the most important people in the story.

Patricia GRACE (1935–) is a Maori and one of New Zealand's most admired new writers. Her short-story collections and novels deal with the Maori, the indigenous people of New Zealand, in their struggle to maintain their traditional culture.

Grace has taught in elementary and secondary schools. Like the narrator in "Between Earth and Sky," she is the mother of seven children. This story, from her second anthology *The Dreamers and Other Stories* (1980), is written in a stream-of-consciousness style and describes the narrator's inner thoughts and feelings before, during, and immediately after the birth of her baby at a nearby hospital.

João GUIMARÃES ROSA (1908–1967) was born in Cordesburgo, Brazil. As a young doctor, he practised in the Brazilian *sertão*, the sparsely settled backlands away from the major cities. In 1943 he joined the diplomatic service, serving his country in Germany, Colombia, and France, and then at home. He wrote in Portuguese and is considered his country's major contemporary writer.

Although he began writing only after he had become a diplomat, Guimarães Rosa's work was inspired by his early experiences in the *sertão*. To him, the *sertão* was more than a physical landscape; it was a metaphor for the "mystery of life." "The Third Bank of the River," taken from a 1962 collection of stories, is set around a river in the *sertão*. Although the story at first may seem absurd, readers will derive greater meaning from it if they can view the characters and the events as more representational than literal.

William George HARDY (1895–1979) was born in Peniel (near Lindsay), Ontario, and made a career as a professor, teaching from 1920 to 1964 at the University of Alberta. As a scholar, his area of study was Classical Philology (the comparative study of languages) and he published many articles in that field.

As a fiction writer, Hardy was best known for his popular novels on Biblical and historical subjects. He also published close to 100 short stories, and it was in this genre that he did his best creative writing. "The Czech Dog" was chosen for the anthology *Best American Short Stories* for 1945.

Shulamith HAREVEN was born in Warsaw, Poland, in 1931. As a child she escaped Nazism and settled in Israel, growing up in Jerusalem where she still lives. She is a writer of children's verse, poetry, fiction, and essays; a translator of literary works; and a frequent contributor to Israeli newspapers.

Her fiction varies widely in subject matter and setting, and her characters are equally diverse, ranging from Biblical prophets to contemporary Israelis. Always, however, they are lonely and alienated, confronting their environment with strain and uncertainty. "Twilight" is from the collection called *Solitude* (1980).

Bessie HEAD was born in Pietermaritzburg, South Africa, in 1937. She taught primary school and worked as a journalist there until the early 1970s, when she moved to Botswana. In Botswana, she lived under the same circumstances as the people about whom she wrote. An interviewer recorded the following: "There is no electricity left. At night, Bessie types by the light of six candles. Fruit trees and vegetables surround the house. Bessie makes guava jam to sell, and will sell vegetables when the garden is enlarged." At the time of her death in 1986, Head had gained international attention and was writing her autobiography.

Her fiction is generally set in Africa and often deals with racial and sexual prejudice and oppression. These themes are grounded in the writer's own experience as a woman of colour living in southern Africa. In "The Wind and the Boy" and her other short fiction, Head sought to blend native folktales with the fabric of contemporary village life.

Liliana HEKER (1943–), a native of Buenos Aires, Argentina, studied sciences at university, but left before earning a degree. Her desire to be a writer surfaced when she was 15. Although writing fiction is her major interest, she has also taught mathematics, physics, and chemistry; coordinated workshops for writers; worked as a translator; and helped to produce literary magazines.

Social injustice is a major theme of Heker's work. She has said that she owes her ideology to her mother: "She has an enormous repertory of songs about starving people, heartbroken lovers, labourers with tuberculosis, and mistreated orphans.... She'd sing as she cleaned the house, and I suffered horror thinking about those ... that's how I received my first lesson in social injustice." In "The Stolen Party" Heker dramatizes a child's discovery that her working-class status will not allow her to be accepted as the equal of her friend who comes from a higher social class.

Ernest HEMINGWAY was born in the Chicago suburb of Oak Park in 1899. His suicide, 62 years later, brought to an end a life filled with adventure, action, and, often, torment. His restless spirit took him to many parts of the globe, while his fiction won him numerous awards, including the Nobel Prize in Literature in 1954.

Hemingway began his professional writing career as a reporter for the *Kansas City Star*, an experience which forced him "to learn to write a simple declarative sentence." He also said that "I always try to write on the principle of the iceberg. There are seven-eighths of it under water for every part that shows." These remarks illuminate two essential characteristics of his writing: his spare, simple language and the hidden nature of his content and meaning.

A major preoccupation was the theme of courage and dignity in difficult human situations. His usually male characters—soldiers recovering from battle, big-game hunters, deep-sea fishermen, boxers—find themselves pitted against physical and psychological opponents. Although "A Clean, Well-Lighted Place" is set far from the battlefield or sports arena, it is considered a classic example of Hemingway's lean, straightforward style and prevailing themes.

Panos IOANNIDES (1935–) was born on the island of Cyprus and educated in Cyprus, Canada, and the United States. Writing in Greek, he has produced fiction, poetry, drama, and documentary scenarios for television. He has also worked as a director of programming at the Cyprus Broadcasting Company.

As Ioannides himself explains, the short story has "a long tradition in Cyprus; it dominates the literary scene, and comes second only after poetry." He says the main reason for this is "the sad reality that in Cyprus a novelist cannot make his living just by writing; therefore, writing is usually exercised as a sideline in the few fleeting hours available in the daily struggle for survival. So the only forms of literature opportune to pursue for a Cypriot writer have been the short story and verse."

The brief, intense story "Gregory" is set during the period of Cyprus's struggle for liberation from British domination in the late 1950s. The story is a direct result of a conversation between Ioannides and a former Cypriot guerilla who had guarded a hostage, a British soldier. Later, the hostage was executed in reprisal for a violent act by the British. "Gregory" describes the well-known "Stockholm syndrome," the phenomenon in which hostages and their keepers develop bonds despite their adversary positions.

Andris JAKUBĀNS, the Latvian writer, explores a familiar topic in his story "A Son's Return": the bonds, and heartbreaks, of family love. The story provides an interesting twist on the Biblical theme of the prodigal son. An old woman lies near death, staying alive only in the hope that her son, who ran away from home, will return to see her. Her daughter is skeptical and bitter, remembering his pranks and seeming carelessness about life. But when the son, Arnolds, does return, the events of the day become the stuff of legend, transforming the drab lives not only of his family but also of all the inhabitants of Linden Street.

Frigyes KARINTHY (1887–1938) was born in Budapest, Hungary. As a young man he studied for a short time to be a doctor. However, he soon turned to journalism, launching his career by contributing sketches and stories to Budapest newspapers in the period just before World War I. Two years before his death he travelled to Stockholm, Sweden for treatment of a brain tumour, but the surgery was finally unsuccessful and he died at age 51.

Karinthy's work is humorous, satiric, and often bizarre. Although his stories are usually set in his native Budapest, they deal with situations and problems universally recognizable throughout the modern world. "Mr. Selfsame" captures some of the realities of modern urban life, and of human response to it. Big-city dwellers, especially, will recognize the situation and the character presented in this sketch. The lengthy subtitle draws attention to Karinthy's satiric intent.

Marie Luise KASCHNITZ (1901–1974) was born in Karlsruhe, Germany. She received no university education but trained and worked as a book dealer. Although she began to write and publish during the early 1930s, her most important work was done at the end of World War II. She excelled as a poet, but was also successful as a writer of fiction, essays, and radio drama.

Two crises precipitated Kaschnitz's best work. In the years following World War II, she was strongly affected by memories of the war itself and by the personal and collective guilt she felt about the atrocities of Nazi Germany. She responded by writing about a world of ruin, chaos, and isolation. The death of her husband in 1958 resulted in another, more personal crisis to which Kaschnitz responded by exploring human feelings of loneliness and loss. Invariably, though, the work arising out of these difficult experiences is marked by compassion for the human condition and hopefulness for the future.

"Going to Jerusalem" is characteristic of Kaschnitz's fiction. The town in which the story is set is never referred to by name, but has a mythical quality about it, and so becomes universal. Its inhabitants, who suffer from an undefinable ailment—less physical than spiritual—are failed by doctors. Their cure is brought about by a mysterious figure who reacquaints them with aspects of living that have been cast aside in their society.

Pär LAGERKVIST (1891–1974) was born in Vaexjoe, Sweden. After a year of humanities courses at the University of Uppsala, he went abroad to study artistic movements such as Cubism and Expressionism, which were then becoming popular in Europe. He reacted to the two world wars with revulsion, becoming an eloquent critic of totalitarianism. He wrote poetry, novels, short stories, plays, and essays, and in 1951, was awarded the Nobel Prize in Literature. Lagerkvist wrote only in Swedish.

The major themes in Lagerkvist's work are the individual's relationship to God, the meaning of life, and the conflict between good and evil. His characters spend their lives searching for meaning and assurance in a world devoid of certainty. These themes appear in "Father and I." Strongly autobiographical (Lagerkvist's father worked as a railroad lineman), "Father and I" describes a Sunday afternoon's outing in the country that takes on a darker aspect.

Margaret LAURENCE (1926–1987) was born in Neepawa, Manitoba, and received her university education at United College in Winnipeg. As a young woman, she accompanied her husband to Africa, living in Somaliland (now Somalia) and the Gold Coast (now Ghana). After the breakup of her marriage, she moved to England with her two children, staying there for 10 years until she returned to Canada in the early 1970s. She spent the last years of her life in the small Ontario community of Lakefield, east of Toronto.

While Laurence's early writing reflected her African experience, her major fiction is essentially Canadian. All of her "Canadian" novels and her short-story anthology *A Bird in the House* deal with life in the fictional prairie town of Manawaka, each book focusing on a female character in the town.

"The Loons" is one of the eight stories that make up *A Bird in the House*, a book whose title suggests the central theme of entrapment. The book's main character is Vanessa MacLeod, and most of the stories deal with her relationship to and remembrance of people she knew while growing up. "The Loons" is told from Vanessa's point of view.

Doris LESSING was born in Persia (now Iran) in 1919, but, as a child, moved with her family to southern Rhodesia (now Zimbabwe) where she lived until 1949. Since then she has lived in England but has always looked upon her first home in Rhodesia as her only real home. "The fact is," she wrote in 1956, "I don't live anywhere. I never have since I left that first home.... I have lived in over sixty different houses, flats, and rented rooms during the last twenty years and not in one of them have I felt at home."

"Sunrise on the Veld" is set on the high Rhodesian grasslands where Lessing spent her youth. It has been called one of the most carefully crafted initiation stories written in English. This craft reveals itself in the story's balanced structure, the carefully observed details, and the parallels drawn to the classical Greek myth of Narcissus and Echo.

Catherine LIM was born in Singapore, an independent city-state situated at the southern tip of the Malay Peninsula. Lim is a graduate of the University of Malaysia, writes in English, and usually sets her stories in contemporary Singapore. Besides being a writer, she is a teacher of English language and literature.

Her stories are noted for their attention to detail, irony, and searing criticism of injustices and materialistic values observed in her native land. "Paper" is typical of Lim's work. The title provides an ironic commentary on the real worth of the material objects for which the protagonists strive.

Vilas MANIVAT, the Thai writer, is best-known for his travel books about London and the United States. He has taught journalism and achieved fame in his homeland as a television personality. He was born in the forested area of southern Thailand, and is very concerned about the preservation of green areas in cities.

His story "Who Needs It?" uses dialogue to make much of its impact. The store-keeper, Nai Phan, known for his generosity, kindness, and ability to remain detached from material wealth, finds his principles put severely to the test when he is confronted by an armed robber. Nai Phan's reaction to the man's desperate actions, and the ensuing relationship between the two men, form the crux of this optimistic story.

Katherine MANSFIELD (1888–1923) was born in Wellington, New Zealand. At the age of 15 she was sent to London to continue her education. Except for the years from 1906 to 1908 when she returned to New Zealand to study music, she made London her home for the rest of her life. She died in a tuberculosis clinic in France at the age of 35.

By the time she was 18, Mansfield had decided to be a writer. Her first attempts at fiction were not successful because they were considered too obvious and simple, but soon critics began to see that beyond the apparent simplicity lay much subtlety and sophistication. "The Doll's House," from *The Dove's Nest and Other Stories* (1923), is one of her many stories with a New Zealand setting. It deals with one of her favourite themes, social snobbery, and explores the sources and effects of assumed class superiority.

Olga MASTERS (1919–1986) was born in Pambula, New South Wales, Australia. She has worked as a journalist in several Australian towns, most recently writing a human-interest column in the Sydney *Morning Herald*. Her work has also appeared in *Vogue* and *Ms.* magazines.

She has said that she finds the lives of poor and humble people her favourite subject and that growing up during the Great Depression provided her with material for her novels and stories. New Zealander Katherine Mansfield's ability to depict ordinary events compellingly was an early inspiration.

"The Rages of Mrs. Torrens" is from the collection *The Home Girls* (1982). The story turns on the reasons for the heroine's rages and on the differences between her and the other wives in town. Kathleen Torrens is a passionate woman, the proud and defiant champion of her family. At the end of the story, her daughter Aileen exhibits these same traits.

Yukio MISHIMA was born in Tokyo in 1925. After graduating in law from the University of Tokyo, and working for a short time as a civil servant, he turned to a full-time career in writing. During his lifetime he founded a right-wing organization dedicated to the re-establishment of Japanese traditions. He also cultivated an image of personal strength and fitness, studying boxing, karate, and sword-fighting (*kendo*). On November 24, 1970, after leading an attack on an army post in Tokyo and haranguing the soldiers there about the military decline of Japan, he committed suicide.

As a writer of fiction and of modernizations of the traditional form of Japanese drama called *Noh*, Mishima became the best-known Japanese writer of his generation. His subjects, like his life, were often sensational, including ritual murder and rogue priests. "Swaddling Clothes" has a less sensational subject and a more muted theme than one finds elsewhere in Mishima's fiction, but it still decries the movement away from traditional values by contemporary Japanese.

Slawomir MROŻEK (1930–) was born in Borzecin, Poland. He studied architecture and painting before working as a journalist and cartoonist. When he turned to dramawriting, his plays *The Police* and *Tango* were seen to be attacks on the Communist regime, and were subsequently banned. Mrożek fled to France, where, living in exile, he criticized Poland's position on the 1968 invasion of Czechoslovakia. As a result, his passport was revoked. The ban on his return to Poland has since been lifted, but Mrożek has chosen to remain in France.

His plays have gained him a reputation as an outspoken critic of pretension, convention, and the abuse of power. Although his stories do not draw the sensational publicity that the performance of his plays did, they are characterized by the same satiric quality.

"The Elephant" is the title story in a collection of short fiction published in 1962. Mrożek's writing generally can be read on two levels. "The Elephant" has much to say about the absurdity of the Polish governmental bureaucracy and the self-seeking of people in power. At the same time, the characters and the situations are recognizable to readers everywhere, making "The Elephant" universal in its scope.

V. S. (Vidiadhar Surajprasad) NAIPAUL (1932–) was born in Trinidad to a Hindu family from northern India. He was educated in Trinidad, and then at Oxford University in England. Describing himself as "without a past, without ancestors," Naipaul has been unhappy about the cultural poverty of his birthplace and about his own geographical and cultural distance from India. Although he frequently returns to Trinidad, since 1960 he has made his home in England.

Naipaul has been called the most talented of the West Indian writers. His fiction deals with people who feel estranged from their culture or society, and who seek a sense of belonging in an indifferent or hostile world. Most of his fiction is set in the Third World, mainly Trinidad.

"B. Wordsworth," from *Miguel Street* (1959), displays Naipaul's keen ear for the speech patterns found in his native Trinidad. Another characteristic quality is the sympathy with which the author draws the characters and the situations.

Jan NERUDA (1834–1891) was born in Prague, Czechoslovakia. He briefly studied philosophy at university and then became a schoolteacher, but soon turned to journalism.

Nowadays, Neruda is best-known for his poetry, but during his lifetime he gained greater recognition as a prose writer, both of fiction and non-fiction. Besides being a literary and theatre critic, he wrote a large number of short pieces, some reportorial, some fictional, portraying the lives of his fellow Czechs and Europeans. These short sketches express various attitudes towards the life he observed: humour, irony, and sadness.

"The Vampire" is one of a number of short stories that came out of Neruda's experiences while travelling in southeast Europe.

Grace OGOT was born in 1930 in Kenya, in East Africa, and has spent most of her life in her native country. As a young woman she trained to be a nurse and midwife in Uganda and England, and worked as scriptwriter and announcer for the BBC. In Kenya, she has served as her country's representative at the General Assembly of the United Nations. As well, she founded and acted as chairperson for the Writers' Association of Kenya.

Ogot's fiction deals with the history and lives of the people of East Africa. She has written narratives in English and also in Luo, her native tongue. "The Rain Came," written in English, deals with the customs of tribal peoples, especially as they impinge on the warmth and closeness of family life. Certain contemporary themes—the importance of the individual, the inequality between men and women, and the seeming illogic of certain superstitious beliefs and rituals—underlie the ancient rites depicted in the story.

Alan PATON was born, of British ancestry, in Pietermaritzburg, South Africa, in 1903. His parents were deeply religious people who questioned the state policy of apartheid, the legal and enforced segregation of races. Paton's own humanitarian ideals evolved from those of his parents. In 1950, he founded the anti-apartheid Liberal party, later became its president, then saw it banned and his own passport revoked in 1968.

In his non-political life, Paton was a high-school teacher for some years until he became the principal of a boy's reformatory near Johannesburg, where he served for over a decade. "Ha'penny," from his 1961 book *Tales from a Troubled Land*, clearly is based on an autobiographical experience. The account reflects both Paton's humanitarian beliefs and social conditions in South Africa.

Paton died in 1988, still criticizing the South African government for not going far enough in its relaxation of the apartheid laws.

Octavio PAZ, born in Mexico City in 1914, has enjoyed a long and distinguished career, both as a writer of international renown and as a public servant in his own country. He was Mexico's representative at UNESCO, and ambassador to India, until he resigned in protest over his government's handling of student demonstrations before the 1968 Olympic Games in Mexico City. Since then, he has divided his time between writing and teaching. He has produced many collections of poetry, essays, and fiction, all written in Spanish. In 1990 he received the Nobel Prize in Literature.

Paz presents a picture of the modern world as dehumanizing and destructive and whose inhabitants are disoriented and displaced. At the same time, however, the author expresses the hope that we can be saved through our creativity and the endeavour to build a more compassionate and life-affirming society. Paz sees his role as a writer to offer enlightenment and hope to humankind.

"The Blue Bouquet" is from *Eagle or Sun?* (1951) and may be viewed as a literary invocation of a nightmare.

Alifa RIFAAT (1930–) is a pseudonym for Fatima Abdallah Rifaat, born in Cairo, Egypt. Her Islamic faith has affected her life as a writer in many ways: when she wrote a short story at the age of nine, she was punished. As an adult, she began publishing short fiction under her pseudonym, but when her husband learned about her literary career, he insisted that she stop writing. After an enforced silence of 15 years, she was permitted to resume writing during a period of ill health in 1973. Since then, she has published some 90 stories. She writes in Arabic.

As one who believes in and accepts Islamic teaching, Rifaat has attempted to write from her religious perspective, particularly as it applies to the lives of women. "Most of my stories," she says, "revolve around a woman's right to a fully effective and complete sexual life in marriage; that and the sexual and emotional problems encountered by women in marriage are the most important themes of my stories."

"An Incident in the Ghobashi Household" appeared, in translation, in a 1983 collection called *Distant View of a Minaret*. The mother, Zeinat, is faced with a problem: her unmarried daughter's pregnancy. In searching for a solution, Zeinat is concerned foremost with protecting her daughter and the life of the unborn child, and only second with preserving her husband's sense of honour. As for Hamdan, the hired hand who is the child's father, Zeinat wryly observes, "His account is with Allah. He's fine and doesn't have a worry in the world."

Gabrielle ROY (1909–1983) was born in Saint-Boniface, Manitoba. She studied to be a teacher at the Winnipeg Normal Institute and held teaching posts in various parts of the province. After studying drama briefly in Europe, she returned to Canada in 1939, settling in Montreal. From the early 1950s onwards, she lived in Québec City.

Most of Roy's work deals with the lives of French-Canadians, although she occasionally wrote about immigrant groups such as the Chinese and the Doukhobors, and about Native peoples such as the Inuit. In her depiction of human life, she strove to give a balanced view: "I have no sooner seen the splendour of life, than I feel obliged, physically obliged, to look down and also take notice of the sad and the tragic of life."

"The Dead Child" is from her collection *Enchanted Summer* (1976). This autobiographical story demonstrates the simplicity and warmth that characterizes her fiction generally.

James SALTER (1925–) was born in New York City, later lived in Colorado, and from 1945 to 1957 served with the United States Air Force. He is known primarily as a writer of novels and short stories, but he is also a dramatist and scriptwriter.

Salter's fiction deals mainly with human relationships and the tensions within people deriving from obsessions, sexuality, ambition, and failure. In technique, the author has been influenced by the painting style known as Impressionism. Salter creates a "literary" impressionism, evoking atmosphere and mood more by subjective observation than by objective description.

"Akhnilo," from his collection *Dusk and Other Stories* (1988), deals with the struggle of a recovering alcoholic, Eddie Fenn.

Mauro SENESI (1931–   ) was born in Volterra, Italy, not far from Venice. After working for a time as a journalist, he turned to fiction, publishing short stories (written in English) in American and British magazines. Unfortunately, a large part of the manuscript of a novel he was working on was destroyed by the Venice floods of December, 1966.

Senesi's stories make use of the long-popular narrative form of the fable. Traditional fables, such as those by Aesop and La Fontaine, were stories about animals written to teach a particular truth. "The Giraffe" was first published in the United States in *Harper's Magazine* and collected in Senesi's *Long Shadows and Nine Stories* (1962). The story's significance turns on the differing impacts the giraffe makes on various members of the town's population.

Elizabeth TAYLOR (1912–1975) was born in Reading, England, and lived all her life in her native country. After leaving school, she worked as a librarian and governess. Taylor began to write when she was very young, choosing as her subject the domestic lives of the English middle class. Her stories reveal a thorough understanding of their ways, and an aptitude for choosing significant incidents, characters, and settings that best represent her chosen world. "The First Death of Her Life" is an excellent example of Taylor's craft.

Yves THÉRIAULT (1915–1983) was born in Québec City, to a Québecoise mother and an Acadian-Montagnais father, who taught him the Cree language. He received his formal education mainly in Montréal. During his lifetime, he held many positions, the most notable being in the fields of filmmaking, radio, and the administration of Native cultural affairs.

Much of Thériault's fiction is set in Québec and features French-Canadian or Native characters. Known for his shocking, often sexually explicit descriptions, the author depicted individuals struggling to control instinctive passions and searching for self-definition and identity. Thériault's output was prodigious: he wrote over a thousand stories.

"The Whale," from *La Femme Anna et autre contes*, is milder in tone than most of Thériault's fiction. Essentially it is a tall tale, a form that has a rich tradition in Québec.

Thomas WHITECLOUD (1912–1972) was born in New York City. When his parents divorced, Whitecloud remained with his mother but spent parts of his youth on the Lac du Flambeau Reservation in Wisconsin with his Chippewan father. As a young man, Whitecloud worked at various jobs from farmworker to boxer. Later, he studied at Redlands University in California and went on to earn a medical degree at Tulane University in New Orleans.

Whitecloud devoted his life to medicine, writing in his spare time. At his death, he left a number of unpublished stories, essays, and poems. "Blue Winds Dancing," one of the few pieces he did publish, was written in 1938, during his final year at Redlands. The story describes a journey from the white man's world of ambition and conformity ("dancing to the strings of custom and tradition") to the simpler joys of nature and family on the reservation. As the narrator rides the rails across the country, his journey becomes a spiritual as well as a physical one. And it is home that defines the end of the journey.

YU-WOL Chong-Nyon, which means "Month-of-June-Youth" in Korean, is the pen name chosen by the young Korean woman who wrote "The Nonrevolutionaries." The pen name refers to the generation of Koreans who became adults during and after the civil war between North and South that engulfed their country from 1950 to 1953.

In "The Nonrevolutionaries" the narrator, who has just returned to Korea from a year's study in the West, recounts the events of a night early on in the Korean war, flashing back to segments of her own experience and to the historical events that made an impact on her native land. On July 27, 1953, an armistice was signed, ending the war between North and South Korea and confirming the boundary at the Thirty-eighth Parallel.

ZHANG Jie (1937–) was born in Beijing, China, and studied economics at the People's University there. After working in the industrial division of the public service, she joined the Beijing Film Studio where she wrote scripts. Since the end of the Cultural Revolution in 1976, she has written short stories that have been widely read and that have gained her considerable attention.

Zhang's stories reflect the opening up of Chinese life to the rest of the world and the tension inevitably brought on by this new receptiveness. It is not surprising that her stories have been both popular and controversial. "Love Must Not Be Forgotten," written in 1979, portrays the trials suffered for true love, and the tension between traditional and new attitudes towards love and marriage.

INDEX OF THEMES AND TOPICS

➤ ACKNOWLEDGEMENTS

Permission to reprint copyrighted material is gratefully acknowledged. Every reasonable effort to trace the copyright holders of materials appearing in this book has been made. Information that will enable the publishers to rectify any error or omission will be welcomed.

The Guest from *Exile and the Kingdom* by Albert Camus, trans., J. O'Brien. Copyright © 1957, 1968 by Alfred A. Knopf, Inc. Reprinted by permission of the publisher.

The Wind and a Boy © Bessie Head, from *The Collector of Treasures and other Botswana Village Tales*, Heinemann Educational Books 1977. Reprinted by permission of John Johnson (Authors' Agents) Ltd., London.

The Rain Came by Grace Ogot from *Land Without Thunder*, published in 1968 by East African Publishing House, Nairobi, Kenya. Copyright by Grace Ogot.

Ha'penny from *Tales from a Troubled Land* © 1961 by Alan Paton. Reprinted by permission of Macmillan Publishing Company.

Sunrise on the Veld from *This Was the Old Chief's Country* by Doris Lessing. Copyright 1951 Doris Lessing. Reprinted [in Canada] by permission of Jonathan Clowes Ltd., London, on behalf of the author. **Sunrise on the Veld** from *African Stories* by Doris Lessing. Copyright © 1951, '54, '57, '58, '62, '63, '64, '65 by Doris Lessing. Reprinted [in U.S.A.] by permission of Simon & Schuster.

Love Must Not Be Forgotten by Zhang Jie, translated by Gladys Yang, from *Seven Contemporary Chinese Writers*, © 1982 by Panda Books. Reprinted by permission of Chinese Literature Press, 24 Baiwanzhuang Road, Beijing 100037, China.

Swaddling Clothes by Yukio Mishima from *Death in Midsummer and Other Stories*. Copyright © 1966 by New Directions Publishing Corporation. Reprinted by permission of New Directions Publishing Corporation.

The Nonrevolutionaries by Yu-Wol Chong-Nyon from *A Treasury of Modern Asian Stories*, edited by D. L. Milton and W. Clifford, published by Plume Books/New American Library. Reprinted by permission of William Clifford, P. O. Box 295, Morris, Connecticut 06763.

Paper from *Little Ironies: Stories of Singapore* by Catherine Lim. Originally published by Heinemann Asia. Reprinted with permission of Octopus Publishing Asia Pte Ltd., Singapore.

Who Needs It? by Vilas Manivat from *Taw & Other Thai Stories* edited and translated by Jennifer Draskau. Originally published in 1975 by Heinemann Asia. Reprinted with permission of Octopus Publishing Asia Pte Ltd., Singapore.

The Vampire by Jan Neruda from *Stories from Mala Strana*, published in 1878.

The First Death of Her Life from *Hester Lily and Other Stories* copyright Elizabeth Taylor © 1954. Published by Virago Press 1990.

Going to Jerusalem by Marie Luise Kaschnitz; **Die Reise nach Jerusalem** aus: *Lange Schatten* © 1960 by Claassen Verlag, Hamburg.

Mr. Selfsame by Frigyes Karinthy, translated by István Farkas. Reprinted by permission of the translator and Artisjus Agency for Literature and Theatre, Budapest, Hungary.

The Giraffe © 1962 by Mauro Senesi, reprinted from the January 1963 issue of *Harper's Magazine*.